GOSPEL

Rumours of love

SIMON PARKE

www.whitecrowbooks.com

Published in the United Kingdom and USA by White Crow
Books; an imprint of White Crow Productions Ltd.

A CIP catalogue record for this book is available from the British Library.
For information: e-mail info@whitecrowbooks.com

Cover Design by Astrid@Astridpaints.com
Cover Image by Harry Parke
Interior design by Velin@Perseus-Design.com

Paperback ISBN: 978-1-78677-147-6
eBook ISBN: 978-1-78677-148-3

Fiction / Historic / Religious

www.whitecrowbooks.com

Acknowledgements

A number of people have kindly read and commented on the manuscript at various points. This remarkable roll call of honour includes Jenny Monds, Rachel Treweek, Richard Addis, Jim Rooney, Shellie Parke, Rachel Atkinson, Rachel Spence, Martin Hoile, Rebecca Parke, Ann Rooney and Clive Williams. For the decisions taken, rage at me – but throw only thanksgiving at them; I certainly do. Karl French was a wonderful editor, a severe mercy to the text and a kind companion to the author. Harry Parke drew the haunting image in the cover design. Jon Beecher made it all happen – he makes a lot of things happen – via the new 'Big Story' imprint. And finally my belated thanks to Professor Gerd Theissen. Over thirty years ago, I read his 'In the Shadow of the Galilean'. I found it inspiring at the time and it sowed a slow seed which has become the book you now hold.

It is not to be doubted a man called Jesus lived and died

The more interesting question is whether he died and lived

And how he believed and loved along the way

It is not the purpose of fiction to provide answers

Only to awaken possibilities from their slumbers

As Picasso reminds us,

'Art is a lie that makes us realise the truth'

Praise for *Gospel: Rumours of Love*

'This beautifully crafted book will not leave any reader indifferent. As Simon Parke seeks to get under the skin of Jesus the man and his early disciples, so this book gets under the reader's skin. I found it both exhilarating and disturbing as the provocative narrative, shot through with familiar words and stories from the Gospels, took me to places of both comfort and objection. Yet through it all I was profoundly moved by the outrageous love of the frequently-raging Yeshua. This is a poignant and mystical story of love which is likely to raise more questions than answers, but then that is not unlike the stories Jesus Christ himself once told.'
~ Rachel Treweek, Bishop of Gloucester

'Meet Jesus unplugged. In a stunning act of imagination Simon Parke shatters every stained-glass window in your mind.'
~ Richard Addis, editor-in-Chief of *The Day* and former novice Anglican monk.

'In "Gospel: Rumours of Love", Simon Parke, a gifted novelist whose time must surely come, has set himself the task of recreating the life of Jesus leading up to the crucifixion and resurrection. The result is a wonderful and profound thing, a book in which the mundane and the miraculous exist comfortably side by side. The book itself sits comfortably alongside – indeed compares favourably to – similar re-imaginings of the life of Christ by Nikos Kazantzakis, Philip Pullman and Colm Tóibín, but it is also a singular and distinctive piece of work, an always compelling, thoughtful and thought-provoking – and at times – a deeply moving novel.'

~ Karl French, writer, editor and journalist

YESHUA

Beside the sea

Perhaps others will write of this, they say they will.
They said all sorts of things on the beach this morning, amid their astonishment at seeing me. Rocky promised a book, 'I will write a book of all this, this must be a book!' ... though he cannot write, as Levi pointed out, 'You can clean barnacles off the keel and stand steady in a storm. But you cannot write.'

Rocky does say things. He has never been measured with his mouth; no hand on the tiller there and caught by every wind. Some say he speaks before he thinks, though I say he just speaks; there is no obvious thought on display.

Though their astonishment, bright-eyed and frantic, scarce equals mine; I laugh inside so much, I cannot quiet it. I laugh as they leap from the boat, splashing and wading towards me, half-swimming. I cannot believe it, this scene before my eyes. I am making a fire, the fire is all I need, it is everything – smouldering wood, smoke and embers, heat in the morning chill and the splash and the rush toward me, the wet sunlight, these mad idiots, my friends.

'It's him, it's him,' they shout. 'Yeshua, is it you!? It cannot be Yeshua! Don't be so stupid! Yeshua, it cannot be you!'

I am ripped apart by amazement and joy ... amazement that I am here, that this is so; and such joy at seeing the sea and these wasters again.

They once ran away, it comes back to me, how they all disappeared, though I have lost my capacity for blame, truly; for we are not where we were, Gethsemane feels a long time ago, and now a different space unfolds. They run towards me, soaked through with Galilee wash and shouting, arguing as they approach and I get up to greet them, to hug and to hold – as close to friends as I shall have, though Miriam is not here. And maybe that is best.

'So where are the fish?' I ask. 'We cannot eat surprise.'

YESHUA

Leaving home

~

I am leaving Nazareth, walking hard from the place and good riddance.

I write of former things, which seem so far away now, but were skin-close then. As close as the wood and nails that passed daily through my hands in the workshop, where my father's tools, may he rest in peace, still hung; and on the door, my new sign:

Yeshua: Carpenter/Builder/Restorer.

It was the second day of the week when I left home, with nowhere to go, but nowhere to stay either, for Nazareth was no friend of mine, not at the end, much having soured. Though you never quite leave, do you? You leave a place, you walk forever, you cross the world ... but past times linger in the cracks and permeate the bones. This we shall see.

And the events of that day, when the fabric was torn, still shout aloud inside me. I remember the harsh words spoken. They return to me as I walk, angry steps, as if my very sandals rage, crunching the space ahead. The earth scalds; each rock and pebble a hot and living thing, with power to wound. And yes, I will miss my wood and the making of things. I say goodbye to that – to my father's tools and to my self in a way; or to a shape of my self, my carpenter self, with no bright star or glistening guide, other than the nous that I must go. When the house is on fire you must leave, with or without a plan. And I felt the fire.

But as the sun lowers now, I am nowhere, stumbling among gnarled stems, grey rock and sad spent feathers, long dead to flight. Plants beg for rain and I beg with them. It is a drying wind, with nothing left to dry but my self and a hawk that hovers overhead. Moses struck rock in the desert and water flowed ... but it does not flow for me, I try. '"Water!' I shout, but there is nothing. Was Moses more faithful than I? Am I not worthy of refreshment?

I have followed some goats for a while, the three of them brisk guides and seeming to know their mind; though they leave me behind now, too agile on the rock to be followed for long, as the stench thickens. The air is still, heavy and awful. It is the smell of death and decay and following the flies, I discover the cause – a discarded mule, pecked and rotting, no further use to the traders who use this way to Jerusalem. For a moment, I even miss Nazareth; a line not often heard. And I am finished, in a manner, as finished as the mule; though only thirty years of age. I am at the end of all I have known with only the dead for company and the rumour of zealots, planning blood and revolt in the caves. These rocks are a good place for their schemes, hidden from busy Roman eyes.

'Are you a zealot?' My mother would ask this. 'Some say you are – a furtive zealot, Yeshua, with too sharp a tongue. The neighbours say, "Is Yeshua a zealot, Mary?" So are you? I sometimes wonder, the way you speak. I wonder if you are a zealot.' But she would not stay for a reply. She would pose questions and then scuttle off leaving the accusation in the air.

I find water in this wilderness. If the goats can live, then so can I. The small pools sit away from the sun, in the cracks and the canyons, where the wadis cut through the rock. I climb down to find them and drink the water of life, chilled by the shadows. It is very good; there is nothing to equal this cool intake. I drink the silence also, and the silence is deep and full of wonder; though I am passed now by traders who prefer noise, hollering beasts and jovial cursing on their way to Jerusalem from the east. They have business on their minds, though one asks me if I am the ghost of John the Baptiser. They had heard of him causing trouble in these parts, disturbing the peace, like a fly on a camel's ear.

'Why does everyone have to cause trouble?' one asks, as they sit and spit and eat their dates, wrapped in careful cloth. 'Everyone has to cause trouble, especially so-called messiahs! Why don't they just go into business, get a job?'

'He hates messiahs,' explains his friend with unhidden admiration. 'Really has no time for them at all; he can't see the point. I mean, fair's fair, they provide a bit of colour and that, something to talk about on a cold night but it's true, absolutely true, that people like that Baptiser fellow, denouncing people and what have you – they're not good for business.'

'Unless you you're a cross maker!' says another. 'There's a string of messiahs on the Jericho road, drying out nicely.'

'They're zealots most of them, not messiahs.'

'And the difference is?'

'A messiah loves himself more.' Laughter ... joshing ... they suggest each other for the role. These traders like the Romans because Romans are good for business, good for the shekel, "good for order, they are, with all those soldiers, and nice straight roads. Have you seen how straight their roads are? They don't like bends, the Romans." And what is good for business is good for Judaea. It is those who disturb the Roman order who they do not like. People like the zealots.

'Messiahs mean followers and followers mean claims, wild claims and uprising – and road blocks.' Road blocks appear the main issue with messiahs. 'There are road blocks everywhere! Soldiers search my mule's arse for knives, everyone nervous.'

I reassure them. I say am not the Baptiser, nor his ghost, nor a messiah. But he says, 'Well, you smell like him!' They all laugh. I am related to John, distantly so, but I do not mention this. It would not help my present cause. And anyway, no one is quite sure how his mother Elizabeth is related to my mother; and my father could never explain beyond, 'a sort-of cousin, I believe.' Again, they complain of the stink, and impute it to me.

'I think that will be the mule,' I say, indicating the corpse upwind. 'One of yours, I presume?' There is no denial. 'And no one smells good when rotting. None of us will be frankincense in the grave.'

I am brief entertainment while they eat; and I do not mind their company, now the goats are gone.

'They say Jericho has the best dates.' I have heard this from someone or other, so I throw it in. Feeling vulnerable, I do not wish things to turn nasty. They like good order for business reasons; not for love of their neighbour.

'You from Jericho then?'

'Nazareth,' I say, fearing the worst and they do snigger. People always snigger. But I am stuck with the fact of my home town; though it ceased to feel like home.

'You ought to see Jerusalem, mate.'

'Not much like Nazareth!' Guffaws.

'Have you seen Jerusalem?'

'I went as a child.'

'The Temple is massive, of course; nothing prepares you for the temple.' He talks as if I had not spoken. 'Nothing prepares you for the Temple, does it, eh?' He looks around and finds agreement, in their eyes and grunts, that *nothing prepares you for the Temple.* 'And those walls! I mean the place is a monster.'

'He's not wrong there,' says another, looking at me. 'It *is* a monster – I mean, a *magnificent* monster, obviously.' *Obviously,* they all nod. 'And noisy as hell.'

'And busy ... nowhere so busy as Jerusalem.'

'Well, it's noisy *because* it's busy, stands to reason. You can hardly be busy without being noisy, that's not going to work!'

'You've never seen anywhere busier than Jerusalem.'

'Caesarea?' says another.

'Caesarea doesn't compare; doesn't compare. But the main thing about Jerusalem is something quite different. Know what that is?'

I do not know what it is, I have no idea, but I pretend thought before saying, 'No, I think you will have to tell me.'

'The dust! The main thing about Jerusalem is the dust,' and again his friends agree.

'Really?' I say.

He shakes his head. 'That's the main thing about Jerusalem – the dust. There's no dust like Jerusalem dust. No dust on earth.'

'I will remember that ... should I visit.'

'Absolute dust bowl, Jerusalem. You haven't been?'

'Only as a child,' I repeat. Why do I expect people to listen?

'Noisy as hell, obviously. It's just noise, Jerusalem – and dust ... and the Temple obviously.'

Soon after, the traders continue their journey towards the city dust; and I am left to myself again and the question of why I am here. I am strengthened in knowing that John was here before me, this distant cousin of sorts. I find here a kind thread of connection in this wasteland; and strange comfort that he found life in this place in which I now stumble. My father asks trust of me – my dear elusive father, I will find a prayer soon. I have lost him in my anger, though maybe he is in the anger; I do not know, for I walk in unknowing. And perhaps trust will arise, perhaps it will be given, for trust is gift and cannot be strained by effort into life. Simple trust is all that is asked and all I ask now. "Your kingdom come, your will be done." See, here in the wilderness dark with only a rotting ass for a friend, I return to my childhood prayer!

Though how I arrive here, I cannot be certain; and how I have left home, I do not know. Many voices speak within, though perhaps the loudest is that of the Baptiser. John is the reason I am here, I think so, though the reason fades with hunger, as reasons do. I have been a follower of the Baptiser, the angry prophet who tears at the guts of luxury and denial – but am now no follower at all, for he is dead and you cannot follow a corpse; that is a very short walk. His head was presented on a plate – yes, presented bloody on a plate! This is the rumour, murdered at Machaerus by Herod – a high-born Jew with low-grade morals. Drink flowing, dancing girls, dancing lust, promises made – and in the cells below, in the dark of the night, the prophet dragged out, my sort-of cousin, roughly held, his neck ripped, his head axed free from the body and lifted up, with his hair as a handle, dropped on a plate in a sea of blood. I do not envy Herod the bodyless stare of John; he was frightening enough alive. It will keep him awake for nights; I hope so.

But is this how Israel is to be? Is this how our leaders are to behave? I think the space around me asks the question; the rocks seem to speak and as I look towards Herod's lair at Machaerus, my blood is angry. As Nazareth dissolves; as my home town melts and all its concerns, rage grows within like the eaglet gasping for food, trying its wings, finding its strength. Here in the wilderness, there is a rage inside me that could pull down the sky. Truly, I feel I could do this. Or is this nothing but a demon?

My mother would call it a demon; for I "always was trouble" … and my brother James would agree. (He stands often by her side agreeing.) The rough truth is, I left Nazareth with no laurels or kind farewells. They said I have a home to look after; a family in need, a business in need. They said many things. "You are the eldest" – my mother never stops reminding me, with disappointment in her eyes. I am the one who must now be father, what with my father gone; this has always been clear, I must replace him … so applause when I left was faint. Though I had to go, and truly, I feel invigorated as I walk, a weight removed. I am a boat without anchor, unwise on Galilee, such storms arise … but good in the wilderness, where I feel light and free.

And I walk and I walk and I walk. I expel breath and take it in, and as distance occurs, my family do fall away in the wind, as if they become hollow. I have been so much with them over the years. Yet as I leave, I wonder if I know them at all … or like them. Must I like my family? Perhaps other mothers await me, perhaps other brothers, other sisters. Perhaps all people are family, and our only father in heaven. Or perhaps no one awaits me. This also crosses my mind. Perhaps I have left the only home I shall know. Foxes have holes and the birds have their nests – but me? I do not know where I shall lay my head tonight ... only that it cannot be in Nazareth.

My brother James was the harshest; a fellow as useful as a splinter. He watched my mother's face, like a shepherd watches the sky, and took her for his lead. She has carved this role for herself – the long-suffering widow. So James was all offence at me, all puzzlement and anger that I should do this – that I should abandon them so. This was his word, for it was her word: "Why do you abandon us, Yeshua?"

But still I walk on. Every step makes more distance from my past and new words arrive in my heart, like an angel. Or perhaps the rocks give me my lines, for someone does. 'You must let me be *Yeshua*, mother!' they say, and I repeat them out loud. 'You must let me be Yeshua, mother!' They were words I could not speak at the time; they were not there, as she pulled at me and wept. She could not or would not let me be, but wept and pulled at me, gripping my arm, begging me to change my ways. I stayed silent, a confusion inside. But now these wilderness words bring peace to my soul, like a father's hug. They arrive as I sit on a rock, minding the snakes, which sneak in every crevice. I shout them back to the rocks: 'You must let me be Yeshua, mother!' and even find an echo. Though what they mean, I do not know. And perhaps – and this arrests me – I must let myself be Yeshua. This may be the truer, if more difficult, call; for who am I now, if no longer a carpenter and no longer a brother or son? Who am I?

And then the light surprises me; a light I had no sense of, not in this form and ferocity. I find myself in a cave; I am brought here in my spirit. The cave is dark and my eyes blind, until a distant light breaks through, faint at first and then strengthening; and in my soul I know this light as the place of my beginning ... I know this. I see my past as if through a fissure in the rock, beyond this wilderness, beyond Nazareth, beyond my birth, way back and beyond. It is pure light which the darkness cannot quench; an ancient light, alive and bright before even the stars ... the stars seem young compared to the light I see in the cave, the light of home.

I stagger a little on the rock, as if hit across the head, as if drunk with wine – such joy! For here is wonder, here in the cave of my spirit, this kingdom within, this ancient light, which I do not wish to lose. Like boat lights in the morning mist, bringing in the catch, here is a joy I have not known, the joy of some bright long ago, some time before my spirit was pressed into flesh. My eyes are opened to the grandeur of myself first formed, dazzling bright and dancing spirit; a time before this dancer was made man and beaten to obedience like a donkey corrected, like a donkey cowed. All become donkeys for a while, this is the way. Only now I will not be so, I will not be cowed by anyone. I will dance.

'You must let me be *Yeshua*, mother!' I say to the wind and it excites me like an unopened casket of treasure. It is as though I wake in some manner to another world. I feel the dance, a true image of myself – a spilling, laughing spirit, anger cast aside. And the rocks sing and the stones smile and the wasteland laughs, for the arching sun demands it. I feel I can move mountains, when two become one in my heart; when all is one, and no longer two. I feel that I reign over all, as some delighted king, I have such strength. And that I come from such light.

'Is he dead?'

There are men around me; I sense them slowly and these are not traders. I find myself on the ground, staring at the sky, though my eyes too salty to see. I stay still for a moment and push the light away, as if a mere dream and no use for now. "It's no use dreaming," as my mother said, and she is right. I am not a dreamer; that has never been allowed. Though what is to be done when the light spills through the caverns inside? I cannot pretend it unseen.

A voice: 'If he's not dead yet, he soon will be ... snake food, this one.'

Another voice: 'Probably a Roman stooge who lost his way ... and on his way to hell.'

'Or crazed.'

'He's a stooge. We kill him.'

The voices are harsh. I am minded at first to give the appearance of death, like a beetle biding its time. But not wishing my body to be tested by a spear, my second thought, I declare life.

'I am not dead,' I say, sitting up. 'Nor a stooge for anyone.' Slowly I stand, holding my hands away from my body, not wishing to threaten; though how I could threaten this knife-ridden band, I do not know. Their blades chime and clatter in the breeze.

'He rises!' They step back a little and one pushes a knife towards me. It catches the sun and glints. I see six or seven men, hardened by sun, purged by discomfort.

'But I *am* thirsty,' I say. I have woken with a terrible thirst which overrides my fear. I know who they are, they do not need to announce themselves; these are zealots. If they are not traders for Jerusalem, using the short route from the east, then they are zealots who chatter and conspire here safe from Roman reach. All know this; even the Romans know this, but mostly do nothing. In Nazareth, they speak in hushed tones of those who "go to the hills", for the Romans do not come this way, which leaves the zealots smug. "No wine, no baths and absolutely *no* chance of a straight road – we're safe from the Romans in the wilderness!" Instead, there is just dry grass, the rumour of Satan and desperate men sewing seeds for a harvest of overthrow and revolt. All of Galilee knows what the zealots want and what they do.

'We want Yahweh's rule – but Yahweh needs help.' And they help themselves with knives placed in Roman necks, above the armour and pushed hard down. I made furniture for this sort in Nazareth, because whenever the revolution comes, everyone will still need a table; and they were decent folk, decent enough – unless you were Phoenician, of course; but then no one had much time for them. Yahweh is an Israelite who does not want visitors, Roman or otherwise. And so here they are, planning the downfall of everyone: the downfall of the Romans, the downfall of Herod, the downfall of the bastard Caiaphas and his Saducee collaborators; and possibly, the downfall of me, now they no longer need a table.

'What are you doing here?' they ask. I need a reason. My mother imagined this to be the cause of my leaving, that I had chosen the zealot way. I called Herod a fox, and such like, for how could I not? But she did not take it well.

'Zealots get crucified,' she warned. 'That's what happens to them Don't think I haven't heard.'

'Mother, Herod *is* a fox,' I say. 'Only a fool would disagree; or someone with an eye to his reputation. Herod skulks around power and feeds off weakness. He is a fox.'

'He is a *Jew!*' She speaks as if the matter is thus closed.

'A Jewish fox, yes.'

She seems to forget the town-talk of Herod. She forgets how he banished his own wife, in exchange for his brother's wife, Herodias. She forgets this is forbidden in Jewish law – when most days of the week, she rather *likes* the law. But she passes by such talk; she calls it 'gossip – *gossip, gossip, gossip!* And I want no part of it!'

She is right. It *is* the gossip around every well in the land, where women like to talk.

'And I hear it was Herodias told him to do it!' they say, in half-admiring tones. A woman with a nose ring and a toe ring who also gets her way? One should not approve, so callous an act, they tut and tut, knowing it wrong … yet something appeals. Herodias is not without her admirers.

'She tells Herod what to do, that one.'

'Really?'

'It's what I hear.'

'Regular old Jezebel!'

'Strong woman, though!'

I remind my mother this same man killed our cousin John the Baptiser – for here is everything needed for offence and upset, surely; the matter as clear as day. 'He killed our cousin!'

'He was a sort-of cousin,' she says primly and then leaves the room and finds herself a job which others have failed to see needs doing. People hear only what serves them, I learn this young. They follow one god in the morning and another in the evening, if it suits. And John's bloodied head does not suit my mother today.

'Perhaps the Baptiser gave him no choice!' she says later. She has been thinking. 'He was hardly a man who spoke sweetly to people,' she adds. 'Not a way to make friends, all that shouting and condemnation. I mean, what did he expect?'

The wilderness does this to a soul, and John was no different. The wilderness does not breed gentle words; and he will not have been quiet in his cell when caught. Yet is not the Baptiser reckoned a good man by our people? Is he not thought a hero? She used to be pleased he was a relation; but maybe I spoke of him with too much awe. Praising another can turn folk away; they in themselves feel diminished. And today, she blames him for everything, as if he is the cause of all trouble in the land.

'So which part of Herod do you admire, mother?' I ask this, though she has no time to answer, with a home to keep and things to do. In Nazareth, I learn that a bad Jew is better than a good Roman.

'And they don't take the bodies down,' adds James, obvious in his intentions; he tries to burden me with fear. The crucified are left to hang, he explains when this I already know. Who does not know this? Who has not seen their bodies, sagging and dry?

'And why *would* the Romans take them down?' I reply. I fight back, I try to sound careless. 'Why would they bother? What's dead is dead. Truly, James, it's not the dead who need saving, but the living. Let the dead bury themselves.'

'Let the dead bury themselves?' My mother arrives in the room aghast, her shoulders tense. She does not like these words, they upset her further; though upset is not my aim. I wish for a peaceable life, but find that when I speak, storm clouds form and war awaits me.

'I sometimes feel stronger than death!' I once said this – no dream, but a sense. I spoke it to James, in a corner, away from the others. It was almost whispered – yet James was public in his response, drawing others in. 'You? Stronger than death, Yeshua? Is this what you really imagine? Every martyr imagines such strength – and each one of them rots. Perhaps you imagine you're better than us.'

'My strength, James, is to know that I am not; and do not need to be.' James screws up his face but makes no reply; he just thinks I am trying to be clever, and maybe I am. And later, as I prepare wood for the following day, rubbing it down and marking for nails, he says, 'Do you *have* to upset mother?'

'Does she have to *be* upset?' I look him in the eye. 'I cannot take the offence of another on my shoulders, or truly, I am crushed before the cock crows.'

'She says you disappoint her.'

I left soon after, on the second day of the week, unsure but whole-hearted, walking hard and following the goats where necessary. In my mind, is the memory of my mother's parting face, all brave for the storm ahead, with loyal James at her side. And I melt a little with absence; my feelings calm, though not much. She keeps her secrets, my mother, as if behind a wall, as if behind a shell. We are not told what lies there, as if she fears blame for all she thinks and knows.

'Not an easy birth,' said Devira, as if letting out a secret.

'Is any birth easy?'

She is a family friend, long-standing. 'There was trouble ... trouble with the neighbours,' she says. But if there was, my mother will not speak of it. And the further I walk, the more I see a woman upon whom blows have fallen. I sense the terror in her hollow eyes; heavy blows must have fallen, though she cannot speak of these things. She appears as a prisoner, separate from me, behind her bars; but quite unable to leave.

'Your mother was a lioness,' says Devira and I know her intent. It is praise of another, spoken as a judgement on me. My mother is raised and I am lowered. Praise the parent to kill the child. 'A lioness for *you*!' She says it again and this may have been so, I can imagine her strong in the fight – though Devira does not name the battle. And my ingratitude shocks her.

'Have you forgotten that your father is gone and your mother left alone?'

Though she was no different while he lived; I do not say this, but it was so. My mother has always lived behind a wall. And now she wishes for grand children, reputation and quiet old age – and I must bring her sorrow in every way. It is the last thing I wish for her; yet the only thing I do.

'Do not be afraid,' I say to her as I leave. 'Do not be afraid, mother. There is no manner of harm for you in this world. Trust the path given you; as I will trust mine.'

Now she kneels, wet-eyed, and looks up at me. 'My son, my son – why must you abandon me?'

YESHUA

Am I a zealot?

'Have you been to Jerusalem?' The zealot leader is stone-eyed as he asks. First the traders, and now the zealots; everyone wants to know if I've been to Jerusalem. Is it the only conversation in Israel? Is Jerusalem all we have to talk about? If it is, I am destined for discomfort, for mention of the city brings heaviness rather than wonder.

'I have,' I say. 'Briefly.' Perhaps now we can move on; or better still, they could let me go. I am glad of the fire tonight but little else; I am a captive not a guest, while they curse and dispute among themselves, as men must do. The flames crackle and snap beneath a black sky, the stars like precious stones. And they are a better theme than Jerusalem, so let us break ranks and talk about the stars, for ever since I was young, I have felt applauded by them; indeed, they were often my only applause at home ... though tonight they seem quiet. I have arrived here by blindfold, the zealot haunt, pushed and harried up a steep climb, along winding and narrow paths.

'Don't want to give a map to the Roman stooge, do we? Who knows what he'll do with it?' I remind them I am not a stooge, in case they have forgotten or misheard me earlier. I expect a nudge into the ravine at any moment.

'So you come to join us?' says stone-eyes. 'Or else what are you doing here?'

I do not come to join them – or do I? I had not imagined joining them. Nothing could have been less my intention when I set off from Nazareth in determined escape. I did not walk as I did to join *in* anything; but to *leave* everything. I did not say goodbye to one odd family to say hello to another – and whose welcome has been short on charm. But what can we say? And is this how things work? Perhaps this is answered prayer. You start walking and see what happens. There is a sense to that. So is my light, in fact, to shine as a zealot, is that why I am here? Is this the strange work of my father in heaven? Are these people the home I seek? They are dangerous friends, who speak warmly of killing. But do they kill well, do they kill for Yahweh, are they good killers, showing me the way?

'Anyone who does not hate his father and mother, his wife and his children – anyone who does not do these things, cannot be as us.' The leader speaks to me as a recruit, and I understand his meaning. How else can a man proceed in brave struggle unless all else is counted as nothing? But I now think of Old Samuel and a wave of fear washes through me. My fireside captors will swoon at his memory, and hear no bad word about him. This is not the place to question the man. Though as a child, and probably ever since, I have always thought him mad. Even in Nazareth today, some call Old Samuel a hero and we grew up with him as our bedtime story: 'Now Old Samuel, he was a true Israelite!' they would say, before leaving me to sleep. But I went to sleep hoping only that I would never be so mad.

The story of Old Samuel came from the time of Herod the Great – father of the present wretch. His soldiers were chasing the Jewish rebels, who hid in the caves of Arbela, where perhaps I now sit. The soldiers could not win from below, but they could from above, lowered by ropes down the rock face in baskets. With fire and sword they entered the caves and subdued those hiding there with terrible massacre. But Herod, according to legend, wished to save some, feeling some guilt as a Jew for this massacre of Jews. So he offered free passage to those still alive; he offered pardon to those who remained.

At first, no one volunteered to come out of the caves; they preferred death to surrender to the filthy Roman collaborator who was Herod. But among the remaining fighters was Old Samuel, who had seven sons. With the offer of pardon, his wife and sons now asked to be allowed to leave; they wished to live another day. They begged on their knees that he allow it. Old Samuel arose and stood at the entrance of the cave. He then invited each of them out to the ledge. When they appeared in the cave entrance, one by one, he threw each of his sons down screaming into the ravine. Herod shouted for him to stop, but he could not stop and he would not stop. Each traitorous son was thrown to his death in the abyss. And when his wife of twenty three years appeared, begging him for mercy, she was sent the same way, tossed firmly over the cliff, spiralling down – before Old Samuel joined them, leaping down himself towards the corpses of his family, shouting 'No king but God!'

'And so it was that Old Samuel's body joined those of his dear family, nobly smashed and broken on the rocks beneath the caves of Arbela, a hero for us all. Now sleep well, my children, sleep well.'

But now, beneath the wilderness sky, the lullaby is real and the leader speaks.

'Jerusalem is where we must strike and Passover is best, the most crowded time. It's chaos. You could come with us, Yeshua.'

'I could,' I say. But Old Samuel has reminded me that I am not a zealot. This chance encounter in the hills is not surprising guidance or answered prayer; and I have no wish to go with them. But neither do I wish to join the ghost of Old Samuel and his family in the ravine. I answer with care, wise as a serpent, innocent as a dove. 'You think a furniture maker would help? Is the revolt short of chairs?'

A sly smile. 'A furniture maker who is good with a knife might serve. You must be good with a knife, Yeshua – strong hands!'

I do have strong hands and a good eye for a nail, hit hard and true. But I had been to Jerusalem as a child and hold no wish to return; once was enough. I remember only the crowds, the noise, the soldiers, the blood, the smell, the animals, the heat ... and the danger. I remember the danger, I still feel it – especially the Temple, a dark memory and unclear now ... though I recall the size of the pillars and the eyes, childish memories but vivid – the hard eyes of the sellers; the cold eyes of Temple aristocracy; the desperate eyes of pilgrims, stooped by fear, hardened by poverty. There was no sign of the holy there and no place for children like me. 'Clear the children!' they would shout. 'Clear the children!' I found it hard to breathe the stale air in Jerusalem; and I believe I was ill on my return, with headaches and nightmares.

'The place was not good for me,' I say. Let this be the end of all talk of Jerusalem. I will not return. 'And the dust, of course,' I add. 'The dust was not good for me. Terrible dust.'

'It's not good for any of us, the dust; chokes all it touches; and smells more Roman with each day that passes.'

'Forever a Galilean, me. Sea air.'

My mother looked frightened in Jerusalem; such is the memory in my body. I remember again the fear. This is our holy city, she said; but held my arm, and held it firm, fearful of losing me. I can still feel the grip. Yet what has the holy to do with fear? This was my thought even then – for holy is a homecoming surely, not terror or panic? And if the Temple is our father's house, it should be the kindest place on earth, surely? Yet there was no homecoming or kindness in those streets, not in my memory. I was the wandering sort, she was right enough about that; so she was wise to hold my arm. But I feel her fingers still; feel her fear – here by the fire, here beneath the wilderness stars, I feel her fingers clutching me. And I was glad we did not go back; nor do I wish to return there in the company of these desperate men.

'So tell me, Yeshua, what is it exactly you are you doing in the wilderness?' The same old question and the question is a threat. I must have good reason; without good reason I am dead. These are black and white times, every village a divide. If I am not with them, I am against them, no space between, no threshold for the unsure. So what is my reason? 'Who are you?'

'I am Yeshua'

'So you say.'

'From Nazareth.'

'*Hah!* Nazareth?!' There is more juice in this joke and he looks around for support. 'Nothing much good comes out of there! It's a piss-hole for Phoenicians these days.'

I'm sure there are bad Phoenicians, though I've never met one.

'And all nations need a piss-hole, surely?' I attempt cheerfulness. 'I have not noticed Jews to be exempt.' I say this as one of them relieves himself into the fire, with hiss and steam. But they do not like my words, so let me move on. 'And I am the son of Joseph, now deceased.'

'So are you a spy, Yeshua?' Snarling faces surround me in the firelight.

'No. As I say, I am from Naz -'

'For Herod or Pilate? Which do you serve?'

'I serve neither the fox nor the eel. I seek only the silence here.'

And this is true, I do seek the silence, but they do not believe it an answer. Who seeks the silence? Their faces curdle. I do not wholly believe in it either. Truly, I do not know why I am here. I am here because I am here, because I had to leave, because I followed the goats, because I walked and walked and walked, because John beckoned, because my father in heaven brought me. But what sort of answer is that when knives twitch and hate schemes?

'Are you an Essene who's got lost?' The question is full of disdain.

'No.'

'The Essenes are soft heads ... collaborators.'

He spits the words as the wind gusts and some logs on the fire tumble. But I am not an Essene – the Essenes are for closing up when I wish to open. They are for separation when nothing is separate. They are for retreat from the world when I fear I must take it on.

'They seal themselves in,' I say, 'with special belief and place. They have short tables for the elect and high walls for protection. But for myself, I wish for long tables around which the poor can gather, and as for walls – no walls at all! How can the people of Yahweh build walls?'

They are not interested and talk among themselves. I am not as them, this is clear beneath the stars. I do not mention this to my companions; but I am simply not as these people sharing the fire with me tonight – for the zealots are just another tribe, caught up in their fight, mistaking hate for hope. A tribe can only hear themselves; they can never hear the truth.

'Is it their peace you fear?' I ask. Let us talk of the Essenes rather than me.

'No, it's their loin cloths!' There is laughter. 'I couldn't be doing with one of them wrapped around my parts!'

Oh, the laughter. 'There isn't enough cloth in Judaea for mine!' More laughter and a small but friendly fight breaks out.

Essenes are widely mocked for their underwear, which rumour says they wear tight around themselves. I do not know. But other Jews, and I include myself among them, see no purpose in such a garment. 'The cock needs to breathe!' adds another.

'And so does your arse!'

These men have been too long from the company of women; and though I smile along, these are not men of the light. Their leader, however, he is not interested in cock and arse and returns us to talk of peace.

'Their *peace*, Yeshua? You like their peace? The essenes sit in the lap of Rome, intent only on themselves! Believe me, they cause Rome no alarm. I do not call their collusion with our invaders "peace".' He spits the word.

'And likewise, I do not name your violence change.' I speak without thinking and then wonder if this is the last thing I will ever say? He is now in my face, holding my neck with rough hands. He has murder in his eyes.

'Pilate killed worshippers while they offered sacrifices at the great High Altar! Did you know that? Of course you know that! Even a bloody Nazarene must know that! Israelites killed by foreign troops! The most sacred moment, in the most sacred place! What do you say to that, Peacemaker? How long can you avert your Roman eyes?'

He pushes me harshly from my rock and I fall. But my nous speaks for me as I get up; I will not be pushed down.

'They sin, you sin – so where to start?' Even the fire seems troubled by my reply; it splutters and pops a little. But I cannot quieten; words arise in me. 'Do we start with them or ourselves? You must choose. Though I say to you "Repent". Here is your first calling.'

'*Repent?!*' The leader can barely speak with shock. 'The children of Israel are to repent when Rome beats us down?! Well, truly we have discovered an idiot in the wilderness today! Yeshua the Idiot! He wants change and peace all at the same time! He suggests a nice word in Pilate's ear after which Rome decides to pack up and go home – oh, and they leave a shekel and a kiss beneath every child's pillow!' They laugh nervously. 'We cannot have change through peace, my friend!'

'But peace *is* change.' Are they stupid? 'Is this not so? I mean true peace, when the heart is no longer divided, *this* is change. Whereas violence in thought, word or deed – this is no change at all. It is what the Romans do, and if we are so like the Romans – if we are such clear echoes of our oppressors – then why do we not order togas all round, build our own straight roads and worship the emperor?'

'Because we are God's chosen ones!'

'But chosen for what? Chosen for violence? If so, we are no light to the nations, this is for sure. And if not light ... '

'We are God's people!' His face is in my face again. 'No Pilate! No king! No emperor! No Temple priests! No king but God!' Others echo his words in mumbles, as though a prayer, "No king but God! No king but God"'

'Amen,' I say, 'amen, I agree,' and he pulls back. He changes tone; he does not now spit in my face. But I need to understand, he says. I need to understand the times; to understand that soon the Roman scum will stop being called "filth" and "oppressors"; that soon Judaea will get used to them, 'soon they shall become familiar as family,' he says, 'and they'll be named our best friends – "our kind benefactors from Rome! Benefactors of the people! Look what they give us!" People will say these things, Yeshua, as the pagan coins arrive with their effigies of Tiberius – they'll be all over the place; they'll be in Jerusalem. And what then? We'll disappear, that's what! We'll be *finished!* For what then will separate the Jews from any other people?' He hardens again, shouting. 'We'll be the same as them, no different at all ... just another conquest, swallowed up and shat out! No king but God!'

'No king but God,' they murmur.

'Herod is a Jew,' I say. 'He is as Jewish as Moses ... yet worse than them all.' His face is in mine again, his eyes alive, his voice dripping with disdain.

'The Romans *allow* him, they use him and his family; they are not true Jews! The Herodians are their Jewish monkeys, imperial tools, always have been.' A pause. 'And so are you, it seems. Well, are you?'

'No. Believe me, I am no Roman tool, I think I make that clear. Did I not make that clear?' I look around. They stare. 'I am not as you, of course; I am not as brave. But I am no Roman tool; they will make nothing with me. And they will not like me much, as you will see, should you allow me to continue my journey. I do not care for those in power, they perform poorly, I find. Whatever they were before, they become liars in power, it is always so. I am a tool of the light – but not a tool of the Romans.'

'You're certainly a tool!' says one, which they all enjoy. 'Pilate will just love you and your "light", make no mistake. You'll do his work – if we let you live.'

Dread invades me, a seeping darkness of spirit. But I speak as I must, for my words count; this is a feeling I grow into. These words of mine have force and truth; I notice this in the wilderness beneath the applauding stars – the belief I have words that count, my knowing, my nous quite free, though my hands are tied. And the eyes of these men, I watch their eyes – they kill me without knives. And a quieter tongue would help, as my mother might say. 'A quieter tongue would help, Yeshua!' And

I do not wish to die. I have seen the light from where I came and I have just begun, surely? I do not know what I have begun. But I know I wish my people better – I know this beneath the stars. I wish my people lives without care and worry, the lives of free men and women, for the birds of the air do not worry, nor the growing grass, so why must they?

And here by the fire, amid the hate, love quite overwhelms me – yes, even for wretched Nazareth! I think of its people making do and getting on, when life breaks them at every step, contorting their minds. The flowers in the field are a wonder – more wondrous than King Solomon in all his pomp! Yet how much more valuable than the flowers, are these people to my father in heaven? Is this not so? And I smile at my captors, each a bag of rage, and I dance a little inside, as though their knives cannot pierce me. The rich and religious – they throttle my people, I see this. But I will ease these harsh hands from my people's throats and make them blessed. I shall return their lives to them and say, 'See, your life returned to you!' ... should present company allow.

In truth, these folk I sit with, they are not much liked; not really. No one loves the zealots in Nazareth, for as the traders say, they cause trouble for the town, bringing Romans and fear. Folk must be careful how they speak, of course. They do not wish to make enemies of the men with knives; but they mutter anyway.

'They go too far,' some say quietly, looking around. 'I mean, who likes Rome? No one likes Rome. But they go too far, them ones. The Sicarii – they kill women and children, some say it. Everyone knows of Ein Gedi and the things done there.'

And Benjamin said the same when I gave him his chairs. 'They're mad, those zealot ones – I'm saying nothing more, nothing more. And did you hear, Yeshua?'

'Hear what?'

'The Yehuda boy has joined them. He's only gone and joined the zealots! Never would have thought that, not the Yehuda boy.' He shakes his head. 'Always a decent enough lad, kept himself to himself. But it's always the quiet ones, eh?'

'His family starved, Benjamin.' I remind him of this, it seems important. 'Yehuda's family were hungry; they starved. That is why he left for the caves. And who made them hungry?'

'I'm not saying they're not brave, Yeshua.'

'The Romans made him hungry and in debt. They are good at that, the Romans.'

'And maybe they are brave, Yeshua, some call them brave; and I'm not saying there's no cause – but they've gone too far. You can't blame the Romans for everything. And what are his parents doing?'

'Presently, too hungry to go looking for him ... perhaps a meal will sort them out.'

And perhaps Yehuda is with me here in the wilderness, as they 'go too far'. Perhaps it was he who pissed on the fire. And will they now go too far with me? I watch their hands. Their hands tell me where the knives are hid, and my neck waits, as soft as fish scale.

'Into your hands, I commit my spirit,' I say to myself, for I see the leader move. Is he my assassin? Am I to be gutted to encourage the others? He takes my arm, lifts me up and stares into my eyes. He wonders. He wonders if I am worth saving. He looks in my eyes for the traitor. Can he see there a traitor?

'Do we let him go?' he asks of his people – and then laughs. I assume my death, but once again, I am blindfold from behind, taken slowly down the mountain, led roughly by hand. I remember the slopes, dust and stones in my sandals, less safe than ever. The fear of the knife in my side, this is constant. I believe they will kill me, to be left by the road, a message, with the mule, to others who come this way. Then I am being lowered down into one of the cracks in the rock, I feel its edge, then falling, dropping without sight, for there is no sight in the harsh grip of the blindfold.

'Stay there!' they hiss from above, as if I have choice.

I feel the cool of the night shadows around me. I lie still on the damp rock, breathing relief. But I cannot stay here, for who knows what's here with me? I listen to them leave, voices disappearing and silence returns ... the scream of a desert fox. I struggle to release my hands from the rope, scraping my wrists on the rock, contorting my arms and finally free, I pick at the blindfold, tight as a fisherman's knot. It takes a while to escape, my hands weary and slow; but my head breathes again. And when I emerge beneath the stars, climbing up and out, they are gone. I never knew my captor's name. I had told him mine, but he did not tell me his; though I believe another bandit called him "Barabbas".

MIRIAM

My family

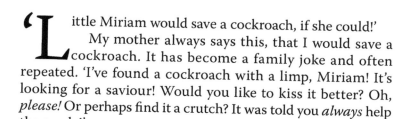

'Little Miriam would save a cockroach, if she could!'

My mother always says this, that I would save a cockroach. It has become a family joke and often repeated. 'I've found a cockroach with a limp, Miriam! It's looking for a saviour! Would you like to kiss it better? Oh, *please!* Or perhaps find it a crutch? It was told you *always* help the needy!'

I don't know why they joke as they do. It is a kind thing to do, surely – to save something? But when in their mouths, it is somehow not kind at all but stupid and cause for mockery. They make me a fool and a reason for scorn and laughter – as if I do not understand the world as others do; as if I am not quite grown up. *Really?* Then maybe I don't wish to be grown up; maybe I don't. Is it only children who can love and save, while adults must become dry and careless?

They don't understand me, but will you? I offer my story and maybe you too will mock. I write in hope you will not; in the hope you will understand, though I scarce understand it myself. How can this story be believed, yet alone understood? But at least come with me to its start, to my home town of Magdala by blue Galilee, though sometimes brown in the storms and rough as a drunkard's temper. Magdala is a town full of fish. My father is away selling melons, because he's always away and always selling, and 'melons travel better than fish,' he says. My two sisters and I are probably falling out, or not talking, and my mother, with her sharp tongue, is making comment about marriage. With three daughters, she thinks about marriage a great deal.

'To catch Miriam a husband, we need find a man who can pin down a swift!' She says this when they speak of my future. Swifts are always flying and difficult to net and she thinks the same of me, as if to fly is a crime. And who wishes to be netted or pinned down anyway? I do not wish this, not at all – though my sister Judith thinks differently. She would not call marriage a net, she would call it 'duty'; and it's a net she wants – she never wants to fly, but merely do her duty. 'And I would feel guilty if I left mother,' she says, heavily. 'One has a duty, Miriam.' Judith says she must stay with mother, and this is great comfort to her, to have a child who will stay. 'You can always rely on Judith,' she says, as if she cannot rely on me. And perhaps she speaks the truth? Perhaps I am like the swift and keep flying because there is nowhere here to land.

My other sister is Berenica, and she'll soon be gone; and when she does go, believe me, she'll feel no guilt; none at all! She is impossible; she will never obey – 'to obey is to die!' she whispered to me once – and she resists our parents endlessly. She may say 'Yes' to ease the path and disappear from view; but her actions will be 'No'. My mother says, 'You are quite impossible!' And our neighbours have no advice to give other than a firm hand. Berenica says she will live in Caesarea, that there is nothing but a dull husband and the smell of fish in Magdala. But good girl Judith will stay, she will do the decent thing ... this is what I see.

'Judith will look after me,' says my mother. 'Berenica's too stubborn and Miriam too worrying. I can't be doing with your worrying, Miriam.'

And I cannot be doing with it either. Who chooses worry for themselves? So I sweep the floor and wash the mat and bake the bread and clean chicken dung from the guest room, where they are also guests – and my mother is happy. Or rather, she isn't happy, but I do try and please her. I try and please everyone! Judith tells me not to get anxious. She says it is stupid and selfish to worry – 'What is gained by your worry, Miriam?' And I believe her, of course, for it *is* stupid and selfish, with nothing changed and nothing gained ... though I am not calmed by such advice, but made more anxious still. I am now anxious that they will see me anxious. Dutiful Judith also reminds me that, like her, I am to honour my father and mother; and this I try and do and will always try and do, though I feel outside this circle. Can one say this? Can I say that I feel an outsider in my own family? I am not able to speak of this, it wouldn't be right. And who would I tell? But truly, I do not know them, or only in passing, I sometimes I feel this. I am a stranger at home. Yet how is this so? How can I not know my mother and my father? And how can I not know my sisters?

I sometimes think my mother did not want children, but Berenica laughs and says I am too much in my thoughts, which is true, for they keep me safe from my feelings.

YESHUA

Am I a Pharisee?

I am not a zealot; time spent in their dismal company proved this. So am I a Pharisee?

I would like it so. It would help me greatly; give me company, at least, for my friends are Pharisees – or those who *were* my friends ... friends come and apparently go. I walk hard and fast away from them now and put distance between myself and Zebedee's boys; but it was not always so. We were close and earnest when young, believing we would mend the world. We met weekly in Nazareth; both I and my brother James would attend. And no doubt he still does, enjoying Zebedee's soup and rolls, while I climb dry rocks, with bleeding feet and a dry throat.

The meetings taught me much ... for a while, at least. Indeed, they taught me all I knew, until the day I knew more. And no one liked that day and there was trouble.

We would meet by candle light when our work was done and our tools laid down. We tugged at our young beards and posed questions of the law, that we might live it better. "To live the law is to live Yahweh. Halleluiah! Halleluiah!" So old Zebedee would say. We asked questions and debated with intent. We would say "How should we fast?" And "How should we pray?" Or we would say, "Should my neighbour be helped on the Sabbath? And should a fire be lit on the Sabbath to save a life?" Another week we might ask "How should we give alms and to who?" Or, "What rules of diet should we follow?" Or, "How shall we know the messiah when he comes?"

Each week we would debate, and I thought I enjoyed such things; yet each week I would leave the meeting angry. I did not notice my anger until James, on our way home, insisted I put on a better face to the world.

'Lose the attitude, Yeshua. It's embarrassing and does not glorify Yahweh.'

'What attitude?' I asked. 'Am I not allowed some silence, James? Perhaps I just wish to be quiet?' But I did not know myself then. I could not see my rage; but James, though blind to himself, saw me well.

'When you are quiet, you rage,' he said. 'I can feel it, Yeshua. Everyone can feel it. Mother can feel it. But why is it so? Why do you always rage, Yeshua, when we study Yahweh's law? Surely it should be a delight to us, a sweet fragrance?' This is definitely a borrowed line and sounds odd in his mouth. 'Yet every week it is so, Yeshua! You leave the group in a rage; I do not understand. And it's embarrassing.' That may have been the most pressing issue, James embarrassed by his older brother, but I did not reply, I could not speak; for beyond my surprise was dread. What or who had I become if I raged at God's law? There must be a special place in hell for people such as me, as one or two had suggested. Yet in the secret place, curtained from the world, discomfort grew until one day, towards the end of the gathering, it took me over, I suppose; anger can do this. It can take you over. And with the candles sputtering, I say to everyone, 'We must stop lying,' because I can say nothing else – and this is the beginning of the end. 'We must all stop lying,' I repeat. They look at me oddly; and none more so than James. Yes, he is deeply embarrassed for his older brother and for himself. But I cannot help speaking and I say, 'Stop lying

– and do not do that which is against love. Is there anything else for the law to say? *Really?* I weary of our debates, my friends, when that is all there is.'

There is silence in the group, though my heart beats loud and hard. It is like I have spoken for the first time in my life, and I wonder if the sky will fall on our heads. I think it will. Then Zebedee speaks, old and kind, but he does like us to agree. So he speaks gently and firmly, as if to a child.

'We are children of the law, Yeshua, so there is *much* else to say.' The others nod; they are glad he speaks in this way, and I quickly feel alone in the circle. I sense a line crossed, and no way back. He continues. 'Yahweh *is* the law, Yeshua. Yes?' He smiles and the smile is the end of my childhood, for the smile casts me out – it is a terror. 'The law is Yahweh among us; the law is the kindness of Yahweh on earth.' He speaks patiently, and continues to smile, but his smile does not laugh; his smile is a rage. He speaks as if all is quite obvious and patience will make it more so. 'If you undo the law, you undo kindness ... and dear Yeshua, you thereby undo Yahweh, the great "I am".'

My breathing is uncertain, like water roughed in the wind. I do not see this kindness of which he speaks; not at all. Rather, I see a weight, a burden ... I see many burdens which people suffer under. It is simple and clear: I now have nothing in common with Zebedee, who, at the candle's beginning this evening, had been my leader. He is not my leader now.

I ask: 'Would not Yahweh wish us to help our neighbour on the Sabbath? Or does he prefer our neighbour to suffer?'

Zebedee smiles again; more rage.

'Some things must be, Yeshua. Some things must be to honour the glory of Yahweh. If we suffer beneath the law, we suffer for his glory – for the law is his glory, is it not?' My friends nod again. They are shamed by me, for Zebedee is not so young and he has done much for us and should be respected. Does he not give us bread and soup every week and does he not give generously to the poor? Is this how I repay such generosity? He continues.

'Is not the law the very *shekinah* of Yahweh on earth, his truest manifestation? And was not the law given to Israel on

Sinai? Yet you, young Yeshua, suggest we now *return* it to him, declaring we have no use for it?!' His voice rises.

I sweat. This is not why I came here; but here we are, and as he pushes me, new words arise.

'I remember ten given,' I say. 'Ten commandments were given in Sinai. Yet we have made ten into six hundred and more. The law breeds well in our hands and now has many bastards.' I look around; I do not win friends. James is aghast.

'The six hundred arise to *protect* the ten – hardly bastards,' says Zebedee, ignoring the shock in the room. 'Or how would the ten survive? As each of us wears an inner garment and an outer garment – the inner garment needing the outer garment, and the outer garment needing the inner garment – so it is with the law. So each is a blessing; each new law an outer garment that protects the ten, like kind armour.'

'If the six hundred laws are armour, they are heavy armour, and not kind – too heavy for the poor to carry.' I feel spite around me, though I continue, I cannot do otherwise. 'The Romans may break us with tax, but we break ourselves with rules – and that must not be *our* way, surely? We are to be a light to the nations – not a prison. Yet we give to the people one law after another, one law on top of another, piled high like heavy stones. And the stones crush us! One law breeds five further laws, and each of those has a child! And our people? They stumble under the weight!'

'No, they are *disciplined* under the weight, Yeshua – disciplined, like wild horses are disciplined, so they may joyfully serve.' Zebedee spits his words; he is sitting forward, his mask has slipped. 'Without discipline, the people die.'

'But surely the Sabbath is made for man and not man for the Sabbath?'

'What! You must be careful, Yeshua, those words are not well-chosen. I believe you blaspheme in my home.'

But I cannot be careful or choose my words. And does not his home deserve the truth? 'It is given as a gift, a day of rest – but becomes for us a difficulty and a punishment, like an over-bearing master. Old Sara was left in the street last week, where she fell. She suffered greatly.'

'Old Sara or not, our respect for the Sabbath cannot be occasional, Yeshua!' It is now Eleazar who speaks, my old friend. 'Old Sara knows that well, she is a true Hebrew. She lay quietly, I'm told, and recovered to an extent – and no doubt praised Yahweh for his mercy.'

'The praise was muted, I believe.'

'But amplified by the angels, I am sure, who sing around the throne. For the Sabbath is not a choice. It cannot be something observed if we so choose that morning to do so! "Perhaps I'll not keep the Sabbath *this* week – but next week, maybe, next week!"' There is laughter. 'Do you hear yourself, Yeshua?'

I have known Eleazar awhile. In our younger days, we both enjoyed wine and the households that offered it, and sometimes we would take James as penance. But then the two of them stopped, and drank from the law instead – while I carried on with the wine. After that, they both rather closed against me, with James in Eleazar's thrall. And now he basks in wise triumph and sits down admired by his peers. Zebedee speaks again.

'Yeshua is a clever young man, everyone tells me so; I am always told how bright he is. "Such a clever young man, Yeshua!" they say.'

'Though a wine-bibber,' says Eleazar but Zebedee hushes him.

'And he *is* a clever young man but thoughtless tonight, my friends; careless with his words and the Law. I truly believe he would have us all as the gentiles! And what then of our faith?'

'Nazareth doesn't want faith,' I say, indicating the town around me. 'You imagine this place wants faith? It just wants its own sort. Well, doesn't it?' I look around, seeking their eyes. 'Listen to our people; listen to them talk. They want their town back and their land back; they want it reclaimed from the gentiles, intruders from Zarapheth and Damascus who have moved into Galilee, who have taken the jobs in Bethsaida and now threaten us here, as if they are demons. That is their word – "demons". Yet in our history, is not the stranger set *above* our neighbour? Well, isn't it? So what faith exists in Nazareth?'

Zebedee struggles to calm himself. 'But what is faith, Yeshua, if not to keep oneself pure in origin? Here is godly faith surely

– purity! We are not as other peoples – this, at least, is true in what you say! Purity is our light! So how could we wish such people among us? For where then is our purity?'

I breathe and I stand. 'You are white-washed tombs, all of you – pure outside and dead within! This is not faith in God. This is a wrecking of faith, a contortion. I tell you, a Phoenician widow knows more of faith than you!'

'A Phoenician widow?' Now Eleazar speaks again, incredulous and drawing laughter. He is excited by the contest, as though he has been waiting some time. 'Just how do you know this, Yeshua? Do you speak with her? Rumours abound that you continue with drink and women.'

'Everyone needs tables and chairs, Eleazar. Even Phoenicians sit down ... even women, I'm told, on occasion.'

Zebedee again ... are they partners? Each gives the other time to sharpen their swords. He now reads from a book he holds. '"He that talks much with womankind brings evil upon himself and neglects the study of the law and at last will inherit Gehenna." I offer these sacred words only as a warning, Yeshua, for we do not wish you there, not at all.' He smiles at me again. 'No one wishes you in hell.'

'I will always talk with women.'

'"Do not sit down with women", it says, "for as moth comes out of clothes, so a woman's spite comes out of a woman."'

'I have found spite in men as well.'

'Oh, so we shall not listen to Ben Sira anymore? Is that your sense, Yeshua? Does wisdom grow stale like bread? Do you somehow know more than the sage, Yeshua?'

I get up to leave. 'I do not know, and I do not know and I do not know – yet still I know more than you.'

I walked home in silence and never returned to the group. I felt every word and look in my body – every sneer, chuckle and attack; as if they were arrows still lodged, arrows which needed pulling out, but that was not for now. James ran after me, I thought he might, a noisy pounding in the dark street – and Nazareth is a deep dark tonight. But I feel no alarm, and I do not turn, for I know it is him. I know his dusty steps, his heavy sandals and the chaotic heart which guides them. He catches me up breathless and I realise he has been breathless all his life. I do not speak, I have nothing to say; but he cannot manage silence.

'I cannot believe the words you spoke.' He is still in recovery; he does not like to run. 'Are you mad?'

'And are you my brother, James?' I stop for a moment, my hands on his large shoulders; I look him in the eye, though his eyes wander. 'Eleazar quotes Deutonomy at me, did you know that?' No reply. I turn and start walking again. 'Probably not, you were nodding too hard to notice, nodding like a puppet in agreement. But the wine-bibber nonsense – he quotes Deuteronomy.'

'So?' He is quite unaware as his lumbering body trots beside me. I walk and he trots. I do walk fast. 'Does Yeshua now ban holy scripture?'

'The Israelites are told what to do with a stubborn son. They are to bring the scoundrel to the elders of the town and say, "This terrible son of ours is stubborn and rebellious. He will not obey us! He is a glutton and a wine-bibber!" And the men of the town shall stone him with stones until he is dead.'

'If it is spoken in scripture ... ' He is working hard to keep up, in every way.

'It's a dangerous friend, James, who wishes your elder brother *stoned*.'

'Then perhaps my elder brother should not be a rebellious and stubborn son.'

We walk in silence. I am not a Pharisee.

YESHUA

Machaerus

I stand amazed, truly. There is nothing like this in Nazareth; perhaps nothing like this in Israel. I had heard, but I had not seen and there is both fear and awe as I behold the fortress at Machaerus.

Three ravines fall away from this monster, they plunge down into darkness, ravines as deep as hell – no enemy could take this. And how was it built? How was such a quantity of stone brought to this place? "You can only build what you can carry," my father would say; and a whole quarry has been carried here. As the rich pray, 'We give thanks for our food and our gold – but most of all, for our slaves.' Giant walls grow from the rock; high corner towers throw shadow on all who approach. Yes, the fortress of Machaerus is a beast. And inside it is Herod the Great's slippery turd of a son, Antipas.

I call him 'Herod the Great'. But Herod the Great was only great for builders. He served the stone masons well, turning Israel into Rome. He built everything – fortresses here in Machaerus and Antonia, in Jerusalem – aquaducts, theatres, whole cities – Tiberias, Caesarea, Sepphoris ... each a Little

Rome in Galilee; each an invasion, each the dilution of faith that Zebedee laments.

So he was a Herod applauded by every builder who could close his eyes and hold his well-paid nose. And good for wedding planners as well – ten wives, they say. Israel counts his wives like they count the rashes on a leper. He murdered one of them, this is known. Her name was Miriamne; though no one remembers the name. He killed her two sons as well, because power destroys the soul. "Power reveals a man," said my father, "and Herod the Great deserves another name."

The rich find happiness impossible, this is apparent to me; and maybe my father knew. They seize but cannot let go; they protect what is theirs but cannot receive life. They force others down, that they might further rise – and this is not living. I see what occurs. It would be easier to gallop a camel through the eye of a needle than for a rich man to find happiness.

But standing here now, it is the dead Baptiser who haunts me, not the dead Herod. We finally met, me and my sort-of cousin, at the Jordan river. It was hardly a family affair. He took hold of my head and pushed it deep beneath the water; too deep. And he held it down with rough hands, longer than he needed, longer than is good for a cousin. I was gasping, drowning ... and then released. I pushed up for air, choking; I came up into the sunlight with a mouth full of mud but a different heart – a heart cleansed in some manner, or refreshed, like wood stripped for purpose. And I felt the light through me, as if I was one with the light of the sun, both old light and new. And so it was that John the Baptiser, my sort-of cousin, took me out of Nazareth; though we did not speak much by the water. He pushed me away; he did not want me near.

'May God give you courage,' he said, but with such sadness in his eyes. 'I call for repentance, which disturbs. But you bring light, which the darkness will curse.'

I did not understand. I somehow imagined that light would always be welcome. Would you not think so? How could it be otherwise? Why would light not be welcomed with joyful cries and excited gasps? Let there be light! But as I see his sadness, and feel his warning again here at Machaerus – where John ended in bloody murder – so I begin. I am thirty years of age, and I begin again ... and there is energy in beginnings.

MIRIAM

The melon trade in Capernaum

My father speaks with the melon-seller across the square; they banter and curse as men do. My father says he is a rascal (in truth, he says worse, a more unpleasant word) and cannot be trusted. 'Trust in God, hard work and the Temple – and in nothing and no one else!'

I have travelled with him to Capernaum. He buys fruit from farmers and sells it for them; I don't really follow. 'Buy low, sell high, girl!' he says and I nod. He has melons in mind today – he deals mainly in melons, as I say, though he has sold dates. And fish briefly. But while he haggles and shouts, I have time to fill, so I wander across the square. I find a tree for shade in the midday sun and listen to a teacher. He sits talking in the market place, seated on a stool, his elbows on his knees – a young man amid other young men and perhaps they seek work, though all focus is on him. Are they his followers? But he is too young to have followers and quite unlike the teachers in Magdala, who are older than Moses – he of blessed memory. And so *interesting* ... and yes, I know it is not proper for a woman to listen to a teacher. So I hang back and stay on the edge, right on the edge;

were my father to look, which he won't, but if he did, I could simply be seeking the shade. And that is all I am seeking, it is no lie, when the teacher begins a story. Perhaps he starts it for me, that I might feel welcome? And I do feel welcome here and not a stranger pushed away.

'So a seeker came upon Rabbi Shammai,' he says, 'and stood on one foot.'

Some laugh a little. I think these are his friends who listen; he speaks as if to friends, though urgent. He speaks urgently. And he is definitely too young to have followers, and without sufficient beard, for as the saying goes, "The beard reveals the teacher" – though I think it a stupid saying. What does a beard tell anyone? And unlike the teachers in Magdala, he is playful with those who listen and smiles at me when I arrive, I believe so; though I'm sure he smiles at everyone; he would hardly smile only at me. And teachers should not look at women, as my mother tells me, lest they are tempted and led into sin. 'Many men are led into sin, Miriam; be not Satan's tool in leading them there.' She invents sin for me long before I get there or even think of it; she always has, as if I was born into it, and remain in the mire, with no chance of being free.

The teacher continues: 'And the man standing on one foot, he says to Rabbi Shammai, "Teach me the whole law while I stand on one foot." But when Rabbi Shammai hears this, he gets angry with the visitor and drives him away, saying he is not worthy of his time. "The whole law explained in such a short time?!" he says. "How could that be possible? Be gone with you!"

So the same man goes to Rabbi Hillel and again, he stands on one foot, and says, "Rabbi, teach me the whole law while I stand on one foot."

And Rabbi Hillel says, "What is hateful to you, do not do to your neighbour. All else is just commentary."'

'What do you think?' says the teacher, looking around intently. 'What do you think?' And no one thinks very much, until a man in the group tries to stand on one leg. He is a large man, with big hands and he sways a great deal, like rigging in a storm. (I later discover he was once a fisherman!)

41

'So teacher,' he says, 'Teach *me* the whole law while I stand on one foot.' But before the teacher can speak, he topples over onto one of his friends.

'I can see I must be quick, Rocky!' says the teacher. 'How did you ever stand up in a boat? Was Lake Galilee calmer than the market place in Capernaum?'

'The land has always moved more than the sea,' says Rocky. 'This is well known.' He then tries to stand on one foot again; he is determined. He balances briefly, his arms held out, while the ground clears around him. No one wishes for this great tree to land on them.

'Love God and love your neighbour,' says the teacher, as Rocky totters. 'These are all the commandments.' Everyone cheers, as Rocky remains standing, though he falls soon after, catching another man with his foot. 'And those who fall shall rise; and those who die to themselves shall live!' adds the teacher with triumph.

'Sorry, Jude!' says Rocky. Jude was the man he landed on. And as I watch, I like these men. The man called Jude is then telling the teacher to get up and move to the other side of the square, where more people gather, due to the melon-seller. Though if my father has success, there will soon be no melons left – he'll buy them all and double the price in Tiberias, where they pay Roman prices.

'Speak near the melon-seller,' says Jude. 'You will get a better crowd. People gather round the melon-seller. He is well known here.'

A new voice speaks up beside me: 'Menahem's better,' she says. 'He gets more of a crowd than this one.' She's an older woman, similar in age to my mother, and very small, standing with me beneath the tree. 'I've heard them all, I have. Not saying Menahem's a *better* speaker, mind. Not a better speaker. Very dull, if truth be known ... but he does get more of a crowd.' I had not noticed her, too caught up in events; but with a busy mouth, she seems glad of my company.

'Who's Menahem?' I ask.

'He's another teacher. Older, more experienced obviously. Doesn't tell stories ... teaches properly, old school. But then

Menahem – you do not know Menahem?' She's amazed I might not.

'No, I'm from Magdala.'

'Magdala?' I don't think she has heard of the place; it is not well known. I always say it's near Tiberias ... "Magdala, near Tiberias". 'Menahem has an aunt there,' she tells me.

'Magdala?'

'No, Tiberias. Or "Sodom", as she calls it. The going's on there, you wouldn't believe.'

I am not interested in Mehahem's aunt in Tiberias. And how Sodom appears here I don't know. 'You live Capernaum?' I ask, politely.

''Course I live here! Where else would I live?' I can think of one or two places but do not name them. 'And so does Menahem's mother, you see, and she has six sisters, and apart from the one in Tiberias, they all live here, with a great number of children, which always helps start a crowd. Family are good for that. Yeshua doesn't live here, you see, and that's a problem if you wish to gain a following.'

'Where does he live?'

'Yeshua? I'm told he moves around ... make of that what you will. Probably a wrong'un ... or maybe he has no family ... or maybe both. ' She doesn't sound concerned. 'Still, he's got a few friends here, which is nice for him and they seem a friendly bunch, no trouble. I don't like to see a teacher teaching to *no one*, because that's just embarrassing.'

'He's called Yeshua?'

'Who?'

'The teacher. You called him "Yeshua"'

'"Yeshua the Nazarene" someone called him, so maybe he's from there, poor sod. Nazareth!' She shakes her head. 'And if he is, I'm not surprised he left; it's a rat-pit. Hardly any Jews left in Nazareth; they say that – been taken over by them Phoenician sort.' She sighs. 'Nothing against them, but it's a shame, because this is Israel, after all. It's not their country and it never will be. And it's hard for a teacher to gain a crowd without family ... a crowd draws a crowd, makes 'em look interesting.'

And then a young lawyer approaches us. I have watched him walk across the square while the woman talks. He stands out in his clean black robe and expensive sandals, which Judith would call "a disgrace". "People shouldn't spend that sort of money on a pair of shoes." He reaches the edge of the circle and addresses Yeshua without delay. He speaks as one with the right to speak; as one who *can* speak – even if another is speaking, he will speak over them. Some are confident in this way; some expect others to listen.

'Rabbi, I see you teach wisdom,' he declares as if the rest of us aren't here.

'How would you know?' asks Yeshua. 'You have never heard me!' People laugh a little. 'I would remember one so freshly washed.'

'He'll be from the synagogue,' says the woman, as if I hadn't guessed. Of course he's from the synagogue! They check teachers, like tax collectors check my father when he travels to Judaea – with suspicion. Though I do wonder at the insult Yeshua offers the man. I don't believe you should insult people, for what does it achieve? And the lawyer blushes, surprised by the words.

'I hear *of* you, Rabbi,' he says. 'Your reputation, it travels before you, like an envoy of fine spices.'

'It is true you can smell the truth.'

'Indeed, indeed. And so I bring a question from the synagogue.' He bows in respect.

'The synagogue wants to know everything these days,' says my companion. 'They're as jumpy as shit, especially when new teachers arrive. They'll want report, and they'll ask, "How did he answer? Does he preach uprising? Which pharisaic school does he represent? Did he mention the Romans? Does he preach a messiah?"'

'A *messiah?*'

'You know Israel, my girl – everyone's asking the same question … and never more so than now, what with the Romans being here; there's a lot of talk and a lot of hope. I'd settle for a half-decent husband myself – but the messiah may well arrive first.'

'So teacher, what must we do to gain eternal life?' asks the lawyer. He seems pleased with his question and I watch. Yeshua looks at him. 'Good question, sir!' he says. 'Perhaps the best question! Perhaps the *only* question!' And then asks with a smile: 'So what is written in the law, my friend?'

'Clever, that,' says my companion. 'That's what Menahem should do. Mehahem doesn't do that and he should do.'

'Sorry?'

'Menahem always tries to answer the question and gets in a twist, goes on too long. But this one answers one question with another question, which is what clever people do.' I do not wish to speak out of turn or offend, but I do hope she shuts up. I want to listen.

'I mean, how do you understand it?' says Yeshua. 'You look like a wise man to me, as well as clean, when most of my friends here are neither! So how do you understand what is written in the law?'

Everyone looks at the lawyer, and I feel sorry for him; his face glistens with sweat. He is young and perhaps expected that he would ask the questions. And now everyone's eyes are on him, expectant. 'Well, we read in the Torah,' he says, 'that you shall love the Lord with all your heart and with all your soul and with all your strength and with all your mind.' He pauses, as if relieved to pass the test. He has obviously studied. 'Oh, and you are to love your neighbour as yourself, yes.'

Someone shouts, 'Well done that man!' and Yeshua nods.

'Well done indeed. You have answered well, my friend – very well. We are all in your debt.' The lawyer eases a little. 'You have answered right and true – and without payment. Are you sure you're a lawyer?!' There is some laughter, but the lawyer feels insulted. I know a man insulted. I have seen my father insulted; you see it in their eyes – plans for revenge taking shape. But Yeshua continues. 'So *do* these things you speak of – love, love and love again, always and every day, love God and your neighbour – and you will live!'

The lawyer nods, preparing in his mind his report to the synagogue: 'It didn't go quite as expected, I'm afraid ... ' But frustration now darkens his face; he has answered aright but is downcast; something grieves him. 'I cannot do this,' he says, choking a little. Indeed, I only just hear his words ... and everyone is silent. The market place quietens, the wind drops; the sky becomes still. Even the melon-seller stops shouting, though that may be because he has no melons.

'Is that so?' says the teacher serenely. The lawyer is like a man with a spear through his leg; suddenly pinned.

'Of course it is so!' he replies. 'For no one can do this! How is it possible? How is it possible for anyone to love, and love and love again, to love God and our neighbour, always and every day? You condemn us all!'

'But that is the law, is it not?'

The man sinks to his knees, dirtying his robes.

'You shouldn't be rude to a lawyer,' says the woman, shaking her head. 'I mean, they've studied, they have; they know things. The Nazarene thinks too much of himself, if you ask me – too young and too cocky by half. He's not a proper teacher like Menahem. Menahem would never upset a lawyer.'

'I cannot do it, teacher ... I cannot,' he says.

I so want to run forward and hug him. Not everyone likes the scribes, whose task is to study the law and interpret the law, but *not* to guide practice – it is for the Pharisees to guide practice, and you don't want to tread on their toes. But he's only young and his only crime, to spend too long inside his scrolls. And now here before us he's sad and I want to help. Yet as I begin to move, I am stopped by Yeshua and the look on his face. It is a look of such kindness, I almost cry.

'This is true, my friend – and neither can you do anything to achieve eternal life.' The lawyer looks like a puzzled dog. 'That was your question, was it not?' He nods. 'And that is the answer: you can do nothing. So forget those who sent you and listen to me. Yes?' The young man nods again and Yeshua gets up from his stool and walks towards him. He holds the lawyers face in his hands. 'I speak to *you* now, my friend, and only you. Forget everything you have ever read and all that you have ever known and tell me: If I give you a fish because I wish you to have one – what have you done to gain the fish?'

His eyebrows are furrowed with thinking. 'Nothing,' he says.

'Nothing, indeed ... you have done *nothing*. Yet still you possess the fish. So it is with your father in heaven.'

I want to hear this teacher again; I want to meet Yeshua.

YESHUA

Word games for glory

Jude remains glum about the numbers. He wants more turning up to listen, more obvious success. He mentions Menahem, from Capernaum, who gets a bigger crowd than me. I do not know Menahem. 'He's local, of course, and his family help,' says Jude. 'Could not your family do the same? If each of them came and brought a friend ... '

'You are my family Jude.' He looks shocked.

'No, I mean your real family, teacher – your mother, brothers and sisters.'

'If anyone comes to me and does not hate his own father and mother and wife and children and brothers and sisters – yes, even his own life, they cannot be my disciple.'

'But..'

'No, they cannot – there is no "but" – for they will always be looking round and about. You must be free of attachments, Jude – free even of the desire for success, for large crowds around us! And anyway, as I say, you are my family, Jude.'

Jude is speechless, though he finds one nonetheless. 'You can't say that, teacher. I know you jest but you really can't say

48

that. That will not win friends. Family is everything! And the Temple, of course.'

'He doesn't mean it,' says Rocky to Jude shortly after. He takes him aside to reassure him. 'Obviously he doesn't mean it. It's just how he talks. And he's just tired.'

I hear him. He tries to defend me; he always does. He has believed I need defending ever since he left his fishing boat and family in Bethsaida in order to journey with me. They were not pleased, but Rocky said it was only for a while. I had asked him to come along, adding 'though I promise you nothing.' And he said, 'That's good enough for me!' as if I had offered him a palace.

'You will now be a fisher of men, Rocky ... a more difficult catch by far.'

Rocky still liked to talk of the sea and its different ways. Everyone likes what they know and he knew of the sea; knew more than anyone. He told me a strong wind could turn the sea upside down. 'Literally upside down, teacher! The warm water on top is sent to the depths; and the cold water below comes to the surface. You can feel it. And the fish don't know where they are! But we do.' He winks. And so I said that we would do the same, we would turn the world upside down and bring those at the bottom to the top; bring the cold into the sunlight and send everyone else plunging down! It's the poor who need raising up!

'Not all of them, I hope,' he replies. 'I've met the poor. And some of them are little shits ... wouldn't want them raised up.'

And he imagines himself the leader of the band. When he is not sulking, he jollies and jests people along; and speaks of fish as often as possible. 'Things shall build, Jude,' he says. 'Just wait and see. Fishing is all about finding the right spot, and only true fishermen know that. You can have the best net in Galilee but if you aren't in the right place, you catch nothing. So we need to be in the right place and people will come, believe it – and we shall change Judea! Turn it upside down!' Jude bows to his enthusiasm and force. He cannot take Rocky on; he is not built for that. He is quick and clever and full of ideas, but I do wish he would *laugh* more. I try to make Jude laugh, to become less serious. He calculates for me – adding our income and subtracting our costs – but I wish him to laugh with me. And I wish him to melt a little; and for his smile to reach his eyes.

'So you are a clever man, Jude.' I say 'Are you not clever?'

'Jude – *clever?*' It is Rocky. 'Clever with words, perhaps – but you can't eat words.'

'Though you must often eat yours, Rocky!' says Levi. He is a new arrival and welcomed by some, particularly Joanna.

'At last! Somebody with some sense,' she says. Levi was the least popular sort when he joined: a tax collector. You cannot get lower. He had collected taxes for the Romans and with a sharp eye for gain. Two for the Romans was always one for him, until I said to him, 'Levi, there is better gain in the world than a pile of coins.' And now his passion is to give it all away!

'He made his money; and now he let's it go,' says Jude, amazed.

It does confuse people, of course, and some do not trust him, including Rocky who offers him no welcome at all. He calls him 'Caesar', to make a Roman of him. 'Hail, Caesar!' he says, in angry jest. But Levi does not fear Rocky. Maybe tax collectors fear no one; there is no threat they have not faced, or curse they have not heard or knife they have not avoided. But he has a battle on his hands. They are up there with Samaritans in these parts, routinely reviled; and Rocky for one does not want him here.

And I remember I played a game with them. It seems a long time ago, but how would we ever be friends if we did not play games? They had so little in common and much to divide; a game seemed good idea. So hear how it went.

I say: '"*ible*" or "*able*" at the end of a word – what does that mean?' They all look blank so I repeat it. '"*Ible*" or "*able*" at the end of a word. What does it mean?'

'Jude doesn't know!' says Rocky, grabbing him and putting his hand over his mouth. Jude fights in vain to free himself; his hands are not as strong.

'It implies expectation,' says John quietly, while Jude brushes himself down. People sometimes forget John is there. He likes the shadows best.

'I was going to say that,' says Jude. Mockery ensues. 'No, seriously, I was – I was just thinking. And then Rocky -'

'John is right,' I say. 'As Jude would have been, had he not been assaulted. Expectation implied. So let's try it out. Laudable. What does laudable mean?'

'The expectation they or it will be praised,' says John, precisely.

'Teacher's favourite,' says Rocky. He says John is my favourite and so attacks when he can.

'Culpable?'

'Someone about to be blamed?' says Thomas.

'Spoken from experience, my friend?' says Levi. He doesn't suffer self-doubt himself.

'There speaks the rat from Bethsaida, of course!' Rocky's words silence everyone. Levi stares at him. 'Once a Roman, always a Roman, as the zealots say. Jewish money taken by "Caesar" here and sent abroad, sent to the Romans. Not good, Caesar, not good. I mean, you say now that you give it all away – but what's done is done!' Rocky tries to smile as he speaks, as if he jokes and banters. 'Or am I being too harsh, Caesar boy? Probably I am, way too harsh. Don't listen to me. I don't listen to myself sometimes! It just comes out, I'm joshing, I'm joshing – nothing meant!'

Levi is furious. 'An accusation made cannot be withdrawn.'

Rocky tries to put his arm around him but Levi shrugs him off. 'As I say, I meant nothing by it, old fellow! You don't want to listen to me! It was just a thought, and probably a bad one!'

'I paid back what I owed; though it's not to you I answer. You spill too much for one so eager to lead.'

'Lead?' says Rocky, as if bewildered. I return them to the game.

'Admirable,' I say into the difficult silence. Sometimes you must just row into the wave and trust the boat.

'The expectation they will be admired,' says John firmly. 'We need not argue, everyone. Why must we argue?' He looks at Rocky.

'Unloveable,' I say. And no one speaks, as if I have spoken out of turn or touched a nerve. 'Unloveable,' I repeat and hold the silence until Jude responds, his throat tight. 'One who expects not to be loved.'

'Exactly,' I say. 'One who expects not to be loved.'

'Like a tax collector, perhaps?' says Rocky.

'Or a fisherman who leaves his family.' It is not a question from Levi; though neither he nor Rocky look at each other.

'But what if we could change that, my friends?' And here is my purpose. Every game has a purpose. 'What if we could help the unloveable *expect* to be loved? Tax collector? Fisherman? Samaritan? Scribe? What if *no one* is unloveable? What if Yahweh is a father who sprints towards us in love whoever we are and whatever we have done? What if no one is unloveable?'

Jude corrects me: 'It is not decent for a man to sprint, teacher.' And when I don't respond he adds: 'It lacks gravitas and is for boys, not men. None of our leaders or elders sprint, it is not the custom, nor would it be respected. It is not decent.'

'Oh really?' I say and Jude nods. 'Then perhaps Yahweh is not decent.'

'We should not talk like that, teacher.'

I like Jude, for I see his soul; though he cannot and lives from somewhere else. And so for all his calculation and all his knowing, he knows nothing.

'If Israel is to be re-born, Jude, this is how it must be among us. No, listen everyone, listen! This is for us all and this is where we start. No one is unloveable, there are no strangers ... only the unloveable loved. Our father rushing towards us, can you imagine that – the wind blowing in his hair, his sandals scarcely staying on! Falling off, perhaps, but he doesn't care, he'll run bare foot! And the unloveable swept off their feet in appreciation!'

A pause and then Rocky wades in. 'Well, that's not going to happen, is it, teacher?' He cannot defend me this time and looks around for support. 'Well, is it? I mean, dream on, teacher, and all that – and no offence, but the unloveable get what they deserve.'

'Speaking as a former tax collector ... ' Levi sets everyone laughing. It is good to see tense hearts eased. 'No, seriously – I did not get what I deserved. I received kindness and hope from this man.' He points to me and I smile; that was a good day in Bethsaida, a life quite changed. 'If we got what we deserved, who would survive?'

'But you're different, Levi.' Jude again. 'I mean, it's not like you're a, well – a Samaritan or anything. You're Jewish, after all.'

'So there's no good Samaritan, Jude?' I say and Jude is frustrated. He likes his judgements and the world neatly sliced.

'Not one?'

'There are probably *some* reasonable Samaritans, who knows? I'm just saying. They have a history and not a good one – not a good one at all. And I mean, who wants to love the unloveable anyway? What's the actual point? And who here loves a Roman?!'

He wants a laugh, but it is not given. 'Your father in heaven, Jude. You ask who loves a Roman? Your father in heaven, where there are no strangers; and as above in heaven, so below on earth.'

There is silence, like the gap between the stars. It seeps between us, like oil leaking from a jar. I see shock and hate. I see run-of-the-mill embarrassment and discomfort and think back to the Baptiser. 'You will bring the light and they will despise you.' Is this a taste? I move to explain. 'When you make two into one,' I say, 'you will be a son of man, each of you – a true son of man, full human. Do you understand? When you cease from splitting and make the two one, you will be a son of man, a child of God. And then, when you say, "Mountain – move!" – then it will move.'

MIRIAM

Never trust a teacher

'So who was it?' she asks, and I do not know what Berenica means. She asks as if I hold some secret back; and she doesn't like secrets. She chases them out of you.

'Who was what?'

'Who was it who made you swoon, Miriam?' She swoons as she says the word, her body crumbling, but I am still puzzled. She has arrived from nowhere with her question, which feels like a trap. 'The sheep in Capernaum were telling me *all* about it, and in great detail. They remember a girl in the market place with a ring on her toe and anklets that tinkle when she walks. Remind you of anyone? Oh, and they remember a man.'

She knows nothing, nothing at all; and there are no sheep in Capernaum, I don't remember any. Berenica must just be bored, for the truth is, no one made me swoon there. She perhaps heard me talking with Judith, this could be the case. You don't always know where she hides in our home and she does 'like a drama', Judith's phrase, and maybe she is right, I see this slowly – as if Berenica needs other people's lives to lift and stir her own. And if there is no drama around – as can happen in Magdala, which is mainly fish – she will stir the pot until some drama appears. She stirs the pot now, I think, but really, it was nothing – and you can't make a stew out of nothing!

'I was with father in Capernaum, as you well know; and he was with the melon- seller.'

'And you left them and wandered off. Or so I hear ... from the sheep.'

'I sought the shade, it was the middle of the day, the heat was heavy and you know father, he never stops. "Poor people stop!" he says. "I never stop." So I just sought the shade of a tree which is not against the commandments.'

'Oh, I'm sure it is, Miriam. There's a commandment for everything, as you well know and one must involve trees at midday.' She pauses. 'And then?'

'What do you mean, "And then?"' I feel flustered, Berenica can do this. 'I talked with a woman from the town – and then came home!'

'You talked with a woman and listened to a teacher. The sheep were very clear on that.'

'Who didn't make me swoon, all right? No one made me swoon! It was just a rabbi, some teacher I had not heard before.' She makes a face, she doesn't believe me – or perhaps she is just playing. I know she loves me; but I don't always know what she thinks.

'I merely said to Judith, by way of nothing, that he was surprisingly young.'

'"Surprisingly young!?"'

'Well, you know what's on offer in Magdala – and that maybe I'd like to hear him again, I may have said that. But how that has become a swoon, I don't ... '

'You wish to hear the "young" teacher again?'

'Yes – he spoke well, he was kind; though rude as well – rude to a lawyer, which is maybe unwise; but it all felt true to my heart.'

'You must never trust a teacher,' says Berenica, and now she becomes serious, as if she looks after me, her little sister. She takes hold of my shoulders and speaks face to face. 'Any teacher who gets near to you, Miriam, whatever they say, walk away from them; walk clean away. Do not allow them power over you, whatever sweet lines they offer. It will not end well, it never does.'

'You sound like Mother.'

'I sound nothing like Mother. Mother makes *you* the sinner, Miriam; but I say it's the teacher.'

'He has no power over me – he doesn't even know me! I went back to father afterwards to find him shaking hands with the melon-seller – and that was that. I did not speak with him or his followers. So you can let go of me, I think!'

She does let go and walks a way. As I have said, Berenica makes her own way in life; and if it isn't her way, be sure she will not take it. She seats herself by the window but will still not leave me alone.

'The first rule of happiness, Miriam, just remember it: never trust a teacher ... *the first rule of happiness.*'

'And of course you are *so* happy, Ber.'

Her sigh is deep, though I don't know what it says. Does it condemn me or her? 'Teachers are too needy,' she says. 'Too needy by far. Who sets themselves up as a teacher, Miriam? What sort of a person? And why would they do that? For attention, of course! And to be in control! To save everyone else because they cannot save themselves! Teachers are shipwrecks, Miriam, advising other boats how to sail. What do you want from your life?'

I'm surprised by this question; I do not know what I want, though I find myself answering straight away. 'I would like to wake up to light blue shutters in my window,' I say, and her eyebrows rise a little; perhaps I have surprised her. But I've always dreamed of these ... light blue shutters, I saw them in a market once; they came from the east, I believe.

'Light blue shutters?' she repeats and I nod. Have I said too much? Or too little? Am I shallow to want this? And will she use it against me? I would hate this to be a family joke, my heart exposed again. 'Then I hope one day you have them, Miriam, truly I do: light blue shutters. But never trust a teacher.'

YESHUA

Sermon on the Mount

I talk with the group. We are sat on rocks outside Capernaum. They call it 'The Mount', though it is more of a hill; and we enjoy the shade and scent of buckled orange trees, bent by the wind and struggling to fruit. It is our story too, as I look around.

'Is it true you can smell God?' says Thaddeus. He remembers my words. People do listen sometimes.

'It is true today,' I say. 'And today he smells of young oranges.' Jude is not here and Rocky is asking after him. 'Where has Jude got to?' Who knows why he likes Jude, when they are so different – and perhaps that is my answer. I like to support him if I can, says Rocky, playing the honourable man. ('Am I *too* honourable, teacher?' he once asked me.) But Jude has clarity and detail which Rocky can only dream of; so the honourable man benefits as well.

'He slept with us last night,' says Joanna, who sorts homes for everyone on the road. Rocky grunts acknowledgement; he is not sure about Joanna. But he likes the beds she finds, night after night and how does she do that? The men complain about who is with who – so many cabals, and cabals within cabals, but Joanna ignores them all. And while they mutter and grumble, they do not take her on. No one takes her on. I do not know how she does it. She simply tells me not to worry, and I happily obey. She has just taken a delivery of some warm rolls, 'but they are for later', she says firmly, which disappoints everyone. 'He was on the roof with Thaddeus,' she adds. We are back with the missing Jude. 'But he left early – I was baking, I heard him on the stairs. He said he was busy with something, some plan or other; he said I should wait and see.' *He's a strange boy,* she whispers to me alone.

'He definitely had a plan,' says Thaddeus.

'Jude always has a plan,' says Rocky, still looking at the rolls. They do smell good and I am not sure they will survive until lunch, unless lunch is brought forward, which Rocky is inclined to do. 'It is not that I cannot wait for lunch – it is that lunch cannot wait for me!' He likes the joke and uses it when he can; his collection is not large, so he makes the most of repeats.

'Jude believes we need more followers,' says Thomas, who clearly agrees with Jude. 'He was saying that to me yesterday.'

'He is always saying that, Thomas.'

'He was saying we need more followers.' He repeats himself. 'That we don't have enough.'

'This is not news, Thomas.' I am irritated. He hides his own will behind another. 'The news will be when Jude stops saying it.'

But Thomas continues, launched on a path that can neither hear nor deviate: 'He says it's no use you talking to a few people in a village square, teacher; that we need larger crowds – or what's the point?'

I ask that myself sometimes, and so I ask Thomas. 'Good question. What *is* the point, Thomas?' Whether he wills it or not, he has reached deep into the bloody guts of the matter – like a priest with a goat ripped open for sacrifice.

'I'm just saying what Jude said.'

'Do you not have a voice of your own, Thomas? Can you not say why *you* sit here under the orange tree? Why Joanna finds a bed for *you* each night? Why we move, with some difficulty, from village to village? Or is it just so you can quote the missing Jude?'

'He's thinking of you, teacher,' he says, with tightened demeanour. 'I mean, obviously he's thinking of you. He's thinking of you spreading your teaching and, well – more supporters would do that, obviously. He says it better than me.'

'I wonder if *he* needs more followers, Thomas ... rather than me?' I pace a little and gesture, as one stirred. 'Perhaps Jude lacks friends and imagines a crowd around me will bring him comfort. Or perhaps he imagines that a crowd makes a speech truer. If a hundred listen then it must be true? Is that what you think, Thomas? Why not trust yourself for a moment, trust your own heart? Why seek the doubtful comfort of a crowd?'

'He says we could do with the money, teacher.' Dear Thomas is uncomfortable and walled up, as though suddenly possessed by an idiot. He wonders whether to flee or to fight and decides to fight. His shoulders tense, his chest expands. 'And he knows about the money; he keeps our accounts, after all. He knows all about the money, better than any of us.'

'So it is all about the money? The money is the point?'

'It's not about the money, teacher, but he does say we could do with more. "If we aren't to work, how will things be paid for? We shouldn't be depending on Joanna." He doesn't think we should be depending on Joanna, you see.'

'What's got inside Thomas all of a sudden?' says Rocky, though I walk away, I have to walk away, I can listen no longer, I have to move from his presence, I must look at the sky, climb a mountain, jump into the sea while the ridicule I feel towards him, and the desire to be alone and to work alone, and the longing to be free of such stupidity – while these things pass through me. After a while, John arrives at my side, but I desire no conversation and signal my wish for solitude; he backs away. And distance heals, slowly; the feelings pass and my breathing settles. I hear Levi confronting Thomas – something about why exactly he is behaving 'like three types of fool', though I wonder the same of myself; wonder at my turmoil and despair at these people, so overwhelming I had to walk away; for when love arrives, everyone and everything is quite well; and when love leaves, all are difficult, and all are at fault and all are tragically to blame.

Yet what am I to do with them? Do I need fewer followers rather than more? We are twenty or so, but is that too many to learn? They exchange such nonsense with one another, trapped in the mad ways of the world. They are like a man caught by the foot in a chariot wheel and dragged along, pulled and turned by the outer events of their lives, by what we shall eat, and what we shall wear and how we shall pay – and quite at the mercy of such things. I watch the clouds, they slow my mind; I turn back towards them and I see. In leaving Thomas, I see him. I see the treasure buried in his frightened soil; buried so deep he cannot find it. So I walk back towards them, meeting John on the way. 'You cannot love what you cannot see,' I say. 'And sometimes we must leave in order to see.'

'Some do not wish to see, teacher,' he says. 'They prefer to imagine things and call it seeing.' I smile. This man is close to my heart; perhaps Rocky is right, perhaps I do love him the best. And together we arrive back with the gang and I ask them to remember the forces within themselves. I say, 'You must pay attention to the forces within.' They do not know what I mean, so I give them a picture.

'Think of light and darkness and how they differ. And remember yourselves, always, as nine parts of light or nine parts of darkness. Do you understand?' Thomas is still sulking; he looks haughty and hurt – but now I see only treasure. 'This being human is like living in a house with nine rooms. Man and woman, they are nine rooms of light or darkness. A good woman, she is perhaps six parts light and three parts darkness. While an evil man, he is eight parts darkness and one part light. So know yourselves, know the nine rooms of your soul. Have no anxiety, but open the doors and windows in each – open them every day, wide open without fear! And so let your whole body be full of light, having no room set apart and sealed away in darkness. Be nine parts light, my friends!'

'There will always be darkness in the world,' says Thomas, never slow to present a problem. His mind seeks them out, a wasp's nest of suspicion. He looks always for the crack and the flaw; and never quite believes the good, sensing it holds a weapon behind its back.

'You speak truth, Thomas; or some of it. There will always be darkness, and I warn you now: if the dark in the world echoes the dark in your heart, then truly you will know terror and spread terror. Herod does what Herod is; that is the way of it. The darkness in him marries the darkness of the world. He knows terror and spreads terror. But it need not be this way. If the darkness in the world finds light in you, then the darkness is lit, and is darkness no more. So find the light daily. Open your nine rooms, Thomas' – I touch his breast, and he jumps a little – 'open them to the light, and take it into the darkness without fear.'

We discover later that Jude has been planning a hilltop gathering, in the cause of more followers. Though I say to him that truth is my food, and truth is my drink and followers are neither.

'A hundred can follow an idiot, Jude; and a thousand can swoon at a fool. Ten might know more than ten thousand – so do not worry about how many followers we have. Only follow your heart. You are still precious whether we are three or a multitude. And remember, we are not made better by others, nor made wiser by them; we are made better by our *selves*, for the kingdom of God is within. Be concerned only that what you say is true.'

But a large crowd has gathered here on the mount, the largest I have seen. It stretches down the hill side and thrills me. Perhaps Jude is right. If Israel is to be restored, it will take the many, not the few. 'They have all come to hear you,' says Jude, clearly pleased. I ask him how he persuaded them. 'I said you are the new Hillel,' he says.

Rocky is excited and pats Jude hard on the back; it is too violent for Jude, who stumbles and almost falls over. Jude is a narrow man, with the lithe body of a money-counter; while Rocky is wide, with hands of great power.

'This is a very good crowd, teacher,' he says. 'Word is getting around. I always thought we could do it.'

'Jude did it,' says Thomas.

'And I say we *all* did it,' says Rocky firmly. 'Though Jude has done well, I grant you. And who is Hillel?'

John speaks. '"If I am not for myself, who will be for me? But if I am only for myself, who am I?" Rocky looks confused.

'That's Hillel,' says John.

'I cannot believe you have not heard of Hillel,' says Thaddeus.

'Did he fish?' says Rocky, stirred. 'Has he been out there in the storms? Has he known the terror of the arching waves? Has he been thrown overboard by the wind and felt the cold undertow of death, pulling him down?'

'Well, no.'

'Then why should I know him? '

'He was a teacher, a famous teacher.'

'So he has soft hands.'

'The Pharisees follow him.'

'While fishermen fish ... and carpenters cut wood.' He nods at me as if I am forgiven for being a teacher, as long as I bring with me a trade.

'And all know we need teachers *and* fishermen, Rocky. And some would say we need fishermen more.'

Rocky is calmed. 'Well, if this Hillel was a proud Jew, then all strength to his soft elbows. But he isn't here now, so it's down to you, teacher. You can see the crowd. And you must send them home proud to be Jewish. That's the game here, I think. If we want to see them again, people need to know where you stand on Israel, "foreigners out" and all that – because there's no fence to sit on.'

He tries to sound cheery, though stubbornness seeps through. He has spoken to me in private about Israel, but now he tries another way; he cajoles me in public, as if the public will change my mind or force my hand.

'I think I will speak about attitudes, Rocky.'

'Attitudes towards the Roman scum? That won't take long.'

'Good attitudes. I will speak of good attitudes – attitudes that grow good things.' I feel energy for these here on the hill. 'Attitudes are the heart beat of our actions, and go before our words – we must look after them.' Rocky shrugs. He has no idea what I speak of. 'They are why I came, Rocky; for what changes on earth without a change of attitude?"

'Well, that's all well and good, teacher.'

'I know.'

'But ... '

'There is no *but*.'

'But no one wants to hear about those, believe me; and we need to give them what they want. I mean, they've come all this way, and really, what have attitudes got to do with anything, when the Romans sit on our heads and Phoenicians take our jobs? Who speaks about attitudes at times like these? It is not a time to be kind, teacher. It's not how things work. They need a clear message.'

'It is clear – though not easy.'

'"Good intentions never caught fish," an old saying that. "Good intentions never caught a fish!"' He is still pleased with it. 'You need a strong net or a sharp hook to catch them! And cunning! A sharp hook and cunning!'

Rocky grows in confidence. He keeps a foot in the sea, it is what he knows best; but slowly he leaves his boat and nets behind and I think he is pleased with his speech. His way is the way of opinion and applause – strong opinions seeking applause. He tells me what to say because he wants people to like me; and also to like him. 'You must say what they want to hear, teacher.' Has he heard nothing? Though maybe I am to blame, I see this. I should not have told him that he would be a fisher of men. Like Jude, he imagines all must be judged by their catch, by the numbers, by things seen. But the kingdom of God is unseen and now I turn to the crowd.

'Welcome to the Mount, my friends, for here is everything! Look around you at the flower, the bird and the child ... and ponder them well, for they know everything! Truly they do! They are not like us. They do not find joy in things, in battle or in status but in life itself, here and now, in the sheer joy of living! If your happiness is sustained by something or someone outside of you, then truly I say, you are imprisoned in the land of the dead. The kingdom of God is within!'

Do people wish to hear this? I doubt it. I hear mumbling, someone calls out. 'How can a good Jew be imprisoned?'

Another says, 'Have you nothing happy to tell us?'

And another, 'How about some cake and wine for us all?!'

I approach the group from where these voices come; they encourage one another as groups do. 'I understand, I understand, my friends. You ask me to give you cake and wine in your prison, to make bad things a little better in your prison; to ease, for a moment, the pain of the chains. But instead, I ask you to *leave* your prison, to get up and leave! Truly, that is what I say to you. But you grimace and twitch because you do not wish to leave, you like your prison too much – it is familiar! You want to stay in your prison! And just want some cake and wine from the prophets to brighten your dark and difficult days. But let me tell you this – it is not the world that makes you unhappy. It is *God* who makes you unhappy, no truly – it is God who makes you unhappy, so that you drop your illusions.'

'God makes us unhappy? What sort of teaching is this?' And now the mount murmurs and some wonder why they have come. 'Why would God make us unhappy?' And 'Who is this man?'

'Believe or do not believe. But there is one among you now who comes not to rock your boat but to *burn* your boat – for its cargo is illusion! I come to cast fire on the earth – and would that it were already kindled! Truly! For you are to be happy not because of *this* and not because of *that* – but for no reason at all! Take delight in everything, in life itself. Then you will have entered the kingdom of God.'

'But who on earth is happy when the Romans dump on us and our own rulers cheat and starve us?'

'Who is happy? You cut straight to the heart, my friend. So let us speak of the happy! Which of you is happy today?' There a few hands raised, but not many. 'Yet do we not all wish to be so and deserve to be so?' Some look at each other, and some look at the ground. 'Do not believe your desires for your desires lie. And your desires make you frustrated. So speak to each of them and say, "Truly, I know in my heart you are not the path to happiness." Say *that* to your desires.'

'How then can we be happy?'

'Desire brings a moment of pleasure; but this is not contentment, this is not happiness. They are not the same at all! Desire is but a brief break in your anxiety, fear and resentment – and very soon they return; very soon. So do not cling to anyone or anything!'

'Who then is happy?'

'Who is happy? The poor in spirit are happy, for a start – the poor in spirit are happy, the doubters who stumble on joy, the crushed who glimpse sun, for theirs is already the kingdom of God.

And those who mourn are happy; those who bury loved ones, who sob at their loss – happy in the comfort found, in the healing torrent of tears.'

There is silence across the hillside, but I continue.

'As Ecclesiastes says, "It is better to go to the house of mourning than to go to the house of feasting. Sorrow is better than laughter for by sorrow the countenance of the heart is made glad."

'And happy are the meek, my friends – do you hear me? Happy are the meek, those with nothing to offer but their beating hearts. Is that you, my friends? Then you are so happy, for in each moment, you inherit the land, you inherit again and again, make it your own and reign over all.'

Someone shouts out, 'The Romans reign over all – and I wouldn't call them meek!'

'They're not inheritors either,' bellows another. 'They're invaders not inheritors!'

The crowd agrees and I step towards them, arms aloft. Jude has done his work well; there are too many to hear me from my mouth. They must help each other to hear, so people pass my words on to those behind – though I get as close as I can. 'Have you not read the psalm, my friend? "Those who wait for the Lord shall inherit the land; the meek shall inherit the land and delight themselves in prosperity." If you cannot hear *me*, then at least hear what King David says.'

They love King David, this I know. His was a time of conquest, of battles won, a time for Israel; 'those good old days', they say, 'such special days they were' – though everyone as unhappy then as now. Do they not see that?

'I'll tell you what I hear,' shouts one. 'I hear Roman feet marching everywhere, stepping on what they will! The meek are doormats, nothing more. They are doormats for the Roman scum to wipe their filthy foreign feet on.'

'Did you hear that?' I shout. 'I think even Herod must have heard! He says the meek are doormats for the Roman feet, but I say the meek are not so. Who are the meek? They are not doormats. The meek are those who are angry for the right reasons with the right person in the right manner at the right moment for the right length of time! Did you get that? So truly, the meek are no doormats, not at all, but happy inheritors of the kingdom –

Like those who hunger and thirst for the saving acts of God. Is that you, my friends? I speak now of the flame-keepers and the hope-makers, the falsely accused, those who cry out for God. When the Baptiser held me under the water in the Jordan River, when he baptised me there, I was gasping for air – I hungered for air with a passion! And in like manner, we seek the goodness of God, thirsting for it like a nomad far from his well; thirsting as you do now on this dry hillside.'

Some reach for their pouches, reminded of their dry throats. 'Yes, let us all drink, the water of life – '

'Speak of the Jewish kingdom, teacher,' mutters Rocky as he gives me a drink. 'They need some encouraging in that direction. Mention King David again; they liked that bit.'

'*You* liked that bit.'

'Anything about King David is good.'

'He was a murderous adulterer.'

'They forget about that because he conquered people.' Rocky senses the need in the crowd, and he senses aright. He has also noticed the arrival of some Pharisees, they loiter on the skyline. He wants it all to become more Jewish. But I do not have the words that he wants. I would have to make my words smaller to speak his little truths. I would have to say goodbye to the light and climb back into a box to speak the things he wishes to hear ... and I cannot do that; too much that is true would have to die. And so I continue.

'I speak of the happy, my friends. Which of you is happy today? Do we not all deserve to be so? You see, I am ambitious for you! So I speak of the poor in spirit, of those who mourn; I speak of the meek and of those who thirst for goodness. Bless them all!

And I speak also of the merciful, for they too are happy. Those who are kind, those who stand for others, who confront the bullying power – for they already know mercy, it is already theirs, shaping their beautiful hearts.

And happy are the pure in heart – is that you? Yes? For they possess simplicity. The pure in heart are simple in motive. They have one motive and will one thing.

So I celebrate them and I celebrate the peacemakers – yes, happy are the peacemakers, my friends, knowing themselves sons and daughters of God.'

And then one of the Pharisees speaks. He has moved nearer the front.

'So is it wrong to be angry, teacher?'

'You must listen better, my friend!' I see him coming; I know where he heads in his big black robe. 'Poor listening is worse than none! God save us from poor listeners!'

'I have listened to you being angry, I know that, teacher. I have listened many times, listened to you rage. And so if my listening is poor, then your rage is worse ... and little given to peace.'

'It is not the peaceful I celebrate, nor the pacifists – but the peace*makers*, those who stick their head in the heat of the oven and make peace where there is no peace; those who build peace and get hurt or killed in this making! They may anger; for there is much to be angry about, is there not? Like religious hypocrisy, like the misuse of power. But their anger insists on peace rather than war. Is that so hard?'

'You speak of another world, teacher; there can be no such peace here.'

'I speak of *this* world, my friend – this world!' My voice is harsh but the man is an idiot posing as the wise. 'And I speak of now. These are promises for this morning, these things are already so, the kingdom is already here in people such as these. So you do not need to search for the pearl of great price. Cease your searching! Truly, it is yours already! Let those who hear me understand!'

As I turn around, for I am done, Jude is not listening. He is speaking with Thomas and his queasy face says it all, as if set for illness. This is not what he wanted when he called me 'the new Hillel'. And I feel strength leave me, as if I am spent. Levi approaches.

'I applaud your courage, teacher.'

'No one listened.' I am not ready for kindness.

'Better the unheard truth than the feted lie.'

'Really?' This is not my present feeling. Levi's face is creviced and hard, it cannot deny his past; yet his smile is as warm as a Sabbath sunset; it lives kindly on his face and offers me rest. 'Joanna gave me these rolls to pass on to you,' he says. 'Fish in one, cheese in the other; she said you will be hungry.'

'I am not hungry.'

'You will be, teacher. And never was lunch better earned than here today on the mount. '

MIRIAM

Rough healing

~

I am hurting.

He holds my head fiercely, his hands are rough. I have not been held by a man before, my hair now pressed against my ears, which feel like they might snap, crushed by the grip. I am trapped and frightened, his face close to mine, with his eyes in my soul like a knife in a wound.

And this is how I meet Yeshua; how first we touch. He is holding my head, like a beam of wood. And some have said it *is* a beam of wood, my father and mother would say so. 'Don't fall near a fire – you may get thrown onto it!' But let it be wood, I don't care; for this is a good holding, though a shock and a terror also; and I hardly know what is happening. It is like I am falling or turning upside down and my neck might break – yet safe; I somehow know these rough hands are safe.

And how am I so? How have I come to this? I had not arrived here with such happenings in mind – that is for sure! I'd been listening to Yeshua talking to a crowd in Magdala. I was standing back, with Berenica.

'So this is the young teacher?' she says, as the crowd pushes and pulls around us, like a restless sea. 'You can see that he is mad, can't you?' She turns and holds me. 'You can see that, Miriam? You can see that he is mad?'

'I love you, Berenica, but I must leave you now.' I have to say this. 'I wish to get closer. Please let me go. We'll talk later.'

And she does let me go, and I do not see her again that day. We part in the crowd, for I can no longer watch others healed while I stand back. I need healing myself and slowly move forward, pushed on by unhappiness, like a hand in my back, pushed on by longing, I see that now. So I had drawn closer, I had no choice ... though fearing also that I was somehow bad to be acting in this way – for who was I to do such a thing? Do you have this feeling? Some push themselves forward, as though it their right; but I do not do this and never have; I watch and I wait. 'Miriam must learn to wait,' they said and I learned well. I have watched and waited all my life.

So on this day, I was sure others needed Yeshua more than I; for who was I to bother him? Until I needed him also and stopped caring about the others ... I didn't care at all but pushed further towards the front. I asked one of his friends, who I remembered as 'Rocky' – the one who stood on one leg in Capernaum! I asked him if I could simply touch Yeshua; I thought this might suffice, I knew it would. I saw others do this, but the man said 'Not now, not now. The teacher is busy.' I begged him, however. I said I must see Yeshua and he said I would have to wait, that the teacher did not have time for me. 'Can you not see how people flock to him?' He then turned away from me, only to turn back.

'I could help you,' he says. He offers to pray for me, he says he can do that – that Yeshua has given him authority. 'It is not just Yeshua who heals,' he says. 'We *all* heal, we all speak for him.'

But I do not want this, and I do not know why. I do not like his tone, though his tone is confident and he is keen that he should help. But he is not Yeshua and I know it is Yeshua I wish to see. Is this wrong? I do not trust Rocky, though as to why, I cannot say.

And now I hear my father. 'You always want more, Miriam,' he would say. 'Nothing is enough for you – you always want more!' But what if I do want more? And who does *not* want more? All of us want more, all those around me now, pushing and elbowing their way to the front – they all want more! Yeshua gives us hope and insists we want more. He says that the thirsty should come to him, and he will give them drink. He says the weary should come, and he will give them rest. He says as God clothes the grass, so will he clothe us, so not to worry about food, happiness or clothes – for our father in heaven knows all our needs! So how could we not want more, for our father in heaven knows us and cares!

'Do you have a demon inside you?' asks Rocky.

I say I am fine, which is so stupid, because I have already said that I'm not, and he moves away with a shrug, I believe he is hurt and I am overcome with guilt that I have turned him down and made him feel bad; so I push through the crowd after him, but when I reach him, he is with another, and so feeling a fool, I turn to go home. I will seek out Berenica, she must be somewhere, when suddenly he is before me: Yeshua.

'I saw you,' he says, 'What do you seek?'

What do I seek? I have no idea at all and can't think, I am too in shock. I face him at last but feel a fraud, for many here have greater needs than me. To my left, an old man is hunched in pain, he mutters for help; and to my right, a boy with no mind and wandering eyes, his body all chaos, held by his mother. But Yeshua ignores them all, as if there is only me in the world. The boy's mother touches Yeshua to gain attention, and he pushes her away. 'Not now,' he says, glancing at her. 'All in good time; but do not touch me now.' And to me he says, 'Why are you here?' And I start to cry, for I don't know why I am here. He holds my shoulders, like Berenica, stilling me.

'How long the fear?' he asks.

How long the fear? What sort of a question is this? And what does he mean? I do not know the answer ... though the answer comes quick and lets some poison out.

'Always ... always.' I feel great relief to say it.

'The fear has always been with you?'

'Always ... all of my life.' And now it seems strange that I have neither seen nor named this until now; though all my life I have somehow been afraid.

'So hear me.' He is calm, though the crowd around pushes. Others demand his attention, but I do not care. He looks me up and down. 'Do you hear me now?' He speaks gently and looks into my eyes. I nod. He is not pleased, I feel this and so I worry. Why is he not pleased? What have I done? He speaks with force, repeating the question. 'Do you hear me?' I don't know what to do. I nod again, confused. 'Do you have a voice?' he asks. I nod again – then quickly speak.

'Yes,' I say.

'You can speak! So I ask again, do you hear me?'

'Yes, I hear you.'

And now he takes hold of my head in his hands. 'So listen. Listen truly! You shall not fear your father! No fear!' His eyes eat me. 'Do you hear me?'

'Yes, I hear you.'

'Nor shall you fear your mother! No fear! Do you hear me?'

'Yes, I hear you.'

'You shall not fear your sisters or your neighbours. No fear!' A pause ... .I don't know what to do, but I can do nothing; I am quite held by his hands. 'You shall not fear Yahweh, do you hear?'

What am I to say?

'And you shall not fear me – no fear! Yes?'

'Yes.'

'And most of all – what is your name?'

'Miriam.'

'Miriam. Most necessary of all, Miriam – where are you from?

'Here – in Magdala.'

'Most necessary of all, Miriam of Magdala – you shall not fear yourself! No fear! Do you hear me?'

'I hear you.'

'But instead – ' the crowd pushes us again, people lose their balance around us, swaying, trapped and pushed by this human tide – 'instead, possess your voice and your strength in delight. Put away your fear – and exist! Exist, Miriam, exist!'

And now he releases my head, pushing me back, and suddenly free, I sway slightly. And then placing one hand on my back, pushing me forward, he presses the other above my breast, and pushes me back, his hand on my heart beat, 'Here is your voice!' he says, 'Here!' He presses at my heart again. 'Listen to your heart, Miriam, the power of your heart – and here is your voice!'

He is fierce, so fierce. Some said he was fierce and I feel it now; his hands and his eyes on fire. The boy with no mind is lashing out beside me. I cannot help him or his mother, for suddenly my mouth is opening, and a voice – not mine – screams out. I let out a scream. I have not screamed before, like a rush of water, some release, some fearless release, a mad noise. It is a voice I had not known but know now; my voice, jerking up from within, pushing out through my mouth, now a broken door, smashed by the force and I am laughing as I fall to the ground, though quite spent, laughing to exhaustion or exhausted with laughter, I know nothing more ...

And when I awake, I am lying inside; a low roof above me. I am laid out in an alcove, away from the others. I hear him talking, I know the voice, though quieter here than in the street. I begin to listen. Yeshua is talking, explaining things to those around him. I drift in and out; it is like the music of the harp; I have heard this played, here in Magdala, by the son of the town's richest fish seller. I hear someone ask Yeshua about the Temple which alerts me; my father loved the Temple. 'Why ask about the Temple?' he says. 'There is no Temple. How can there be? The Kingship of God is inside you and all around you,' he says, 'not in some mansion of wood or stone. How could it ever be contained in that way? The rich live in mansions of stone; but that is not Yahweh's way.' He laughs, though no one joins in. I sense discomfort in the group, for some of them murmur and

I feel discomfort myself. We must surely trust in the Temple? My father trusted in the Temple.

'Yahweh's kingship is found wherever you are and in whatever you do,' says Yeshua. 'Split a piece of wood and the kingdom is there, lift a stone and it is there! So what now is the Temple?'

There's puzzlement around me, this is how it feels; or maybe admiration, I do not know – but all is subdued. I smell a fire and I smell food; there is smoke, and a woman walking by; I have seen her with Yeshua. She has a bracelet of gold on her wrist and bold hoop-like earrings worn around her ear on a small chain, as if she does not care what people think. She is everything I wish to be.

'You wake,' she says as she returns, and I smell her saffron perfume. 'You have Rocky to thank.'

'Rocky?'

'He carried you here when you fainted. I believe Yeshua prayed with you?'

'Oh, well, sort of!' Do I blush? 'He shouted more than he prayed. Though perhaps that is how he prays? I mean, obviously I'm grateful ... '

'My name is Joanna,' she says. 'I help with things ... help get things done.'

'I'm Miriam. I like your earrings.' Is that the best I can do? She must think me a fool.

'A present from my husband, who chooses well only by mistake. Is that henna on your toe nails?'

'It is, yes.' Does she disapprove? She doesn't seem bothered, but I'm on my guard, wary of judgement.

'Very nice; it suits you. Now we'll find you some food.'

Wherever I am, I do not want to leave. Something is over. I will not be going home; that path, in this instance, has been closed off. I have left home now; and this is all I know.

'Is there any way I can help?' I ask. 'I mean, support what's going on – help with things, help get things done – like you?'

Truly, I do not know what I ask.

YESHUA

The whore of Nazareth

~

'She did not even *come* to the synagogue, Devira. She chose to be elsewhere.'

'She had her reasons, Yeshua.'

'I am invited to speak in my home synagogue yet she feels unable to attend, unable to hear her son, who is such a disappointment, of course. She finds so many ways to be angry.'

'She is not angry.'

I smile rather than scream. 'She is angry, Devira, but she cannot speak it.'

'She was scared of what you might do, Yeshua, what you might say – and not without cause. I mean, you brought the house down – and not in a good way. Look at what happened, for pity's sake! Would you wish her to see that?' And then, as an afterthought, 'Why *do* people hate you?'

It is true, my return to Nazareth ended in violence; Devira is not wrong. I was chased from the town by mad men and very nearly killed. I have often seen hate in men's eyes but never such hate as that; I picture it now, a Nazarene hate, it disturbs me still.

'I merely read from the book of Isaiah. It is not a crime.'

I had read it in the synagogue in Nazareth, invited to do so. 'The Spirit of the Lord is upon me and he anoints me to proclaim good news to the poor. He has sent me to announce liberty to the captives and the recovery of sight for the blind, to set free all those who are bruised and oppressed – to proclaim the year of the Lord's favour.'

I then closed the book and said, 'This is here and this is now. In your hearing and in this place, is this scripture fulfilled.'

And then the murmuring began. 'Is this not Joseph's son – the one who left here in disgrace?' And, 'Physician, first mend yourself before bothering us!' And, 'By what authority do you speak? And why is your mother not here? Are the rumours true?'

I should not have returned to Nazareth; I see that now. Perhaps I had dreamt of a homecoming. But you cannot go back, even with truth in your tunic. Never go back. But such violence in their eyes as they came after me! And I am sure – but for some kind Pharisee friends – that they would have killed me, with God on their side, of course. 'Our hate is God's hate!' I melted away while they argued with my jackal-eyed pursuers. And my mother stayed away from it all; I'm not sure whose side she would have taken.

But now I sit safe with Devira on the Sepphoris road, with the smell of Balsam, olive trees and some goats. Devira's family farm this land; and I built the hut in which we sit; hastily done but a decent enough job.

'Glad to see it's still standing,' I say, but she is not concerned with our shelter.

'You do not win friends in Nazareth.'

So we are to talk of Nazareth? Then let us talk of Nazareth. 'Nazareth is a snake pit, Devira.' I will be clear. 'How will Yahweh's rule arrive there!? Not by invitation, I can tell you.' But Devira is not interested in Yahweh's rule; she is interested in her olive crop and my mother ... though in my body, I am still in the synagogue with the arrows of hate loosed from their eyes. 'You know the history of this place, Devira – a settler town for Jews, fearful of the gentile invasion of Galilee. And yes, that *is* what they call it – "an invasion." "We are more Jewish than Jerusalem," say the Nazarenes. So they liked my words as much as they like the Phoenicians.'

Devira considers me. 'You need to speak with your mother.'

'And they need to apologise to my father.' I will not let the vermin go. 'Did you hear them?'

'I heard them.'

'"Is this not Joseph's son?" they bawled. '"Is this not Joseph's son?"' And they laughed and mocked as if my father was an *idiot*. As if Joseph's son had no right to speak in the synagogue! Was my father such a fool or cause for laughter?' She sighs. 'Why do you sigh?'

'You do need to speak with your mother. They mentioned her as well – and don't pretend you didn't hear.'

'Do you sit on some knowledge, Devira? My mother pushes me away.'

'*Hah!* You push yourself away, Yeshua, with the way you behave and the words you speak. You cause such offence you *demand* people push you away. It would give *any* mother sorrow, frankly, and if you do not know this, you know little.' Devira now turns on me, it seems. 'And she has to *live* there, Yeshua, she has to live in the place. She has to buy food there, sit by the well, hear the tittle-tattle – while you scuttle from village to village like a rat after food ... .it is not easy to find you, you know.'

I am glad at this, for I do not wish to be found. I avoid the towns. I made an exception in Nazareth but will not do so again. Towns are not safe, I am not ready; though my friends think otherwise. They want me to go to the towns.

'Sepphoris is just over the hill.' Rocky keeps saying this to me. 'We should go to Sepphoris!' But I do not go there – though I built a good half of it. Or Miriam: 'Tiberias – it's not far from Magdala and I have friends there. We should definitely go. I want Berenica to hear you!' But I do not go to Tiberias either. I will stay with the villages, where I can speak and heal, unknown and unhindered, safer ground.

'That woman needs no more grief from you,' says Devira.

'Grief from me? Truly, my mother would have me have me in a box, where I would die.'

'You don't understand, do you? You imagine you do, all that cleverness, but you don't. You do not know the abuse they took.'

'Who took?'

'Your parents. You were young, of course; but so were they … too young, really. She hasn't wished to speak of it and why should she?'

'Speak of what?' My frustration grows. 'I have never stopped her from speaking. Truly, if she has not spoken, it has been her choice.'

'I will say only this, and I say too much: you were lucky with how they spoke in the synagogue; very lucky.' She is troubled in her breathing, disturbed within; I feel a storm approaching. I feel the sky darken and the swirl of large waves building in the distance. I am on a flat plane with the rumble of flood water sweeping toward me, I sense it. 'Your mother – and I do not want to be the messenger – but your mother was known as "The whore of Nazareth."' I had heard this myself from one of the vermin, once the crowd got confident, but thought nothing of it. 'So now do you understand, Yeshua?' I understand nothing and remain silent. 'The thing is – and you must hear this carefully – she said she hadn't been with your father.'

There is a silence between us. I hear the goats call and the wind in the trees.

'I don't understand.'

'She said she hadn't been with your father, bodily, when you were born.' She pauses as if her work is done. There is some relief in her, as if a tooth has been pulled. 'So make of that what you will, everyone else did. I'm just saying. Better you know than not know, Yeshua. Just stay clear of Nazareth. And spare your mother any more grief. You're not all bad.'

She is quickly up, gives my forehead a dry kiss and makes for the door. Before leaving, she turns to me and says 'Bethlehem.'

'Bethlehem?'

'Little place south of Jerusalem. That was where the trouble started.'

MARY

Memories of better days

~

I will speak with Yeshua; it is the right thing to do.

I have spoken with James and he is of the same mind. One cannot behave like this, and he the eldest. It is not perceived well by those around; he upsets people and it is best he ceases now. I do not sleep well, my guts churn and Devira says it is not surprising: 'For it's the mother who takes the blame!' And this is how it feels sometimes. She asks me if I am angry, and I say I am not angry, but disappointed, as a mother – and who would not be, really? He goes his own way, but then he always did. I could not control him as a mother should.

'It wasn't always like this,' says Devira. 'Do you remember, Mary? I remember. I remember the girl you were and the thrill she felt when she fell with child?' I feel my eyes water, I wipe them with my sleeve, for Devira mustn't see and we cannot live in the past, there's no value in that. I *was* happy, it's true, I'd forgotten but remember now – yet that was all a long time ago and I need to get on with things now, remembering solves nothing. 'You were *so* happy. Despite everything,' she adds. 'The gossip, I mean.'

'I have lost them both,' I say, 'they are quite lost,' for there is
no value in this; no value in glances over the shoulder. What is
there to look at over the shoulder? That young girl is long gone;
she passed through me and left – and the thrill? The past is
another land and one where we cannot live. One must simply
get on with it, I can hear my father saying that: 'There's no use
in tears, Mary. What good is there in stupid tears? They achieve
nothing but a smudged face. You wish for too much, that's your
trouble. Wishes are for fools.'

And he's right; and I will not be the fool. Though something
is awakened by Devira's words, as if a wall is broken in me and
memories flood through; like wreckage in a storm tossed toward
shore, I cannot control them, for this is not what I imagined,
not what I was led to believe in the dream – no, a vision more
than a dream – when such special things were promised of
his birth. Such things were promised! And I was frightened
at first; who wouldn't be? But then so happy. It was as if *I* had
been chosen, as if I was good and my face shone, I know it did,
everyone said so. 'Your face shines, Mary!'

'You were such a happy girl then,' says Devira and it's true,
I had quite forgotten. 'I've never seen you happier than those
times!' They were different days and I so new to the world, a
young and silly girl, I have no doubt – but willing to do my
part, willing for it to be so, according to the words given, and
yes, I believe there was joy there, for I too was caught up in the
hope – felt raised up by it, when all my life I had seemed to
be put down. These memories are suddenly strong and arise
unbidden; I cannot push them down. Perhaps Devira does not
know the effect of her words and I shall not tell her. But one
must be cautious with hope, this I have learned, and learned
well; it can pierce you terribly, and when it leaves, the room is
cold and you feel a fool. And I will not be a fool.

I will find Yeshua, speak firmly with him, speak some sense
into him and bring this family shame to an end.

MIRIAM

Yeshua's rage, I can't believe it

~

I do not like the scene in Chorazin; I feel the danger.
Yeshua speaks with the crowd, small at first, hardly a
crowd at all, for village life goes on, the olive crusher's stone
still rumbling and crushing and the ritual bath house busy with
soap, cleansing visitors to the synagogue – 'everyone here needs a
wash' says Rocky, who grew up nearby and 'never liked the place.'
Some look across as the Pharisees loiter – they loiter like vultures,
and I am sorry if that is rude, but that is how it feels. They snoop
on us so often I begin to recognise some of their faces, which
could do with a smile. They seem always to oppose, and all the
more since events in Nazareth – word has travelled like a rabid
dog, barking and determined. Jude says we need the Pharisees
on our side, while Rocky – he calls them 'The Robes' – thinks
they're harmless, and perhaps they are. But I sense trouble today,
for Yeshua is far from calm in the shadows of the synagogue, the
largest I have seen – truly, it is a size in black basalt stone, the very
rock a shadow and a threat and that's Chorazin for you. Rocky
may be right. Earlier, Yeshua chatted with one or two of them,
trying to jest, trying to draw them out, he does this. He wants

the robes to laugh! But now his head is up, like a dog sensing danger. He tells people to be wary of who they follow and who they listen to, 'for there are many false prophets and teachers not worth the name.' And Berenica would agree.

Someone asks: 'But surely we are to obey the Pharisees and teachers of the law, Yeshua – for who else will teach us?' I believe the question is aimed to cause discomfort; I have learned that this occurs. Some questions are like knives, looking to fillet. But Yeshua seems to welcome the attack.

'Indeed, indeed!' he says. 'You must obey them here in Chorazin and do everything they tell you ... *everything.*'

He smiles at the robes and I do wonder at his meaning.

'Everything?' asks another.

'Of course! For they sit on the Seat of Moses, do they not? The Seat of Moses in the synagogue here, you know it, a very fine seat, reserved for the esteemed in your magnificent synagogue, a stone chair of honour! So do everything they tell you, for I have sat with them, talked with them and they are most wise, *most* wise.' Now he pauses and crouches down, as if gathering us around him. The sun is high and the crowd increases, slowly and without noise – people wander from their homes, women put down water jars, tradesmen pause, while the olive crusher ceases to grind, his stone made quiet. Stepping away from his oil, he tells his boy to stay and watch, to keep guard, for Chorazin is light-fingered, everyone knows, no matter the synagogue's size. He will hear this man, what can be lost? And the man continues: 'But do not do what they *do*, my friends – do not do what the Pharisees do!' Yeshua stands up and wanders, moving in and out of the synagogue shadows. 'For these people, they wear fine robes, we can all see their robes, but they do not practise what they preach – we notice this also, do we not? Yes?' He demands we agree, though some hold back. 'They tie heavy loads on people's shoulders – but are unwilling to lift a finger to help them as they stagger! And so, my friends, the bruised are bruised again and their dreams quite crushed.'

He now staggers himself, as if weighed down by great weight, and then falls down. 'Crushed!' he declares from the ground.

'These people ... ' And now he waves at them, he points towards them, as he gets up off the ground. ' ... they love their holy clothes and marvellous tassels; they love their place of honour at banquets and the respect offered in the market place. Oh, how folk bow and scrape to them!' He bows low, and then bows again. 'Who would not like that!? I would not mind some bowing in *my* direction, not at all! *Some*one ... *any*one!' There is some laughter in Chorazin now, he stirs them a little.

'But this is not how things are to be among you! You are not to be called "Rabbi" or by any fine title – for you have only one master, Yahweh ... and you are all brothers. So set no one above yourself. No one! The greatest among you will be the servant; and the least among you shall be the best! Can you not see that? Even the synagogue lions can see that – and they're not alive!'

The two stone lions had struck us all when we arrived here, sitting on guard – 'ridiculous', said Levi, 'eerie', said Thomas – watching and waiting at the synagogue entrance. And they may only be stone and quite dead, but they heighten the danger I feel, the sense of dread, as if the synagogue prepares to attack. The Pharisees speak among themselves, perhaps the lions make them feel strong; and then one steps forward into the silence. How silent the place has become – and no cloud in the sky; even they have stopped, sensing the air, wary to pass through.

'You are a false teacher, Yeshua – an abomination in God's presence.'

'Why, thank you.' Yeshua smiles for a moment, always a sign of danger. 'God's mouthpiece speaks, though whether God does also?' And then he starts, forgetting others who listen, aiming only at the robes.

'So woe to you teachers of the law and Pharisees – hypocrites all! Yes, *you* – hypocrites! You shut people out of the kingdom of heaven. You slam the door in their faces.' He acts this out, the slammed door. 'And you yourselves do not enter, oh no! Yet you block the path for those who try to!

So I say it again, woe to you teachers of the law and Pharisees – your hypocrisy is a festering sore in Israel's side! You travel over land and sea to win a single convert! Oh, how you love a convert! Have you found them here in Chorazin? "We have a convert!" you declare. Yet when he becomes one, you make him twice as fit for hell as you are!'

Now he moves closer in the market place dust; his voice drops a little.

'So woe to you blind guides. You say, "If anyone swears by the temple, it means nothing. Yet if someone swears by the *gold* in the temple, he is bound by his oath!" Can this drivel and nonsense be believed? Yet it is what you say and do – a fine council of fools! For tell me which is greater: the gold – or the temple that makes the gold sacred?'

'You mock the law, Yeshua; and so you mock Yahweh. Let the blasphemer be stoned!'

"*I* mock the law, my friend? *I* mock it?' He is incredulous. 'You have lost all sense of it! You give a tenth of your spices as an offering – mint, dill and cumin. How virtuous and holy! Yet you neglect the *heart* of all law, which is justice, mercy and faithfulness. Exchange your pinch of dill for a pinch of mercy and kindness, my friend – that would be a start!'

He walks away from them. I have not seen such disdain in people's eyes. They hate this man; but then he is speaking again, this time to the crowd.

'These men, people of Chorazin, they are blind guides, do not follow them. They strain out a gnat but swallow a camel.' And now he walks back towards the Pharisees, with second thoughts, as if he has not finished.

'And woe to you, and I say it again, woe to you! You clean the outside of the cup but inside, you are full of greed and self-indulgence. First clean the inside of the cup, and then the outside will also be clean.' And then to the crowd: 'See, I give you lessons in how to wash plates!'

Jude is shaking his head. 'He upsets with this outside/inside talk,' he mutters. 'It doesn't advance us, really not.' But Yeshua upsets again, as if one telling is not enough, as if we might have missed the point – though if you do not hear it the first time, I am not sure you ever will.

'And know this – know this, truly, that neither your robes nor your titles give authority. They give you no authority for you are like white-washed tombs, do you hear me, white-washed tombs –

'Here we go again,' says Jude.

' – which look so fine on the outside but on the *inside* – on the inside, they are full of rotting bones and the stench of death. You are snakes, a brood of vipers, with only poison to offer. Just how will you escape being condemned to hell, you who snuggle so deep in Satan's pocket? So deep and comfy, how will you escape?' He looks questioningly at them, and then smiles. 'Though who knows, we might throw you a rope and haul you out if you ask nicely!'

There is some laughter, though the atmosphere chills as another robe steps forward. He is a different robe, higher class, more distant in his manner and happy to stand alone, as if his status demands it – though he has the same hostile smile Yeshua always receives; the smile that precedes assault.

'A Sadducee,' says Levi to me. 'Now *they* are close to the seat of power. They run the Temple, this lot.'

'We are all admirers of Moses, I am sure,' he says with snake-like charm and I dislike him immediately. 'Are you not an admirer of Moses, Yeshua? You must be so?'

'A great man in our nation's history,' says Yeshua. 'And the Seat of Moses in the synagogue is here to remind us. Chorazin is doing its best to remember!'

'Indeed, indeed – but a great man who leaves me with a question ... well, leaves us *all* with a question, I imagine.' Yeshua stands still and waits. I watch him wait and would love to know his mind. 'For Moses said if a married man dies leaving no children, his brother shall marry his widow, and have children on behalf of his brother.'

'Indeed.'

'So imagine, if you please, seven brothers! The first dies and the widow marries the second. But then he also dies, poor man, and so she marries the third brother. And then imagine that this happens with all the brothers, she marries them all in turn, this is her life – and then the woman dies. And so to the question on all of our minds: in the resurrection, of the seven brothers, whose wife will she be? For she has been married to them all!'

'Is this the resurrection you Sadducees do not believe in?' inquires Yeshua quietly.

'I believe my question still stands, teacher, and should not be avoided, whatever your wild suppositions.'

'The Sadducees don't believe in the resurrection,' says Levi, offering commentary to this ignorant girl from Magdala.

'The dear people of Chorazin wish to hear what you say, teacher, for who knows, they may be that poor widow? Or a brother?'

'We are all grateful for your concern, my friend, touched to the core. But you and your fine robes are mistaken, so *profoundly* wrong, for you know neither the scriptures nor the power of God – which is a bleak place to be. For in the resurrection – which you do not believe in, but which the rest of us hold dear – they shall neither marry nor be given in marriage, but all are like angels in heaven. This is how it will be, my friend, so your question is a fool. You know nothing of heaven and its wonder. *Nothing!* But here on earth you tire me with your ignorant attack; indeed, I am sure you tire everyone! You lock things down and I must unlock them!'

Jude is agitated by this drama and keeps muttering 'He's a Sadducee, he's a Sadducee!' until he can wait no longer and steps out into the space to calm Yeshua down. He says in his ear that enough has been said, he believes enough is enough. 'This is not our battle, teacher. And these are powerful men who we will need.' But Yeshua ignores him, he looks through him – it is a most terrible gaze – and Jude turns and walks back towards us, shrugging his shoulders, but in shock I think. And now Yeshua moves towards a child. He softens in manner and bends down to his height and blesses him.

'Hello, my fine fellow,' he says and the little boy smiles. 'Truth at last!' says Yeshua as he lifts him onto his lap. 'And what is your name?'

'Benjamin, sir.'

'Here is the excellent Benjamin and here is the kingdom of God, my friends! No one is closer to the kingdom than he. Benjamin is closer than us all! So become as a child, each of you here in Chorazin. And harm no child in your care. Harm one such as him and you harm our father in heaven. Lead one such child astray – and it would be better for you to be thrown in the sea with a millstone round your neck! So yes, let the robes return to their judging huddles – but let the children come to me, for here is the kingdom.' And slowly other children appear from behind the coat tails of adults, a little army of the small – previously hidden and previously in fear. But now they converge on Yeshua, adults hurriedly following, and he is engulfed by the crowd and children's shouts. Rocky steps quickly in, forcing his way through to pull him out.

'Careful now!' shouts Rocky. 'Careful now! Let the teacher free!'

Joanna looks on with concern. She tugs a little at her braids when nervous, I have noticed this, and now she signals to Levi, who moves towards the rumpus and when Yeshua emerges, pushed and pulled about, Levi guides him quietly away; I do not see where. Rocky remains in the crowd, for now there are others there, those less pleased by Yeshua, and I see him disputing with someone. And no one knows what to do, for some are happy and smile at Yeshua's words and some are angry. Neither do I know what to do, for who speaks like this? Who offends like this?

'He cannot keep doing this,' says Jude to Joanna. 'He really can't. You'll have to tell him.' Jude is embarrassed at being ignored by Yeshua. I stand nearby, I cannot help but hear. 'He'll have us all in trouble.'

Joanna looks at him. She is not given to a warm spirit at the best of times; and replies coldly now. 'He speaks from his heart, Jude. Would you have him close it up?'

'I just – well, I would have him use his head as well.'

'Like you use yours?'

'You know the danger he invites, Joanna ... danger he invites on us all. It's not just him, you know. We are all in danger!' Jude is animated. 'He cannot promise heaven to everyone, yet

curse such people as these. He just cannot! You should speak
with him.'

'And what would I say?'

'That he cannot – *should not* – upset these people, it is not
our purpose!'

'And what is our purpose, Jude?'

'Nothing is gained by hostility. That's all I say.'

And when I find him – for I search straight way – Yeshua
is slumped down and quite without life, in a home nearby. A
woman leaves as I enter, it is perhaps her home, I do not know
but know I must be here and I am shocked. It is hard to believe
... so hard to believe that this is the man I beheld just now in
the market place. I stand in the door way; and I say nothing;
I do not know what to say or whether even to enter. He leans
forward, head in hands and quite broken. I wish to be nearer;
I move across the room and kneel before him.

He lifts his head and looks upon me; or perhaps he looks
through me. His silent eyes do see through ... though perhaps
I imagine this, for I fear my shame being seen.

'I am spent,' he says quietly, with a hint of a smile. 'I had to
speak. I could do no other ... '

'You were magnificent.' This may be true, though I say it to
encourage. 'No one could believe what you were saying!' This
is certainly true. He breathes slowly and deeply, as though his
body carries a pain.

'I have done enough here in Chorazin to be believed, I have
done enough; but I was not believed ... '

'Are you all right?'

'Their anger – it lodges in me.'

'You are tired.'

'I am poisoned by their rage ... I am like a sponge soaked
in poison.'

I do not mention that his own rage might lodge a little in them
as well. I cannot imagine where his fierce speech comes from.

'Many *weren't* angry, teacher. Many smiled. Only the robes
were angry ... one or two others also, but mainly the robes. And
they are always angry, from what I can see.'

'I need the hills, Miriam, I have lost the light.' I do not know what he means, but he says it again. 'I have lost the light, quite lost it. These things – they must pass through me, but I need the hills, to be alone. Do not tell them where I am gone.'

'I won't tell.' This at least I can be sure of. His strong hands sit on his knees. Without realising, I put my own hands on his – and stroke them gently. Do they feel me? I wonder if he will pull away ... but he does not move. He remains still and I continue to stroke, as with a baby, when coaxing them to sleep, one stroke after another. He does not sleep, for he sits alert, almost a supplicant, as one receiving a blessing. I do believe I bless him. And in time, he lifts his large hands gently and leaning forward, he kisses me on the lips. We pause, perhaps in surprise; I have not yet opened my lips to him – or to any man. But with our second kiss, longer and fuller, I do ... though this cannot be, for my family must know. How will I tell them without rage and attack in return? I cannot tell them.

'Thank you, Miriam' he says, getting up. 'Thank you.' He smiles, like one at peace. 'And tell no one where I am gone. Apart from Joanna, Joanna can know ... but no one else.'

I wish to ask 'What now?' for I am startled and falling apart inside; if this can be said. But I fear his reply, so remain silent. And hearing voices approaching – it sounds like Rocky – he moves quickly to the door, but turns before he leaves.

'We shall be as one, Miriam, whatever unfolds. We shall be as one.'

YESHUA

The ant and the louse

The leather strapping snaps as I near the cave, leaving only a useless wooden sole. It has been threatening to break for a while; Joanna has mentioned it and even measured my foot, to compare it with Chuza's, saying she will find something similar.

But that is no help for now, so I throw the sandal away, hurling it towards Jerusalem, hurling it towards the Temple, and as I do, I decide also to let go of my clothes. If my feet are to be naked, let my whole body be so. I remember my words in Bethsaida. 'You are naked before heaven,' I had said, 'you are naked before heaven, so what you hide will be revealed, and whatever is covered will be uncovered. But bring forth that which is within you, and truly, that will save you. But if you do not bring forth that which is within you – if you hide it and seal it in – then it will kill you.'

I wish nothing hidden, nothing sealed in, but all things brought forth and all things uncovered, so I start with my body. I waver on the seething stones, hot and sharp, standing, when possible, on my right leg, the one with the shoe; and undoing my cord belt, I lift off my outer tunic. I lay it down on the rock; it is heavy with sweat and dust. I stand now beneath the heavens in my inner tunic, with only holes for arms and a lighter garment by far. But while I am naked now in the eyes of the law, I am not naked enough for myself. So I remove also my inner tunic and now know only my vulnerable skin, the big sky and warm breeze on my back.

'Who am I?' I ask and a single cloud passes above.

I make my careful way forward, choosing the flat stones and dry grass for my weight, and then hot sand between my toes before the deep shadows of the cave, I stoop a little to enter, the sudden cool, and all that I am, and all that I do, is quietened like a child. I sit down and feel the rough grit on my arse; and know that I had to come, that I had to be here, naked and alone, in solitude and homecoming. This is what I feel. The world and its noise is left behind; and all uncovered, all unhidden.

I enjoy the silence for a while, with empty mind. Here are no needy hands grabbing at me or dark-willed jibes ... here, no thing is asked and this is heaven. I stop and I breathe ... I watch an ant at work moving a dead louse, which is carried on its back, bent legs in the air. I like the ant. It is hard work removing the louse and I know how he feels; truly, I have met the louse ... and his friends.

It took me half a day's walk to be free. Half a day's walk to be clear, to feel the space grow inside me again, to feel things left behind. But I am slowly restored to joy in the stillness; a joy somehow started by a kiss, the blessing of a woman, kind hands and soft-lipped. I have not known this. We must speak together, though what do I say? I know the blessing but not the future, or how one thing becomes another, or what it becomes, though for now, like a plant beaten back and trampled down, I grow again; this is so. I recover the space sometimes lost – like an enslaved village evicting a tyrant: 'Be gone – we would be free!' And when space appears, so too does joy – how can it not? And quietly, with gentle footsteps, the past also returns, my father and I, preparing the land before building.

'It's all in the preparation,' he would say if I complained of the work. 'You cannot build on mud; and you cannot build on mess.' We would clear the space – pulling up, ripping out and taking away; then dig to lay the foundations. Some builders would avoid such labour, if the ground was hard. In the summer months, the sun-baked earth looked a solid enough base, and they would treat it as such. 'Why make a problem, Joe, when there's no problem there. The ground feels like rock to me!' But my father would shake his head. 'There's no rock there, Yesh; they're building on sand and there'll be nothing left standing when the rain comes. Give us builders a bad name, that lot. Everything needs a foundation.'

But it was always the space, and not the building, for me. While those who passed saw the building we made, I saw only the space that held it. A building has shape and time, a beginning and end ... but space is eternal, like the light. I said this to my father once and soon wished I had not. 'You been listening to the Greeks or something? If space is eternal, Yeshua, we don't get paid! Space is there to be filled, my boy.'

It was good for trade that I learned Greek; and in Sepphoris, it was much spoken, which made the zealots rage; they liked God but did not like migrants. But on one day, as we spoke, there was something more than the Greek, for my father wasn't done. He warned me against dreamers; spoke up for getting on with things, as though suddenly, he was making a point, making a speech that had been waiting inside him for years. 'Sometimes life is a bastard, Yesh ... a proper bastard. You don't know where you are or what's happening and everyone has their say – and don't they just? But you have to get on with it, Yesh, you just get on with it ... and not mind what people say. You do what you think is right; that's all you can do ... just do what you think is right.'

Was this about Bethlehem and events there? I do wonder now. So much to speak of, and nothing quite said by either mother or father. He was a cautious man, my father – cautious of people and life. He watched for danger, eyes on the horizon, like a watchman on a tower – as if he had been battered in some way; as if cut and hurt by past events. And everything led back to Bethlehem; though no one spoke its name.

'Believe me, you never know what's coming your way, Yesh. Things happen you couldn't imagine. Nothing prepares you, we live life blind. So you keep your head down and your eyes open.'

And once, a few weeks later, he looked at me as we ate our rolls, surrounded by timber and nails. He looked hard and long at me, his eyes holding mine, as though he knew me for the first time; as though only now could he look. This is how it felt. And he said 'Your mother and I, there's something you ought to ... ' – but he said no more. Someone shouted a greeting across the street, 'Hello there, Joe! Still in work, you lazy sod? So miracles do happen then!' And he waved in return, as it made for peace and he liked peace. 'Happy are those who work for peace,' he'd say. 'Now *they* will see God.'

He was always working, my father; keen not to waste time but to get the job done: 'Anyone can start, but few can finish.' So he'd say 'Hello' to folk and exchange brief words – and then return to work. Though I remember children could slow him for a while. 'Let the children come to me,' he would say. 'It's no bother to see a small one.' And he would be on his knees to greet them, to make sure his eyes met theirs. 'Kids, eh?' he'd grumble when they left, as if they had been all trouble and nuisance. 'Little trouble makers! Now let's get the cross-beam up, Yeshua – or the *patibulum* as the Romans call it. You see, you're not the only one with brains.'

But as my memory of him fades, I feel the space ... the space that held the building; the building borrowed the space. In the end, only the space remains and I know the space inside me now. The emptiness feels endless. It goes back before time and forward beyond all horizons. It consumes everything, as a lake consumes a raindrop. To walk in such space, this is to be free. The fear and rage, they pass through me, they dissolve, for they are not the space, and the space is prior, and the space is stronger and the space is light.

And into the cave, the light spills again. As in the wilderness, it appears through a corridor of time, before all things – as if to go back to the beginning would be a walk into dazzling bright. And the desire in me is strong, the desire to go there, to cease this work, to leave it behind and to hide ... the temptation is to walk back, to give up, to know my God again in ease of life. I have surely done enough? Have I not done more than enough? This thought strikes me. I do not even know what I do anymore. What do I do? If a teller of truth, I have found few who listen; and fewer still who understand. I sing a song and no one joins in. And how can I explain what I know? What story can suffice? When I tell a story, each hears another, with their own meaning. So why do I bother?

'You must speak plainly, teacher!' says Rocky and I try to speak plain of un-plain things; but nailing the breeze to a pole would be an easier call. For the kingdom is like a breeze, I have said this to Rocky: 'The kingdom is like a breeze. It cannot be caught by the hand or thought by the mind. It can only be known, it can only be felt.'

Some say I allow Rocky too much of a voice; some, that I am too close to John; and others believe Miriam is allowed too near. Some mutter that I keep myself to myself; that I am distant from those who follow me – and some say I am too near by far. 'You should not cry,' say others. 'Teachers do not cry.' Yet they turn away when I laugh, drink and dance. 'Teachers should not do such things!' *Hah!* What is it they want from me? What is it *you* want from me, father? I bring forth that which is within me ... and find a prayer at last.

Here in the cave, I wish to return to the light, the sense is strong; to give up and to go back. How I long for this! But my naked limbs do not take me there, nor can they; there is no going back ... and no giving up. I watch the ant moving the louse. He orders the others; he is a busy ant and the louse is shifted. Is he free? He is free to be an ant, free to move the louse; but not free to be a mule or a zealot ... or Yeshua. We are not free; though free to be ourselves ... free to stay close to the light, whatever the dark; free to guard the flame. Though from here on, I do not see clear. If I wished clear sight, this cave offers none. The way ahead is veiled ... like the sun in the dawn mist, shimmering and vague. I come from light, but where I go, a cloud obscures my sight; and I know, I know – it is not given us to know these things. It is not given to us to know who and how and when. Who dies early and who dies late? Who by water and who by fire? Who by famine and who by thirst? Who in comfort and who tormented? We cannot say who shall find peace and who shall be denied peace. Who applauded and who reviled? Who shall have children and who shall be stoned? Who will dance and who will hobble? We do not know and cannot tell. Though lead me not to the time of trial, dear father, for I am weak ... and your kingdom come, your will be done – and as it is above, so let it be below.

I lean back against the rock and sit for a while in silence, which is stronger than an army. Something is decided, something understood; I allow the unknowing like a farmer must allow the soil and plant wisely ... and perhaps young John understands, and perhaps Miriam, and maybe Joanna – but Rocky, *never!* Rocky has other skills. He could mend a net while ordering his crew in a storm. Neither John nor Miriam could do that! And he still keeps some of his large metal net needles.

'They might do for a Roman one day,' he tells me. I often wonder what he hears me say; but his hearing I cannot help. And now the sound of voices outside, they get closer; the world presses on me again. It is time to leave the cave, and exchange one light for another, greater for lesser, such light here in the dark. Rocky and Jude lead the pack approaching me. When I step out and greet them, they are shocked; their hands go to their mouths; some laugh. I forget I stand naked before them.

'Teacher!' A cloak is quickly wrapped around me. We build a fire and set olive bread to bake in the sand. No one seems eager to speak; they are subdued. Perhaps they remember events yesterday in the cursed Chorazin. Perhaps they do not like such speech from me; such attack on others, such offence caused. Perhaps they wonder if I come here to repent of my harsh words?

'We wondered where you were, teacher,' says Rocky.

'I was here, as I had to be.'

'Alone?'

What does he imagine? 'Many stand at the door, Rocky – but only those who are alone and solitary can enter the bridal chamber.'

'We have been searching for you the entire night.' It is an accusation.

'We set out at dawn.' Jude corrects him. He likes accuracy, while Rocky sees less need; truth for him is a blur and imprecise. I look around at them, hungry and thirsty after their travel; and feel sad. 'Can you not be alone?' I ask. 'Or allow me to be?'

'But why do you escape from us, teacher?' says Rocky. He is hurt; he cannot understand. 'When we have left everything to follow you!'

'You have left nothing to follow me, Rocky, because you do not leave yourself. You leave your boat and your family, but you do not leave yourself, so you have left nothing. If you leave yourself, then you have left everything.'

Rocky looks lost. 'But how do we leave ourselves, teacher? Do I pull my arms off? Do my legs and arms say goodbye to my head?'

'Wouldn't be the first time,' says Levi.

And I say: 'Create vacancy, Rocky – this is what you require ... vacancy, for still you carry everything within you, when there is nothing to carry. You are like an old soldier who demands his armour and spear. He does not need them, for he does not now fight – yet insists on weighing himself down. He staggers under their weight as he drinks wine at home with a friend! There is no need. So create vacancy like the night sky above us, Rocky. For see what glory it holds!'

Above us, the dark blanket spills with stars.

MIRIAM

These stupid men

'If it's the kingdom of God he describes, then heaven help us all! Yeshua's dream is a fool's paradise, a land of sweet never-never!'

And I have to listen to this! I'd prefer to throw a cake at them; or perhaps for the house to fall on their heads, and it's quite a place, way beyond what I have ever known ... though Joanna called it 'tawdry, my dear, tawdry' – which was not a word I knew. But it has rich red drapes on the walls and pottery so finely painted, I have not seen such things – a whole set showing a woman with snakes in her hair. 'Medusa,' I am told, but who is Medusa? I never heard of her in the synagogue. Was I not listening enough?

The owner trades in grain, the steward says, 'very big in grain, he travels a lot, picks up all sorts of things and the Pharisees don't need to know.'

'About what?' I ask.

'About the snakes and Medusa – it's just the bloody Greeks for you.'

'What did she do?'

'Medusa? She turned people to stone. But it's a long time ago.' And I will not tell the Pharisees, I owe them nothing and I merely serve wine here, the pottery is not my concern while I listen to some young men talk – though if I was Medusa I believe I'd turn *them* to stone. They are from Sepphoris, I imagine ... or Caesarea ... or Tiberias. There is something of the Roman about them and something of the Greek, something of the city. They're Jews ... but Jews who like Rome and who like Greece and who like themselves. I don't take to these arrogant, stupid men, in their little alcove in the grain seller's house, where they gossip and guffaw; and I can't help but overhear them; and can't help but listen. They speak of Yeshua, which pulls me up; and they speak as if they know him. Well, they know *of* him, this is clear, they have gathered information; but they do not know him.

One says, '"Have anxiety about nothing, my friends!" No, seriously, that is one of his lines!'

Another, 'Like that's going to happen. Anxiety's the only thing holding me together!'

'He is peasant class,' says another, 'that's what they say ... probably nothing more than a whingeing zealot. They do so whinge, the zealots!'

'Oh, definitely peasant ... his father was a cheap builder, who we *never* used, by the way.'

'I know someone in Sepphoris who used them. They actually thought Yeshua was the better carpenter. So if you need a new table ... '

'So he's basically a labourer.'

'He hasn't studied?'

'*Was* a labourer, he's given that up ... .he builds stories now.'

'I'd get more use from a chair.'

'It's true, though. Ask him a question and he'll tell you a bloody story! "What does life mean, teacher?" "There was a man travelling from Jerusalem to Jericho ... "'

'Not a story man myself. I prefer facts. I mean, a story can prove anything, can't it? What does a story prove? It's just something someone's made up! No need.'

'Though he tells them well, to be fair – I mean, for a builder.'

'That's a fairly low bar, Ishmael ... almost touching the ground.'

'Have you actually heard him?'

'Yes, I have actually heard him – *actually*! Everything is *like* something with Yeshua. He's interesting. He has a metaphoric mind.'

'A metaphoric mind?!' They are hooting with mirth. I don't know what it means but I hate them. They mock each other; but mainly they mock Yeshua.

"A man without love is like a river without water," – that sort of thing, he's very good ... no really. I mean, he's bright.'

'So is Satan. You're not a secret follower, are you Ishmael?' All eyes are suddenly on him.

'No!' He waves the idea away. 'But he experiences God, you can tell that.' Ishmael is serious. Perhaps there is hope for him.

'How?'

'Well, he talks of light as if he's actually seen it, rather than read about it.'

'So he's a good actor.'

Another pipes up and I'm afraid I don't distinguish between them, they all sound the same: 'Don't say he's one of those ecstatics?' The young man starts waving his arms about, eyes rolling and full of groans and the others join in. 'The sort who swoon a great deal.'

'Swooning? No need for it – really, no need. Not for men. I mean, women can swoon – but men?'

'I don't think he swoons,' says Ishmael. 'I haven't seen him swoon. He heals, of course.'

'Oh yes, the world and his wife thinks he healed them, his reputation grows like the emperor's wine cellar! Can't move for weird and wonderful healing stories.'

'He healed Rocky's mother-in-law, I hear.'

'And they still talk?' More guffaws.

'Rocky is a head-case anyway. Do you know Rocky? The biggest mouth in Galilee. He left his family to follow Yeshua around. And why would you do that? Why would you leave your family for, well – *this*?'

'Perhaps he doesn't like them very much. There are members of my family I wouldn't mind leaving.'

'Now, now!'

'I once met his wife, Sapphira – she was happy with the fishing business; and it was not unsuccessful. He was a worker on that boat, out all hours. And then he sold it all! He sold the bloody boat and followed Yeshua! And she's not happy about it.'

'"Avoid healers and lepers," as the sages say – "particularly healers."'

'He's an aggressive shit, though; I've seen him at work. He commands the demons out – have you seen him?'

'It's true.'

'He shouts at them. No, really – he literally shouts at the demons, a friend told me, he saw him – saw him rubbing saliva into the blind man's eyes and pressing his fingers down the ears of the deaf! Seriously deranged.'

'He shouts at Pharisees as well, mind, which is at least mildly entertaining.'

'Oh, and whisper it quietly in the synagogue, *sssshhh!* – but he also offers forgiveness! No, he does, he absolutely does. He offered forgiveness to some bloke on a stretcher.'

'He *what?* That's blasphemy!'

'He may not have meant forgiveness as such, because obviously no one but God ... '

'No, I'm sorry, but I'm serious now – that is blasphemy, however you dress it up. To offer forgiveness is blasphemy.' Everyone mimics shock at such behaviour.

'We're doing our best, Moses!'

'Blasphemy isn't funny – no, really.' And then something catches his eye. 'Oh it's *him*, is it? He's the one?' He points through the window to the crowd outside where Yeshua is laughing about something. His friend nods.

'That's him. And that's Rocky beside him.'

'"To enter the kingdom of God, you must become as a child."'

'What?'

'That's another one of his lines. *Become as a child.* He wants us to un-grow ourselves! Any volunteers?'

'"And the first shall be last and the last first," – contrary to all evidence available! You have to wonder who he thinks he is?'

'He's a blasphemer, that's who he is – he should be stoned.'

'And his family might join in. No, seriously! I mean, I don't know about the stoning, but have you heard them? His sister thinks he's crazy. Ayla, I mean. You know Ayla? She calls him "a flowing fountain of nonsense" ... says he has caused no end of trouble at home.'

'Doesn't look good if your own family don't trust you.'

'It's what I hear.'

"He'll fade, obviously. Attention-seeking preachers – they do come and go. So forgive me if I couldn't give a flying shit about Yeshua! I mean, why are we talking about him? Remember Zeki?'

'Zeki!?' They all break out into laughter. 'No, we shouldn't laugh.'

Though they do laugh, as they remember the old man who died in Tiberias. He burned himself to ash after telling everyone he would rise again and overthrow Israel's enemies. He died in agony and didn't rise again, because no one does. And the Romans are still here.

'Poor man ... mad as a goat with a stutter. Now can we talk about something else?'

The mood quietens.

'One rabbi told me he was a sorcerer.'

'Wouldn't surprise me.'

'When I said "something else" I was including the topic of Yeshua.'

'Jude Iscariot is one of his followers.'

'And I know Jude. We talk ... he tells me things. He's impressed – I mean, he has some issues with him obviously ... '

'Just "some"?'

'I knew Jude at school. Clever boy, he was. Surprised he's caught up in it.'

'He does the accounts. He says I should join his band.'

'You, Ishmael? And are you tempted?'

'No!'

'Not just a little bit?! You are the following sort, so why not the insane and blaspheming Yeshua?'

'*Piss off!*'

I approach them with wine, their cups empty, drained to the dregs. I cannot be quiet; I really cannot be quiet.

'I have been listening to you, gentlemen; to everything you say.' They quieten and look at me as an oddity, as entertainment. They have not noticed me before and, like a dog, cannot believe I speak – for a woman should not speak openly with men or she will be named a whore. But then maybe they wish me to praise them. Even a woman can offer men praise; it is her duty. 'I have been listening to your wisdom with amazement, gentlemen; and with wonder.' They soften. 'And I have been carefully adding up all that you know.'

'Adding up all that we know?' They are intrigued.

'And now I've done it; I think so. And it comes to nothing. All that you know comes to nothing, maybe less. You do not know Yeshua at all; you have not the faintest clue. More wine?'

MARY

In search of reunion

~

James tells me Yeshua is in Magdala, speaking to crowds from a boat; he has always liked the sea, though I remember him being quite sick in a boat.

'Go to the water, James, and it will tell you everything,' he once said. And while he joked with his brother – I know he joked, that was his sort of humour, though not to my taste – I think something inside him may have believed it. That was the sort of thing he believed, he could be most contrary. He will say such things about Galilee; yet he is full of contempt for the Temple! Why not say the Temple will tell you everything? Yet he cannot do that, he is too stubborn, I could never correct that in him. And he will discover for himself when he is a parent and cannot get his own way. Everyone thinks it is easy until they do it themselves. He'll learn; one can be sure of that.

So now we seek him out, the authorities think it best – and poor old Zebedee, as if he is to blame! Some say he encouraged Yeshua, and now call him a faithless and dangerous teacher. But I know this to be false; James has been very clear. He says Zebedee was patient with him, yet firm; that he attempted to guide Yeshua, but that he just wouldn't be guided – and there is no surprise. And James' friend Eleazar confirms this. He is often around at our home now and seems a most polite and sensible sort; the son I should have had, perhaps. I don't mean that, of course. But James clearly has great respect for him, so one must count one's blessings, that such a person visits and befriends one's family – and at least puts one of my children on the straight and narrow.

But Eleazar is not with us today; they say he goes sometimes to Jerusalem, and to other towns, to teach the faith – he is clearly considered very top-drawer by the authorities. Instead, it is Ayla and James who share the journey with me to Galilee, and we arrive in Magdala mid-morning. They know Yeshua better than anyone, of course, and Ayla is not shy with her opinions. 'He has betrayed the family,' she says, and while I try to temper her tone, I cannot disagree. 'He cannot be considered a teacher. How can one who betrays his family be a teacher?' She sounds like my mother, who takes the same view. And on arrival, I find I do not care for Magdala much; it compares unfavourably with Tiberias, which I hadn't thought to like, but it quite turns the head, being such a new city. We stayed the night there in clean-enough lodgings, perfectly decent, before travelling on the few miles which brought us here.

There is nothing wrong with Magdala as such – as long as you like fish! And I have no wish to judge, it is not in my nature – but it just seems rather pleased with itself, and rather busy with itself and with no time for anyone. And when all's said and done, they are hardly the only town to salt and dry fish. They're busy, I grant you. The harbour is teeming with traders, and all making a great deal money, no doubt – though there are others elsewhere working no less hard and equally deserving of income. It has not been easy of late, without the building and carpentry business, which was something Yeshua *could* do. He wasn't a bad carpenter and must have done something right, for he was always employed. We walk around the town a little. Ayla says she has never seen so many fish; and you smell them long before you see them. We agree to stop talking about the fish.

We go to the synagogue, where they know of him. And some say he teaches well – 'He speaks with such authority!' they say. But others are less charitable and confirm my fears. We do not reveal ourselves, so we hear honest opinions, with more than one saying he is possessed by demons – 'and he scoops up the poor in his pocket. They love to hear him, though he poisons their minds with promises.'

I do not like to hear these things; they wound me, as they would wound any mother, surely? No one wishes to hear this. But I keep my counsel, for what is one to say? I can only stare at them as they tell me – Ayla tells me I am staring, before she pulls me away.

'We just need to speak with him, mother.' She feels that if we speak with him, things can be settled; and we are told he has left the boat and is now teaching in the market, 'or in a home which opens onto it – he was there yesterday, quite a crowd.' And now that I am here, now we are close to seeing him, I become quite worried, for I do not know what I wish to say to him. Ayla says she will do the talking for me, bless her, but she won't do the talking, because James then says that he will do the talking, that he will speak with Yeshua, that it is the man's role; and that Ayla must be careful. A woman can speak in the home, and Ayla speaks clearly enough there, but not in the market place, not in public. 'Leave this to me,' says James and I am impressed. I believe Eleazar has made James more confident, when before he was perhaps bullied by his elder brother.

'I am not sure he will like our visit,' I say, but James has already sent a messenger ahead; he tells me not to worry, which I find reassuring. Some from the synagogue have followed us. I do not wish to appear foolish in their eyes, but Ayla calms me.

'You need not look so anxious, mother,' she says, though I believe she frets a little herself, for suddenly we see him, as if a stranger. As we were told, he is talking to a group on a balcony, busy with his hands, intent on his speech, and there are many below as well, pushing forward to listen. We cannot get near. And I have to say, I can hardly believe this is my son, my first born, and once the source of so much joy. What has occurred to make it so? I do not know. But really, why must I stand here in fish-filled Magdala and demand my son gives up his foolishness and come home? Why must I do that? Is that fair? No parent should have to do this – *no* parent. We do it for his own good, this is what Ayla says – 'we do it to save him from himself.'

Somehow the messenger has pushed through. He has climbed the stairs and now moves towards Yeshua. He touches his shoulder, Yeshua turns, he speaks with him, he is telling Yeshua we are here, as James instructed. But James is now talking to a man in the crowd, pointing at us and then pointing at Yeshua. Yeshua stops, he looks out across the crowd, his eyes searching – and then the man in the crowd shouts out: 'Your family is here, Yeshua. Your mother, your brothers, your sisters! They want to speak with you. Hear them, please!'

The crowd is silent; all watch Yeshua who stands up and is quite still. James pushes his way back to us, covered in sweat but pleased with his work. Ayla holds my arm.

'And so my family are here!' says Yeshua. 'Perhaps your family are here too? But who is my mother? And who is my brother and my sister?' Such silence ... this man does command silence, and I am frightened. And now he swings round, his arm out, pointing to all. 'Look! Here are my mother and my brothers! Whoever does what my father in heaven wishes – they are my brother, my sister and my mother!'

And I die where I stand, my guts churn; Ayla holds me in her fury, squeezing my arm.

'I want to go home,' I say. 'I want to go home.'

YESHUA

Nicodemus by night

~

He comes by night; he does not wish to be seen. Shameful deeds are performed in the shadows, away from public view. And it seems I am a shameful deed.

'I come on behalf of Pharisees who wish you well.' This was his message, written in Greek and passed to me yesterday. 'Sadducees also. Those better-born than some others, the Temple sort; we need not clash. I wish to inquire and support.'

Some are worried that I meet him, both Thomas and Rocky fearing a trap. 'You have to wonder what he wants?' says Thomas, who trusts no one including himself. But John and Joanna know of him and believe he could be a friend. 'They are a significant group in the Temple,' she says. 'And Chuza has seen them at the palace; they speak with Herod, quietly.'

'No one should speak with Herod,' says Rocky. 'He's a false Jew. May he and his household rot!' He attacks Joanna more than Herod with these words. He has recently discovered that Joanna's husband works for Herod; that Chuza actually runs his household. This did not go down well and sets the group apart in some manner.

But on arrival, Nicodemus carries his wealth simply; he was born into it, so there is no need for parade, he has nothing to prove. I watch him enter and in the lamp light, see a careful man. Susanna greets him and sits him down. He is unsettled by her presence but I wished for Susanna to greet him. We must live in the light and not bow to darkness.

'Yeshua will join us shortly,' she says. 'Some wine? We have a recent delivery from Crete.'

'We should not be alone, woman,' he says testily. 'It is unseemly. I believe you must leave.'

'This is my home, sir.' He is surprised. 'You are welcome here; but I will not be leaving. That would be odd, would it not? To walk out my own front door on the bidding of a stranger. Though if *you* wish to leave ... '

'Then I must apologise, of course. I understood it was the home of one of Yeshua's followers – not that of a woman.'

'I see you are from old Israel,' says Susanna. 'Yeshua would like a new one.'

'Greetings, Nicodemus!' I say, stepping forward from the shadows. There is relief in his face. 'You have met my friend Susanna, who kindly offers us her home.' I sit down opposite him and Susanna brings us wine. 'It is from Crete, she tells me.'

'So I hear.'

'Thick as the blood of a minotaur! Herod imports it ... but maybe that does not commend it to you. Well, who knows? Is Herod a friend?' Our guest smiles nervously as I chat, waiting his moment. He wonders if Susanna will leave; he is made awkward by her. 'You must say what brings you at this time of night, Nicodemus. I have only your written message. And please sit down.' We sit opposite each other, silent for a moment, sipping our wine. 'You come to offer support, perhaps – you come as a friend?'

'Oh, quite, quite – I mean, well, who knows, as you say; but yes, a friend, I believe.'

'But a friend who does not wish to be seen with me ... you choose the shroud of darkness.'

'These are uncertain times, teacher, and we must all be wary.'

'Must I be wary?'

'There is no peace in our politics, as you know. It makes everyone on edge and no one able to listen. This is dangerous, without doubt. Everyone shouts ... including, if I may say so, yourself, Yeshua.'

'I may have shouted quietly on occasion ... but I shout only the truth.'

'Well, I believe you know the trouble you cause; of course you do.' He smiles. 'But we also know that you are admired as a teacher, by some – we know that. The crowds come to hear you.' He nods as if to agree with himself. 'And God is with you, I am sure ... in a manner and up to a point.'

'And where is the point where God leaves me?'

'It is just a phrase!'

'I testify to what I have seen and heard; nothing more. What else is there to do? We testify to what we have seen and heard.'

'Quite, quite – though you speak differently from others; you say different things. But then perhaps you see and hear different things – who knows? It may be this that upsets, of course; that you hear and speak differently ... and disturbingly.'

'Around me, I see and hear lies, Nicodemus – lies and more lies. They are like the flies that gather on a dead dog. There are so many of them, buzzing around us, and all so busy, one cannot help but see and hear them. I'm sure you see them too.'

'Well, we must indeed beware of the pagan lies ... '

'In my experience, they buzz mainly around synagogue and Temple.'

'Ah, well ... ' Now he breaths deeply, shaking his head, much unsettled. 'I don't think those are fit words, Yeshua. Not fit at all. You compare the Temple to a dead dog – not fit words, I think.'

'But are they true, Nicodemus?'

'True?'

'This is all I ask when someone speaks. Not "Is it upsetting?" or "Is it fit?" – but "Is it true?" For if the words are not true, then they are a lie; and nothing strong or good is built on a lie. But if they are true, then whether they are fit words matters not at all, surely?'

'The truth and the lie are so easily discerned, Yeshua? I wonder if it is so simple.'

'The truth sets us free – and lies enslave. This is how we know, how we discern.'

'They are words of danger, Yeshua, much danger – which you should not repeat in public, if you wish for my opinion. I suggest you be most careful ... and I speak as a friend.'

'And I likewise and I say to you, be born again, Nicodemus – be born again.' I drink some wine. The Cretan red is warming on this cold night, but my guest is confused. His caution thinks hard; this does not proceed as planned. He looks at his sandals. 'Do you hear me, Nicodemus?'

'I hear you, Yeshua ... which is not to say I know what you mean; the two are rather different. How can anyone know what you mean, when you say that ... '

'You must be born again, Nicodemus – and Israel must be born again, starting with the Temple.'

Nicodemus sips at his red. 'A very pleasant wine,' he says, 'very pleasant. The Cretans have done us proud ... for pagans. And how shall this *be*, exactly – this being born again?' He speaks with a chuckle, as if to a child. 'Can an old man enter again the womb of his mother? A rather unseemly sight, I think you will agree. And not one I relish!'

'*You* are a teacher and you do not know this, Nicodemus?' I am stunned by the stupidity in one so lauded in the Temple. Is it not obvious that all must be born again, starting with the Temple, starting with his heart? Is this not obvious?

'I know the Law of Moses, Yeshua.' He coughs, as if this hardly need be said. 'And, of course, I admire much of your teaching, greatly admire it. You speak plainly and with no little courage. But you choose battles you cannot win, which is unwise. Rather, learn patience, my friend, patience! Patience is bitter, as the saying goes, but it has sweet fruit.'

'I see only rotten fruit.'

'Yeshua ... '

'The same rotten people telling the same rotten lies. You come here in fear, Nicodemus, and beg the night to hide your steps.' I pause and reach out for his hand; I wish for his friendship. 'But you come also in courage, my friend, which

I admire. You applaud my courage and I applaud yours. You feared to come, yet you conquered your fear. Truly, you are a seeker after truth – impatient even, or why else would you be here? And so I say to you this: I say that those who seek must continue to seek until they find.' He nods. 'And on finding they will be disturbed.'

'Disturbed?'

'Of course! How can the truth not disturb? It is like a large animal in a small room. It will knock things over and bring calamity. But on *being* disturbed, Nicodemus – on being disturbed, you will marvel and reign over all. That is how it will be, Nicodemus. Keep hold of your courage and you shall marvel and reign over all! So where now is the darkness?'

His eyes wander in discomfort. In his heart, he begins to leave. He seeks to find, I know this – but does not wish to be disturbed. I see his heart look for the door. 'We must speak again, Rabbi,' he says as he puts down his wine – but I do not wish him gone.

'You are a ruler in Israel, Nicodemus – you and your friends are rulers. Is this not so?'

'Well ... '

'And you know that Israel's hope, our Passover hope, has slipped from our grasp. You know this, Nicodemus! Everyone knows this! Ponder our history and our visitors. Assyria, Babylon, Persia, Greece, Egypt, Syria – and now Rome! We have lost our way, have we not? And the question on everyone's lips, "When will Israel be free from such harsh bonds? When will the tyranny end? We must reclaim ourselves, be born again!"'

'These are difficult times.'

'So could not you and your friends be midwives – midwives to the Law of Moses reborn? Is this so difficult to see?'

'Midwives?' He knocks over his wine, Cretan blood spilling onto the tiles.

MIRIAM

What Phillip saw

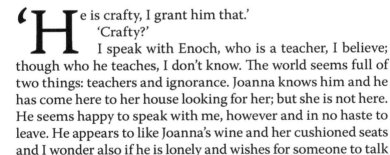

'**H**e is crafty, I grant him that.'

'Crafty?'

I speak with Enoch, who is a teacher, I believe; though who he teaches, I don't know. The world seems full of two things: teachers and ignorance. Joanna knows him and he has come here to her house looking for her; but she is not here. He seems happy to speak with me, however and in no haste to leave. He appears to like Joanna's wine and her cushioned seats and I wonder also if he is lonely and wishes for someone to talk to; especially a young woman from Magdala, who, having an unimportant voice, allows more space for him and his words, which are eager to get out. Yes, I am angry, and perhaps it shows; but interested as well, so I put on a smile, I do this well, pour him more wine – and bring nuts for good measure. I hear Berenica saying, 'always trying to please, Miriam.'

'A different sort of Hasid, I like him,' says Enoch, putting too many of the nuts in his mouth. He chokes a little, they are dry, but recovers. He sips again at the wine. 'Yeshua teaches the little people, you see, which makes a happy change … .no really, one cannot fault him on that score. He doesn't mix with the big people, not interested; and I don't know what he'd say to them if he did! Something rude probably! With Yeshua, the big people ... '

'The big people?' I don't know who he speaks of; I think he speaks in code for attention. Joanna warned me: 'Nothing excites Enoch quite as much as his own voice; though someone did say he was the cleverest man in Israel.'

'The rich, Miriam, the *rich*,' he explains. 'I call them "the big people", those who can look after themselves. The only conversation Yeshua has with the rich is how exactly they shall look after the poor! Who, by the way, he calls "Happy". I do like that ... I like that very much. "Happy are the poor!" he says. You see, I did say he was crafty – because that's a bit of a twist on the usual narrative ... though out of touch. He has clearly never been poor.'

'Have you listened to him?' It's a challenge.

'I have listened to him most closely, Miriam.'

'Well, so have I ... and he healed me also.' But Enoch is not concerned with my listening or my healing. On the subject of Yeshua, he wishes only to hear from himself, and I submit; and as I say, I do not mind. I am happy enough to hear the view of another, especially one as wise as Enoch. Perhaps it will be interesting ... certainly more interesting than me! And yes, here I am, hiding again, losing my voice, as probably you noticed.

'The thing is, Miriam – and this is where he differs from others – he gives to the poor the privileges of the rich, which is a bit of a stunt to pull off.'

'How do you mean?' I don't know what he means. Yeshua has no money to hand around. So what privileges can he bestow?

'Well, think about it for a moment; *think* about it, girl. For surely it is the rich who are supposed to live without care and without worry? Is that not so?' I see what he says and wonder if that's why Joanna seems not to worry at all, for she is rich – when I have always worried. 'But Yeshua says the *poor* should do the same! "Live without care!" he says. "Do not be anxious about your life! Trust your path, as the flowers of the field trust theirs – and all shall be well!"'

'I have heard him speak like that.'

'And, of course, the rich hate it!'

'But why? For then everyone is happy, surely?'

'But they don't wish the poor to be happy! Or certainly not happier than them ... or what's the point of being rich?' He laughs. 'He's a rascal, young Yeshua!'

'I don't believe so.'

'Then you should listen more, my girl! Your adoration is obvious and touching to behold, but you are as blind as the dead if you do not see how he undermines everything.' A harder look crosses his face and I feel my own face drop. 'He says the Kingdom of God is not something we must wait for, not some future arrival; but rather, that it is here and now, within each of us. He says that.'

'I know he says that.' Of course I know he says that. 'But I don't see how those are the words of a rascal.' Enoch's eyebrows are raised. 'I mean, why is something so cheerful declared dangerous? Is this not good news?'

'You clearly don't mix much with the Sadducees and Pharisees.'

'He says they are like white-washed tombs.'

'He is friend-averse, is he not?'

'Some say he is John the Baptist come back to life.' I press on him, like I press on a lemon, to receive all the juice. I do not believe Yeshua to be the ghost of the Baptiser, though some do say that. But neither do I expect Enoch's answer.

'They are fools,' he says, picking up a pastry from the tray. There is always pastry around when Joanna is in the kitchen. 'John was a shouty man, he liked shouting; a sledge hammer, you might say ... very shouty. We do not miss him, frankly; no one needs shouty men, though of blessed memory, of course, very blessed memory. But this man, Yeshua, the one you dribble over – well, he is a knife, and a sharp one. He will hurt many, be very sure of that, Miriam. I would keep your distance, as I'm sure you are advised to do. He will hurt many.'

And later, in Joanna's house, I hear Rocky and John the Elder talking; though they are hardly friends. He is the other John in the group, which does confuse, the elder one, hence his name; but he is from Jerusalem, not Galilee. So some say he's not one of us: 'A Judaean is not a Galilean and never can be.'

'We are twelve,' says Rocky, who wishes to be away. He is impatient and ready to leave and stands in the doorway to show this. He probably does not wish to meet Joanna, he never comes here normally. 'Like the twelve tribes of Israel, John. This is how it must be. We will speak always of the twelve, all right?'

'But how can you say "we are twelve", Cephas, when we are many more than twelve?' John joins us when he can. But Rocky is one of those who doesn't think he counts as much, because he is not from Galilee.

'Twelve men good and true,' he repeats, as if this settles the matter. 'Like the twelve tribes of Israel. It has to be twelve.'

John laughs in disbelief. 'It has to be twelve, even if it isn't twelve?' Rocky shrugs.

'It has to be twelve.'

'But you know we are more than twelve, Cephas. We are many; that is a fact.' He does not call him 'Rocky'. He is wise to the offence that will be taken, for only the Galilee crowd call him this. 'And I suppose I am not in the twelve – or Lazarus or Nicodemus or the others who support you all?' Rocky doesn't answer. 'Do you not trust those who live around Jerusalem? We are not made bad by our birth place, you know.'

Rocky doesn't trust them; he trusts only Galileans – and not many of them. 'Of course I trust you!' he says. 'It isn't that, John, not at all. I trust you absolutely!'

'And your twelve also forgets the women, Cephas. Are they not good and true and loved by our master – Joanna, Susanna, Mary, the mother of James ... young Miriam?'

He has no time for this. 'They serve and serve well, John. The women serve us well.'

'They serve Yeshua.'

'They serve us all. And yes, Joanna is very useful.' He nods at his own thought, considering the woman; and then suddenly he sees me, and adds. 'As are others, of course; they help ... very good with the cooking and the flowers. But women cannot lead, John, this is obvious. No sane Jew would wish to be a woman, this is well known, so how can they lead us? That is against Yahweh.'

I disappear from his sight, withdrawing myself though not my ears.

'Yet our master gathers them around him,' says John. 'He gathers women around him and speaks closely with them.'

'But in a different manner, John ... in a different manner! He gathers them to *serve*. We must not be misunderstood, believe me, or we'll be sunk – sent to the bottom of the sea with the fish bones. You must understand that. Our master must be protected from gossip. People see the women listening and speaking; they see the women who follow him – and they make up their minds, decide things ... falsely, of course. But you know what they say. They say he, well – converses with prostitutes! And we cannot have such talk, it isn't helpful to the cause. So twelve men good and true, that's how it must be, like the Israelites ... '

'And Miriam?'

Rocky pauses. I hear him look for me, wondering if I still listen. He answers with a low and awkward voice. 'I do not wish to speak of the Magdala woman, John.'

'But he speaks closely with her. And you know what Phillip saw ... '

'I know what Phillip *thinks* he saw, which is not the same thing at all. Very probably mistaken. We are twelve, John; that's how it will be ... twelve men good and true.'

MIRIAM

Around the chicken soup

I cannot cook, though I know women are meant to; but it seems a waste of time, when I could be listening and talking. I mean, no one can enjoy cooking; my father only complained about what was on his plate, always finding fault – so why bother to put it there? Yet my mother stayed silent and carried on.

And I am trying, I am trying to learn; I do my best with Joanna in the kitchen and today we are making chicken soup and stirring hard. My arms ache but I keep going, not wishing to let Joanna down. So we work together but dare I speak? I prefer to speak than to cook. And while I admire Joanna, I am frightened of her and do not wish to offend. Yet the question remains: why does Joanna, the wife of Chuza, who is Herod's man – his head steward, I believe – why does she protect Yeshua as she does; and ensure he is funded and cared for? Because this *is* what she does, this *is* what she chooses. She could live in more comfort and with less trouble; yet risks a great deal on a nobody ... which is what people say Yeshua is. They say this to me in the street, if they hear I am a follower.

'He is a jumped-up nobody,' they say. 'You're wasting your time, girl.' And in the end, with the stirring done and Joanna's bracelet returned to her wrist – she doesn't wish it to fall in the soup – I tell her this.

'A nobody?' She laughs, as she takes off her apron. 'They say he's a nobody?'

'They say other things as well.'

The fire needs more logs; it is clear-skied and cold tonight. I wonder if she'll call a servant to fetch some. I begin to take off my apron, but she tells me to keep it on as I need to keep on stirring. 'You keep stirring,' she says, 'and I will get some more wood.' Joanna does not need to be making the soup or carrying logs. There are others who could do this. But she wants things done right, and tells people so in a straight manner. 'Do you understand what you have to do?' she says. 'If you don't understand, I will do it myself. I don't need people who don't do their jobs.'

I like this, in a way. Joanna is not above us and happy to labour as we do; though I don't do as much as others. As I say, I am not drawn to the kitchen; I am drawn to Yeshua and his teaching. But Joanna starts in the kitchen because, she says, 'Everything starts in the kitchen; you know everyone's just a meal away from a mood.' She returns with some wood and re-sets the fire. I carry on stirring though my arms hurt.

'Have you listened to this "nobody"?' she asks.

'Of course I have listened.'

'And what have you heard him say?' And then she starts to echo his words. '"Truly I say to you, we lay burdens on the people, one heavy law after another!" I am amazed at how she speaks. She mimics him! '"Yet we murder those who speak against such things, we kill them at Machaerus, we kill them in the synagogue! But in truth, it must not be this way among you, my friends. You are to love those who hate you and do good to those who wish you harm!" She pauses, removes her bracelet again and returns to the stirring. 'Are those the words of a nobody, Miriam?'

I cannot believe she has mentioned Machaerus. Is that not Herod's fortress, where her husband works? And then she echoes Yeshua again.

'"The rich steal life from my people – and I give it back to them! Whoever would be first, let him be last and a slave to all."' She pauses again. We stir together for a while. 'No one else says such things, Miriam. No one! And don't be fooled, there is more to come, much more.' And now she faces me over the soup and I feel disturbed. 'He stands in a boat on Galilee, you have seen and heard him there – but though he stands in a boat, he speaks of the Temple in Jerusalem. Do you understand what I say?'

I am filled with dread. 'Well ... '

'Wherever he is, he's never far from the Temple. He would dismantle it stone by stone if he could. He believes the Temple holds Israel back; he believes it to be a ghost of a time now past. For a "nobody", he's really quite something.'

I am appalled. 'That cannot be right, Joanna. I mean, the Temple – how can that be a ghost?' These things cannot be true; he cannot mean them. My mother and father journeyed to the Temple every Passover, at great sacrifice to themselves. The journey from Magdala was not easy for them; nor the expense. We have our differences, but was all this for nothing? It seems disloyal even to speak of it. I have stopped stirring the soup. I feel sick.

'Your eyes display terror, Miriam, but you must know these things.'

'I ... '

'Yeshua claims the law is his master; he always says this. "I have come to fulfil the law, not to change it," he says.'

'I have heard him say that.' I gather myself a little; maybe it gets better.

'But he doesn't believe this, not for a moment.' She looks hard at me. 'Yeshua sets his own thoughts above the law. You must see this?'

I am confused and overcome with fear; I can hardly breathe. I step away from the soup and wish to return home – but would my parents have me now? I find a stool and rest a moment. I seem to shake; Joanna's words have made me so. Maybe I have known these things, but not wished to know them. Joanna sees more clearly than I; she has clarity I do not want. Her words fill me with fear.

'So what is he?' I ask. 'Or who is he?'

Now she stops stirring. 'You like him, I see that.' I feel the heat of my face; though I am far from the fire, I am burning. 'And he likes you, that is quite clear.' Is it so clear? I have never thought it clear. It is not clear to me. And does she approve? I am unsteady, yet elated. 'But you must be careful, Miriam.'

How can I be careful? Though now I wonder many things.

'Is he a good man, Joanna?' I need her to tell me. I know he is so; but then how can a good man think such things of the Temple? 'I believe I must return home.'

'And where *is* your home now?'

'I don't know.'

'"The good man brings good things from the good stored in his heart." You have heard him say that?' I sob a little, my breathing shallow.

'I have, yes.'

'And what does his heart speak of?'

'I don't know – but my heart sings when he speaks.'

'Miriam, come with me.' It is a command; she turns and I follow.

'What about the soup?'

'The soup will survive; forget about the soup. We will ask Marcus to look after the soup. Marcus!' A young lad runs in from the court yard. 'Marcus, look after the soup for a moment.'

'I was just feeding the dogs ... '

'The dogs can wait, Marcus. They know how to wait. And keep stirring or it will burn, so don't fall asleep.'

'I won't, mistress.'

'Miriam – come.' We walk up the stairs to the roof where some chickens strut and peck. The heavens above us are black, the stars bright and we so small. It is quieter here and more private; perhaps she wants this. Everyone knows that kitchens have ears. My aunt used to say this. "Kitchens have ears. To make something known, you whisper it in the kitchen." Now Joanna sits me down on the bench and we look across the roof tops to the olive grove. I wonder why we are here. Joanna does not talk like this; we have never talked like this.

'You like Yeshua; you want him to be good.' I nod – though what I assent to, I am not sure. 'But be warned, Miriam: if what he says is good, it's a very different good to the good that you and I were taught. This is good that rips up everything.'

'How so? I mean, how can good be different? Good is good, surely?'

'Miriam, you really don't listen!' She laughs in astonishment. 'He is the devil!'

'The devil?' I am stunned; no, appalled.

'He claims to fulfil the old prophecies, you have heard him.' I nod again. I am becoming a puppet. 'And yet he drives a cohort of legionaries right through them! The food laws, the Sabbath laws, laws of retribution, sacrificial law, family rules – he turns them upside down, Miriam. He tells the story of the son who leaves his father – perhaps you have heard it?'

'I have heard it.' It is a shocking story, though beautiful as well.

'So you remember that the boy insults his father, storms out, takes his inheritance with him, squanders it all in dissolute living and loses everything. Yes?'

'Yes.'

'And then in desperation, with no other options, he returns to his father, expecting rage.'

'I would expect the same. Or worse.'

'But what happens? His father runs down the road to greet him – yes, *runs* – hugs him and welcomes him home with a massive feast! So what are we to make of that? It's a disgrace! The boy should never be allowed back! *Never*. The family, the neighbours – they'll think the father weak, stupid. But Yeshua doesn't care, he undermines us; he undermines everything. "The answer is here," he says "but it's not what you thought." She pauses, as if weighing the moment. 'He says our God is old and tired. The God of Israel old and tired!'

'He says that?'

'Our *picture* of God, yes.' She pauses. 'He must be careful, of course, Miriam.'

'I haven't noticed him being careful.'

'"Old and tired" – he said that to me ... quietly.'

'He doesn't say it to others?'

She laughs. 'How can he? The Pharisees in Capernaum, in Nazareth, in Chorazin, in Bethsaida and Nain – they spend their waking lives trying to catch him out, and with good reason. How can a holy man question our laws, the very manifestation of Yahweh – and get away with it? But know this: none of our traditions are safe in his hands, Miriam – *not one*. He says it is attitude which counts, not our laws. "Beautiful attitudes" he calls them. So what part of our faith is left standing? And you wonder at the offence he causes. Truly, he is the devil.'

'Do you really believe he ... ?'

She cuts across me. She tramples over me like a bull. 'Do you not see why he tells stories, Miriam?'

'Well, everyone likes a story ... ' But I know I'm to look stupid again.

'He tells stories to disguise the revolt. But to those who have ears to hear, to those who listen to them, Miriam – well, he praises the Torah while burning it!'

I find myself shaking again. And then I wonder what Joanna herself thinks? Does she tell me these things to turn me away? I have to know this. I fear she disapproves of me. And does she herself now turn against Yeshua? It is not unknown among his followers. They start out keen but drift away, finding him not quite to their taste after all. Perhaps Joanna is the same.

So I ask her: 'These things you describe, Joanna, these things Yeshua says and does – do you also take offence? You say he is the devil. I imagine you must take great offence ... '

'Do you?' she asks sharply with a stern face. 'Do you take offence, Miriam, given everything I have said?' She looks hard at me. And then merriment breaks out in her eyes; delight I have not seen before. She smiles! And I cannot help but laugh.

'Come, let us return to the soup,' she says. 'Marcus' arms must be tired. And the devil needs us.'

YESHUA

Do you want to be healed?

'**S**o do you *want* to be healed, Shimon?'

We meet beneath the midday sun in Nain, where the people like me; or some at least, those who were there at the funeral. They still speak of the widow's son, Jeremiah, who I restored, just round the corner. He was being carried out beneath a white sheet, when I paused the weeping procession to say goodbye. His mother wept terribly and I knew Jeremiah. My father and I did work in Nain, it was nearby; and he was a tiler and a good enough man, honest with all. So I pulled back the cloth and bent down to kiss the pale forehead ... and feel warmth. And I wonder: is this the remnant of something lost or a sign of life still here? I hold the base of his neck, lifting his head, and gently rub his cold heart. His head is heavy and still as can be, and I begin to lower it down, a letting go; when suddenly his eyes open, and I start to laugh, mostly in surprise. He begins to speak with a wispy voice, not quite his own yet. I bend down to listen, more words are said, his awakening strengthens and then very slowly, he lifts himself up on the pallet. He is now sitting. The bearers stand awkwardly, not knowing what to do, for they come to carry the dead, and the dead are now alive; they have not practised for this; while around them, there is too much shock for joy; too much disbelief. And some are angry, for this is a funeral procession, the paid wailers in black, crying to the sky. No one wishes to wail in vain. Though his mother believes and runs instantly towards him, tears of happiness now, 'My son, my son!' and she takes him in her arms, hugging more life into him, while I melt away ...

So there are some who like me in Nain, especially the large family of Jeremiah. But that was then and I am now faced by Shimon, a very different sort, alive but bitter. He calls me over to him today, as he has done before, many times; though often only to mock. He gestures to me from his stool, as if it is a throne, from which he sneers at my prayers or keeps himself apart. He always makes himself known, and usually to destroy.

'He heals others but he can't heal me! That's Yeshua for you! Raises the dead but can't help the living!' He shouts this at passers-by. 'And all you who can walk, praise God, praise God, for I cannot! And kind shekels in my bowl please – and give 'til it hurts 'cause my legs hurt more!'

He has collected coin in Nain for many years, his twisted leg on show; while the rest of his body contorts around it, as does his mind. One twist leads to another; and one pain to another. I feel the disturbance, the demons gathered within and I have no time for this man. Yet I am here, asking if he wishes to be healed – your kingdom come, father, I would see him free.

'So do you *want* to be healed, Shimon?'

'Of course, I want to be healed! Who wouldn't want to be healed!?' He speaks to the crowd, a comedy turn. 'All I need now is a healer! Do you know one Yeshua?'

I kneel down beside him in the dust. He stinks. 'So I ask you again, Shimon, "Do you seriously wish to be healed?"'

His voice snarls. 'You're a piece of shit, Yeshua, I knew it! You don't ask that of others, do you?' I look at him, his face in mine. 'Well, do you? I've never heard you ask anyone *else* if they wish to be healed. Did you ask that Jeremiah fellow? I don't think so, not with his family watching.'

'He was asleep.'

'But you ask me, you ask me – Shimon of Nain! I've been here fifteen years and you ask if I wish to be healed.'

'So do you?'

'Fifteen bloody years!'

'Then bless the kind people who support you.'

'*Kind?* I was abandoned and not given a chance. These people say they've never heard a story like mine. *Never!*'

'And I'm sure you tell it well. But I say to you: forget your story now.' He looks at me with hatred, but I reach out and touch his shoulder, seeking his heart. I would like to reach his heart but he recoils from my touch. I need to reach his heart.

'Forget my story? That's easy for you to say. You walk easy – too easy perhaps! You walk out on your family, I hear.'

My God, I could do without Shimon! Contain him, Yeshua, contain him – I speak with myself, advising myself, calming myself. He stirs a storm in me and I am to contain the storm. 'I seek God's path as I'm sure you do, Shimon ... so forget your story. You wear it out by constant telling, it is threadbare, so let it go. It's like an old cloak that no longer warms. It does not serve you, but holds you back, like the chain on a slave. See what holds you back, my friend!'

'I am no friend of yours.' He whispers it, but as a curse, like spittle. I do not listen; I still reach for his heart; I need to find his heart.

'Your story is past, Shimon. Do you understand? It is not now. So un-fence your mind, my friend, and free yourself from ... '

'It's my leg that cripples me, not my fucking story. What are you talking about? Are you mad or something? Someone said you were mad. Or bad. Who knows?'

'Do you wish to be healed?' I ask him again. His hate can be held; I can hold his hate for now, I believe I can. 'But remember this: If I heal you, you will need to speak differently with people.' I see his plate is full of coins; not gold or silver, but enough to live. 'Oh, and you will say goodbye to such coins. Do you have a trade, Shimon?' He looks down and hastily gathers the coins together. He puts them in a leather pouch round his waist. 'Do you have family?'

'It's not fair, Yeshua. One day you'll discover that – that life is unfair.' He is in my face, but I laugh.

'If you wait for fair, Shimon, you will wait a long time. Many winters, many summers for *nothing* is fair ... nothing. Never imagine anything is fair; all is unfair.' How can he not understand this? 'Though blessing appears.'

'I don't know what you're on about.'

'Fairness is a tyranny! As if my father in heaven can treat two people the same. He greets the first and shuns the second. Then he breaks the first and gives silver to the second. Do you not understand? How we live and how we die – nothing is fair! Though blessing appears.'

He eases away from me, shuffling on his stool, pulling his leg with him. He sneers again. He grips onto all that is unfair, I see this, he cannot let it go; he holds it in his heart like rotting treasure.

'I must have the wrong voice, Yeshua ... or the wrong look? Which is it? Or perhaps I don't say how wonderful you are, like all the others? Perhaps I don't kiss your arse enough – or, and here's a thought – perhaps I'm not a woman. They say you like the women, how they follow you around. Or perhaps you follow them, who knows? Perhaps if I was a woman you would handle me a bit better!'

I feel a terrible rage; no light ... only rage. It holds me, I cannot move, I cannot speak. I look in his eyes which dart around like fish in the shallows; but I hold my stare as the storm rips through me, uncontained, everything overturned. I wait for it to pass, wait to be left alone and free from its hold. I manage a prayer, "Deliver me from the time of trial."

'Perhaps I'm my own man,' he says. He sees me shaken. 'Well, I've had to be, haven't I?'

'So perhaps you don't need me.'

'Perhaps I don't need you, no!'

'So do you want to be healed?'

We return to the start, like wrestlers resuming their pose.

'Perhaps you *can't* heal me, Yeshua! Perhaps that's why you're so full of shit, with all your questions. You're no healer at all, are you?'

Rocky steps forward. He is a bigger man than the cripple, bigger and stronger by far, and over-bearing.

'You shouldn't talk to the teacher like that, you vagrant! You should show some respect to your betters! Manners of a bloody pig!'

'Oh, I see your fat monkey's here, Yeshua ... '

'Rocky – leave us alone.' I do not look at him, but hold out my hand. I stare only at my present foe. Rocky doesn't move – but I will not back down, I will not allow him here. 'Leave us!' He will be angry and all shall know it; but he returns to the crowd, which has grown around us; I feel it keenly. We have become as two warriors, fighting to entertain.

'Come away,' I say and point to a quieter place. I need to reach his heart.

'"Come away?" What's that supposed to mean?' And now I face one who is no longer himself, but a second self, who acts a part. 'Do you fear what people will see, healer man?' He asks and smirks at some who watch.

'Let us end this in a quieter place,' I say. 'Where we can be ourselves ... I will help you there.' We are in the valley of decision; I do not know which way he will take. My own heart beats wildly. He longs to be well – yet fears it above all things. 'Let go of your story.'

'You come here to judge!' He turns on me again and then to the crowd: 'He comes here to judge me, I see that now! He knows nothing of my suffering! Nothing! Let the good and generous people of Nain see that Shimon has been failed again, abandoned again!'

He shuffles away, feeling his money-pouch, back to his place by the wall. The crowd is disturbed. Rocky is the first to step forward to help me; and I am grateful for his arm. He lifts me up from the dust where I have knelt and guides me to the shadows behind the pillars; and there I hold onto him or I will collapse.

'Where shall we go, teacher?' asks Rocky. I cannot speak, my body too punched and battered, my spirit mauled, as if by a lion – I am destroyed by hate. 'You don't need his sort, teacher. You just don't need them.'

MIRIAM

Yeshua's shame

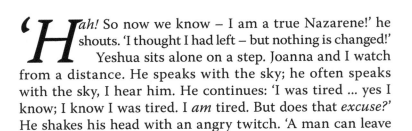

'*Hah!* So now we know – I am a true Nazarene!' he shouts. 'I thought I had left – but nothing is changed!' Yeshua sits alone on a step. Joanna and I watch from a distance. He speaks with the sky; he often speaks with the sky, I hear him. He continues: 'I was tired ... yes I know; I know I was tired. I *am* tired. But does that *excuse?*' He shakes his head with an angry twitch. 'A man can leave Nazareth but ... '

He sits in the courtyard, as the shadows lengthen, the day done. We are in the district of Tyre and Sidon and they have been busy days; too busy. Everyone is tired and no one has time. I have been with the group, and large unpleasant crowds have swirled around Yeshua. So many demands on him, I wonder how he goes on! And now it seems he's snapped. Rocky doesn't help things right now. He questions why Yeshua spends time in such places – places filled with foreigners, 'when it's the House of Israel we must speak with, teacher. Why do we spend time on the others? They are nothing.' And perhaps tonight Yeshua wonders the same. He is upset; I have not seen him so disturbed.

Joanna and I find him sitting hunched forward. We sit down with him, though not alongside; but a step or two up.

'And no one is best when they're tired,' says Joanna firmly. She is practical. She does not linger on matters, when lingering achieves nothing. Yeshua does not respond. 'No use bathing in shame, Yeshua,' she says. 'I have tried that way all my life. It's the worst bath of all.' But in the dry blowing of the evening breeze, Yeshua still wishes to bathe.

'She was asking for help,' he says. He half-speaks to us, though offers only his back. 'You will have heard.'

'We all heard her, yes – she had an annoying voice,' says Joanna. She won't be kept out, though he tries. 'And she was pressing you, she wouldn't let you go. People can't press on you like that; they can't be allowed to do it. If she'd treated *me* like that ... '

'She only wanted me to help her daughter, Joanna.' He is matter-of-fact. 'What mother would not? What mother would not want that?' He shakes his head.

'And you *did* help her daughter,' I add. I have to say something. He seems to forget this, making everything dark and difficult. And I do not like to see him so low; I do not like seeing any one so low. 'You did help her. In the *end*, I mean ... ' I confess to being shocked by events, I won't pretend all was sweet. Yeshua sounded like my father when he spoke with the woman, which is not praise – far from it.

And now Yeshua insists on reliving it, as if this will somehow mend what's done. He does not look at us; but looks straight ahead, speaking to the courtyard wall. 'She asked me to help her daughter. And what did I say? I said, "It's not right to throw the children's bread to the dog." That is what I said to her, just like a true Nazarene!'

And I heard it all, he remembers it right. Rocky had then told her to move along, saying the teacher didn't have time for Canaanites, that he came for the Jews – and that Canaanites should look after themselves. But she didn't move along. She stood her ground like a rock in a sand storm; the insults just flew past her.

'I called her a *dog*!' says Yeshua. He cannot put it down; he is disgusted with himself. '*A dog*!' Joanna and I look at each other across the step, but say nothing. He does not ask for our help; nor do I believe we can give it. He speaks to himself of things done, this is his way; he does not seek soft words from us. 'She asks me for help and what do I see? I just see a gentile, a Canaanite – pressing, insisting, demanding; and I hear voices from my past, Nazarite voices ... and I call her a *dog*.' He pauses. 'In Nazareth, they used to call Sepphoris the 'City of Dogs' – the city where everyone speaks Greek and visits the Roman theatre. And there was Nazareth, only four miles away, quaking in its Jewish boots. "What happened to the Promised Land" they asked. They were bitter in Nazareth, so bitter – and today in Tyre I joined them. I joined the bitters. I called her a dog – and in my heart, even as I said it, I saw her face and was already asking forgiveness.' He shakes his head again. 'And then she says to me,' – and now he smiles – 'she says, "Even the dogs can eat the crumbs from their master's table." That's what she says, quick as you like, strong as you like, as if my insult is nothing, as if she is *used* to such words. She who is familiar with insult – and I insult her more, exposed as just another man who knows nothing but shouts loud ... just another man from Nazareth. God help me.' He looks again to the skies.

'And what did you say to her then?' I ask, but I will first tell him. 'You said, "I like your faith, woman! Your faith shines. Where is your daughter?"'

'I did say that, yes.' He remembers with relief. He tells it only one way in his mind, and needs other tellings.

'And then you went and helped her,' says Joanna. 'You gave the woman what she wished for, you *healed* her daughter. I don't know what you did but I know you healed her, because her mother glowed like an angel by the throne.'

And so gently yet so true, a smile creeps across Yeshua's face as he remembers, I love his smile ... before punishment returns. 'Yet tonight there is only shame, Joanna. You cannot rush me to happiness. Forgive me, father, I do not know what I do.'

'We are born into shame,' says Joanna, with anger. 'You know this better than anyone!' She gets up and confronts him.

She faces him now, filling his view. 'Listen to us all! Listen to our parents! Listen to the rabbis! The child is not told, "That is wrong." The child is told "Shame on you!" It is shame or honour – and usually it is shame. We are born into it and we drown in it. And did she not forgive you, Yeshua – as you would forgive her? Yes?' He nods – and I like Joanna when she speaks like this. 'I had to leave to arrange accommodation in Sidon – we have some, by the way. But the events I saw, though speckled with your history, were kind. You were a good man today; you were kind! Let not shame blind or disable the joy.'

I think Joanna speaks of herself, for shame often arrives at her door, she has told me. And when it does, she just puts on more jewellery. Yeshua, though, doesn't move. I reach out, touch his shoulder ... and he weeps. Suddenly he is weeping, heaving and weeping, though whether in sadness or joy, I don't know.

I hold him, as slowly his resistance lessens and his sobbing body finds rest.

YESHUA

The adultery girl

I sit with Miriam.

We are in Julia's home in Jerusalem. Joanna also stays here with Levi, Susanna, Phillip and young John ... but it is early and we are alone. Phillip wonders if people should see what we do. I say to him the light sees all things, and I do not fear the light. Miriam rubs my hands with oil. She does it slowly, working each stretch and crease of skin; this is skin I scarce knew I had before she touched it. It soothes me beyond telling and gives what I have never known. I could never give as much as I now receive. I am revived and all melts away, even Shimon of Nain.

A man bursts through the curtains from the street; sudden violence in the room and everything wrecked.

'Yeshua with his whore!' he shouts. I push Miriam away – away from the man and his people outside; I see them. I am caught out and unready. 'Tell Joanna!' I say to Miriam, as two others enter the room; there are now three of them before me. They are men of middle-age and sweating, wild eyes. He grabs me by the arm, the leader, and I struggle. But other hands drag me across the floor. 'Hater of Yahweh!' he shouts. 'Hater of Yahweh!'

'Adulterer!' screams another.

I have seen him before; I know this man, it comes back to me. I saw him yesterday in the market place. Picture the scene, for he pictures it now and it eats his face with rage and finds me guilty. 'Libertine!' he keeps shouting and others join in, as they drag me struggling and wrenching towards the door. I am stronger than one, but weaker than three.

'Libertine! Libertine!' they chant.

'So our daughter can do what she wants?' he grunts in my ear as I am forced through the curtain and into the sunlight. 'Then perhaps we can do what we want!'

His daughter, I met her yesterday. I was in the market place buying fruit when I found her alone, though not alone, circled by men. And dropping my oranges, I step into the circle. She is tied and kneeling, about to be stoned and my only thought is: 'I must join her.' So I step forward, enter into the circle of judgement while men finger sharp rocks in the sun. I look in their eyes, feel the disturbance and the hate like a desert wind, and it makes me stumble. I gather myself. The girl's head is covered, her hands roped behind her back. I am told to step away by the Pharisee Club who oversee events.

'You?' says the rabbi, as if breathless, as if punched. He does not expect me; nor me him. Before me, and clearly leader of the pack, I see Eleazar, from the Nazareth group, older, harder, the years have not softened his soul. *'You!?'*

And I am more amazed. He has wandered some way from Zebedee; and his father and grandfather are date farmers, so how is he here? Why is he not harvesting? But he is here with power and keen to offend – I note he grants me no title. 'There is no doubt as to her sin,' he says, 'none at all. There were relations between them, adulterous relations – between her and a man.' He walks towards me. 'And I suppose you might know a little about that, wine-bibber, given your family history.' He looks at me, as if a secret has been shared and he has triumphed. 'In this instance, the law of Moses could not be clearer, really not. There is no debate to be had ... only right punishment, which we will bestow.' He speaks as if weary that all is so clear. Everything has always been clear to Eleazar, but it is also clear to me. I feel the space inside me. I feel the corridor of light within; and cannot help but laugh. 'You laugh, Yeshua?'

At last, I am given a name! 'What else could I do? I just wonder how you miss the joke, Eleazar. And about "the man" you mention ... I do not see him here. He is held up perhaps, his arrival delayed?'

'He will be dealt with according to the law. Now if you just ... '

'But not *here?* And *not* in like manner?' I spit these words, pure spit. Eleazar looks at me and then looks away.

Someone in the circle shouts, 'Get out of the way, wine-bibber – or you'll get the same as the whore!' Others join him: 'Get out the way!' and 'Move!' The circle closes round me.

Eleazar: 'You best be on your way, as the man suggests. Whatever the failings of your mother, the law is our light, we agree about that.'

'The law is king, Eleazar, but a tired king. The law is a worn-out fetter, do you not think – like an old donkey rein. It can save – but it cannot save. It can heal but it cannot heal. Do you understand? '

'I understand you blaspheme and deserve the stones yourself.'

And now I laugh again; the girl looks up, her eyes have died. She does not expect laughter but I would give it to her if I could; I would give her some mirth. 'Do you not think we should all be laughing?!' I ask of those around and I ask it loudly. 'No, really! Do you not think we should all be laughing?! Yet such sour faces all! A synagogue of sourness! Do you know what you are like? You are like those who, given a garden to enjoy, set loose wild dogs and bandits with knives, that they might know only fear while walking there. Your father would have you *enjoy* the garden – yet you make it a place of terror, for yourselves and for others!'

I wonder if the stones will now start their murder, and include me in their flight. Eleazar and his friends survey events – they watch, but do not declare. I continue.

'Truly, we should laugh, my friends – laugh that it has come to *this*, to a judgement so skewed! I can scarcely believe we stand here! Really, I cannot!' I hold my hands to the sky in wonderment. 'I mean, how is it so, fellow Israelites, fellow chosen ones?' I walk forward. I watch the stones in their hot hands. They have chosen from the pile, small and large, round and sharp. My father would always use cut stone, I remember; it gripped better in the wall. Round stones slid, we advised against it – though cheaper homes used them, they had no choice. Cut stone was the sign of a rich man's home.

But these are stones for killing not building ... for blinding, for stunning, for breaking, for cracking, for maiming, and for murder, though I am still laughing. I laugh at these people and the stones they hold, as if the stones make men of them, make *holy* men of them, caught up with heaven in their offence at this woman.

'It should not be like this among us,' I declare. I want the whole town to hear, I do not hold back. 'You are called to be a light to the world, but you have turned this light into darkness! Do you not see the judgement coming? This is not how it should be among us!'

I stop my pacing and walk back towards the girl. I do not laugh now; I have arrived at a place of rage, which becomes contempt. I feel the heat of the circle, and see the father of the girl. He leads this pack of wolves; he is swaying. I bend down and kneel on the ground. I kneel near the girl, so she is not alone.

'Here is someone's daughter.'

'She's no daughter of mine!' shouts the father and others agree. 'No daughter, no daughter!' they chant; and then 'Hater of Yahweh, Hater of Yahweh!' I wait for the first stone. They look to the Pharisees who consult among themselves. Eleazar's hand is held in the air. When the hand drops, the stoning starts, this is how it is. And bending down, I write in the sand with my finger, THE LAW SAYS KILL HER, which causes comment. But my course is set; as above, so below. I slowly stand in the windless silence.

'We who would be holy, we who would keep the law – we must weep for our sins, must we not? Yes? And having wept, make due sacrifice at the Temple?' Some nod, though others glower. 'But is it possible there is one here *without* sin? Is that possible, my friends? And could that person be you? We who would be holy must weep for our sins. But imagine if there is one here present who is without sin, without blemish! We would all like it to be so, would we not? How we would admire that man and beg him to come to dinner that we might ask how he is so free?! So, reveal yourself now! You must do this. Reveal yourself! Let him who is without sin cast the first stone this day, that we might wonder and bow!'

I move away from the woman. I watch Eleazar's hand held in the air; it remains in the air. I watch the father. The family look to him and he looks to Eleazar. He is not sure and some grumble. The circle thins a little. Some stones are dropped to the ground, I hear them fall. The silence continues, unsure of itself.

'The stoning is postponed,' declares Eleazar. 'To be reconvened, according to the law of Moses.' He raises his other hand, holds them up and brings both down to indicate the end of the matter. There is muttering in the crowd. Someone shouts, 'This isn't right! The law of Moses is abused!' And now I feel fear and the closure of space within me. I feel life draining away as the crowd disbands; I am diminished. As the scribes and Pharisees leave, one of them spits on my neck.

'Hater of Yahweh and food for Gehenna!' he says, before turning away. But I cannot quite let them go. I cannot let them go without words, for I rage too much inside at all that is done.

'The Queen of Sheba will stand up and accuse this generation, truly she will! She will accuse you all! For she came from the ends of the earth to hear the wisdom of Solomon and know this – something greater than Solomon is here! Something greater by far!'

Though no one listens; and Eleazar, who has remained quite still with his cronies, shakes his head, disdain in his eyes, turns and walks away.

The woman and I are left alone; but I am too tired. I sink into the sand and crawl towards her, like I used to crawl in the wilderness when overwhelmed.

'If they do not condemn you, then nor do I.' I free her, untying the harsh knot from her wrists. Her eyes are quite dead and she is rigid in her body. I help her to her feet slowly.

'Where will you go?' I ask and she smiles as if this is the question of a fool.

'Where can I go?' she says.

And so the following day, her father and two sweaty ruffians are dragging me into the court yard, where other family await; I see them as I struggle. A servant screams, though no one listens, and someone asks what they should do with me. 'Take him out of town,' says a voice, 'we can deal with him there!' This is madness, but I have no power. I am like a lamb to the slaughter, pulled and held. And then Rocky, James and Jude arrive. I am grateful beyond words to see them; never more so. I am still held for a moment; they do not release me. But Rocky and Jude have knives in their hands. They tell me I should carry a knife, for safety; they have always said that.

'Release him!' says Rocky and I see in him the hunter. Every fisherman must be a hunter; they track, they trap, they seize and they kill. Rocky, when angry, could gut a man as well as a fish, I have no doubt. But I am still held by my neck.

'Release him,' says Jude – a quieter voice, but no less firm. He holds his knife before him.

'What's this?' asks young John, arriving on the scene. He cannot believe his eyes. Rocky ignores him. 'I'll take your ears off,' he says to the one who holds me. 'And then your other parts.' I feel the grip loosening. I am pushed nastily aside.

'Another day,' says the father. 'She will not live anyway. And nor will you.' Hate looks at me and walks away.

We recover slowly. Joanna has joined us. We are invited inside to break some bread together. 'You must be careful, teacher. That sort, they are not good enemies,' says Jude as he watches them leave. 'We cannot be seen to be against the law;

we simply cannot. It turns people against us. What occurred today, this is not good news.'

I sit them down in the courtyard. Susanna brings us some wine, bread and fish. 'Mullet,' says Rocky. He cannot help himself; he has to name the fish. He perhaps does it without realising. He simply says 'sardine' ... or 'mullet' or whatever. These were his main catches in Galilee, wet and thrashing in the sun. Though once, in disgust, he shouted, 'cat fish!' and pushed the plate away. Catfish cannot be eaten, forbidden to us, for they lack scales and are scavengers.

'They wasted my time – for what Jew will buy them? Though the Greeks in Bethsaida, I discovered they didn't mind, they bought the shit – so the gentiles are good for something!'

Some say, in a small room, he still smells of fish. And today Joanna gives us mullet, while Julia brings a cloth and some water for my head. I wash my neck as well, still raw from rough hands. And in response to Jude, I tell them a story.

'A man had a horse; but one night, his horse ran away into the hills. The following morning, the villagers came to him and said, "Bad news about your horse." And the man said, "Could be bad news, could be good news."

Two days later his horse returned – but with twenty wild horses. So now he has twenty-one horses. The villagers are very pleased for him. "Good news about the horses!" they say. "Could be good news, could be bad news," he replies.

Later that week, the man is breaking in the wild horses when one throws him off and he breaks his leg. The villagers are upset, and say, "Bad news about you breaking your leg." And he says, "Could be bad news, could be good news."

A short while later, soldiers come to the village, recruiting for war. They press all the men into service, but because he has broken his leg, he stays at home in the village. The villagers are delighted for him, and say, "Good news about you being saved from the war!" And the man replies, "Could be good news, could be bad news."

Do you understand? The kingdom of God does not proceed by the judgements of men, Jude. Good news? Bad news? Only God knows. Do not judge the day; and you will not be judged.'

But Rocky cannot hold back.

'When the messiah comes, he will overthrow the Romans, rid us of their armies and re-establish Davidic monarchy. That is the kingdom – is it not, teacher?'

Has he understood nothing? His love for me is clear; and today he saved my life. But truly, he has understood nothing.

'If those who guide you say, "Look, the Kingdom is in the sky!" then the birds are closer than you. And if they say, "Look, it is in the sea, then the fish already know it." The kingdom is inside you, Rocky, and it is outside you – like the food you have eaten and the food on the table. Like the food you chew and food you reach for, the kingdom is everywhere.'

Rocky and Jude are closer now than ever; though whether they help each other, I am not sure. Not all friendships bless – some put fences around the other's mind. And do I help? I think of the woman in the square, untied and free, the stones unthrown; and I hear her words again.

'Where can I go?'

MIRIAM

By the nous

We are alone.

I bring him oiled bread with hyssop; he likes hyssop. And I ask him about his followers; I do wonder about them. I don't wish to appear rude or forward but they do not seem very wise to me. 'They are like little children, Miriam,' and I say, 'I know they are like children!' for this is obvious. And he says, 'They are like those who have gone into a field to play. And when the owner returns and says "Give us back our field," they will remove their clothes, see themselves naked before the owner – and leave the field to them.'

'They will give up?' I ask. 'They will give up and be ashamed,' he says, 'I expect so – though truly, the field is theirs.'

'I will never give up; I will never do that.'

'Say not what you will do, Miriam; future words are coins without value. We are all heroes of intention. Live only today and its worries, they are enough. This bread is good.'

'But surely we must plan for what is to come, Yeshua? There is tomorrow as well as today!' I find comfort in plans, as if something is made sure by them. But he laughs.

'We can say to the sky, "Tomorrow you shall be this," or "Tomorrow you shall be that," – but we only know the colour of the sky today.'

'And Nicodemus? Is it true?'

'Is what true?'

'Is he really a follower now?' Others have told me of their meeting; that Yeshua had high hopes for him, though Susanna says it ended badly, with wine spilt. She says Nicodemus ran away.

'The Temple is done, Miriam,' he says and gets up to pace the floor. I feel hurt by this, though Joanna has warned me. 'They must see that. If they cannot see that, they cannot see anything. It is a graveyard which holds only the bones of old ways. The Temple is done, quite done ... it will fall.'

It shocks me to hear such things – but shocks me less now. Indeed, it almost seems simple as he says it, as if the huge walls will easily crumble, strong pillars falling, while Caiaphas and his crowd dance for joy at their collapse!

'Susanna says that one day we will have hearts and not rules.'

'Then Susanna knows everything,' says Yeshua.

I am now jealous of Susanna. And then he sings to me quietly, a lullaby song.

'Hook, line and sinker, they will struggle and fight.
With a splash and a rattle, will the council of fools.
But hook, line and sinker, their time has run out.
One day we'll have hearts and not rules.'

He smiles. Does Susanna know this song also? Is it from Galilee? I wish someone had sung it to me. I gather myself, for now is the time.

'And what *is* the kingdom that you wish for, master? People say different things. Many say it will happen here in Judaea.'

'The kingdom is not a place, Miriam ... it is a way, a state. It is the presence of God in a soul, in a look, in an action.'

I wonder at this and seek it. 'And how may I know this presence?' He hesitates; I see he holds back. 'Am I not worthy to know?' I ask. This is my first thought; I have always felt unworthy and feel so now. 'Give a fool wisdom and he turns it into lies,'

I've heard this. Perhaps he thinks me too much of a fool? Or too much a woman? But he shakes his head, as if to reassure.

'I have not spoken of this, Miriam, for you do not throw pearls before swine. The pearls will be trampled on and lost. But I will speak of it now, for perhaps you are ready to hear.' He pauses again, as if still making up his mind. But then he starts, speaking slowly. 'The energy of God is found not by seeing, Miriam; nor is it found by feeling. Do you understand? I believe you will understand; I believe you are ready to receive these things.'

'The energy of God is neither in seeing nor feeling?' I repeat his words for I am confused. 'Then where is it found?'

'It is found by knowing, by the nous.'

I do not understand but cannot admit it. I feel frustration, for where is this nous? I want a simpler path. 'But where is this knowing to be found, Yesh, if not by seeing or feeling?'

'You have a quick mind and quick senses, Miriam; but these are not your way into the kingdom. You think fast and feel quickly. But beyond seeing and feeling, there is a hidden door, a thin fissure in the rock of your being, through which knowing is found, where nous is found ... a more ancient light which is not seeing, and neither is it feeling. It is knowing.'

Again, I do not understand. I think too fast, he is right, and my thoughts take me past this hidden door; they cannot stop to enter, I watch this occur – though I long to understand a different land. And I wonder if I know this man at all, such distance between us – yet sometimes, no distance at all, as now, when he kisses my head and strokes my hair.

'You have angels in your hair, Miriam – beautiful angels. And one day you will share these things I have told you, for only you can. It will be your treasure to share. But now ... ' – he stops for a moment, he almost chokes, tears arise – ' ... now it is horror or it is joy ... for what started in Galilee must finish in Jerusalem. I know this now. So let us hope for joy, Miriam ... and for Nicodemus.'

YESHUA

No house of prayer

Rocky surveys the temple; he has awe in his fisherman's
eyes, for until now, he imagined Bethsaida a busy town.
But compared to this, Bethsaida is silent. We stand in the
outer courtyard, a distance from his past life – neither boat nor
mullet in sight. 'It's a size, isn't it, teacher! The very heart of Israel!'

'I've seen more health under a stone.'

'Then why are we here?' Rocky is nervous. I have stood for
a while and watched this Passover scene – the reek of blood,
the push of bodies, the clinking coins ... the shouting orders of
soldiers, priests and builders – 'Mind that bull!'

'Let the stone mason past!'

'The money changers are through the gate on the right.'

'Only doves bought in the *Temple*, do you understand? Only
doves bought in the Temple will be accepted!'

'But they cost the earth in the Temple. I can't afford ... '

'Perhaps God *wants* them to cost the earth! It's a sacrifice,
remember!'

Childhood memories return, the fear, the shouting and the
violence; though no violence at all, as it is usually known ...

only violence against truth, against the spirit of truth, violence against the holy, like a dead dog blocking a stream.

'I come to warn of judgement, Rocky.'

'But not here surely?' Why do I still expect him to hear? Words leave my mouth with one set of clothes; and he gives them another set entirely.

'Judgement is coming, for the place is a disgrace. Do you not think so? I mean, what do you see before you, Rocky? This place – this place is a highway, a building site, a contortion of power. They are rebuilding the Temple, do you see them? They are re-building the Temple – when the Temple needs to fall!'

'It's only repair to the stone work.'

'And that will make it well, will it? A little fresh stone will make all things well? You cannot cleanse a sewer, Rocky, or dry out the sea. We gaze not on a house of prayer, but on a counting house, the home of thieves and crooks with grasping hearts. This Temple is a conspiracy against the poor, a feeder for the rich and an insult to Yahweh – and I will pull it down.'

'Who the hell are you?' says a builder. I step out and stand in his way. Everything begins somewhere, and I begin here, this stepping out; and with a huge heave, I turn over a table to block his path. I lift it high, then let it crash and fall, and then another one, lifted up and over; and another heave, coins piled high go flying and the money-changers turn on me. But I carry on, taking hold of another table, more money falling, the changers are shouting, the tethered doves squawking, and someone grabs me – but I pull away, I am in a rage, I knock them down, more tables tumble, more coins rolling on the ground, men on their knees scrambling, animals screech – and I am alive! I feel so alive.

'This is a house of prayer!' I shout. 'A house of prayer! Yet God is not here! God has left the building! So just who is it you worship in the Temple's dark corners? For no one is here to listen! God is elsewhere in Israel, he makes a new home! He is where the carpenter shapes wood, the path-maker breaks stones and the flame-keeper lights the stove. He is where the women draw water, the debtors weep and the children play. He is with them in the sand and the dust, in the sorrow and the joy; yes, God's garments are covered in muck and dust! Unlike the Temple, God's clothes are unclean with the love and care for his people!'

The temple guards approach me, with spear and sword. 'Stand back,' I say, 'stand back!' There is silence for a moment; I have only a moment. The crowd gathers but holds; I am encircled. I say to the soldiers: 'I have no gripe with you.'

'You disturb temple business.'

'And so do you, my friends; so do we all.' I quieten a little. I do not shout now; my breath settles. 'You disturb the business of prayer – and what other business is there?' These soldiers do not know what they do; they do not realise. 'You guard the Temple with weapons of iron, but I guard it as well – I guard the light, I guard the flame. I guard the Temple as a place of prayer.'

'But by what *right* do you do this, Yeshua?' A fresh voice, one with authority; a Pharisee has arrived, like a wasp on a grape. All look round and *By Blue Galilee!* – it is Eleazar. I am shocked.

'You follow me like an unfortunate smell, Eleazar.'

'But God's law is a sweet smell to the faithful, Yeshua. The stench perhaps is yours; and it seems you have some tables to mend.'

'I would prefer Israel mended, Eleazar.'

'You cannot mend that which is not broken, Yeshua. You best stick to tables. And I return to my question, simply posed: By what right do you do this? By what right do you behave in such a criminal and violent manner?'

'You speak shit, Eleazar. Your mouth is like a camel's arse. Shit comes out of it, spilling everywhere – and never in such quantity as today. You Pharisees, Eleazar – you are like the dog in the cow's manger. He cannot eat the straw – but neither will he let the cows eat it. This is how it is with you! You cannot find God. Yet you stop anyone else from finding him!' Still the crowd holds back, and Eleazar does not move.

'You will answer my question, you son of a whore! By what right do you disturb the Temple and desecrate the holy of holies?' He points to the Temple facade which towers above us.

He supposes he frightens me. But no thing frightens me, not in this moment, least of all this black-robed turd.

I say, 'The holy of holies, Eleazar, is yourself – and there is only one who can desecrate that place. The kingdom of God is within you ... yet you make such distance. The kingdom is here – yet you make it there. God is closer to you than you are to yourself! Yet you look the other way and strain your eyes not to see ... and strain your heart not to know.'

'And my question, Yeshua?' His voice gets higher with rage. 'Let us debate the question, like we used to in Nazareth, before you gave up the one thing you were good at – making chairs.' He turns to the crowd. 'His father was a labourer, you know! A third-rate builder!'

'And yours a date farmer, another fine trade – we all enjoyed your family dates in Narareth. Yet just when you should be helping with the harvest, you are here in the temple talking shit.'

'His mother was a well-known whore, who thought she could hide away in Bethlehem!' There is chatter around us and I raise my hands in the air, I feel such rage, my blood is too hot in my body. I could pull this whole Temple down around me.

'No, no, *no!*' I am appalled at Eleazar, appalled by his mouth in the Temple. 'As the prophet said, "The Lord is in his holy temple. Let all the earth be silent towards him! *Silent.*"'

And suddenly they are quiet; I shout them into silence. Miriam said I can be fierce, but I now quieten too. 'You do not need all this, my friends, neither the stone nor the silver, for neither can speak and neither can bless. Instead, exchange sacrifice for repentance as John the Baptiser said; and when you pray to your father in heaven, your heart is enough – you need no Temple. Can you imagine that? Your heart is quite enough. So creep away, listen to the sky, find a secret place far away from here. Go there, close the door behind you and pray like this:

Our father in heaven, may your name be honoured,
your kingdom come and your will be done,
on earth as in heaven – as above, so here below.
Give us today our daily bread, for we hunger quickly;
and forgive our offence, as we forgive the offence of others.

Preserve us from the time of trial for we are weak;
and deliver us from stalking evil.
And that is enough, my friends, whispered in your secret
place ... that is enough.'

'Seize him!' shouts one of the priests.

'How did you escape, teacher?' asks Thomas later, as we gather in
an upper room, hidden away and in fear, like mice in a cupboard,
with a cat pacing below. Others also wish to know, for there is
only fright in their eyes. Word has travelled concerning events
in the Temple. Perhaps they wonder how they will escape when
their time comes. It seems different between us now; more
subdued and fewer jokes. Rocky is silent, Jude avoids me, Levi
upset. I wish to encourage them but do not know how, as if
they are all let down.

'I simply asked him to answer a question, Thomas.'

'What question?'

Rocky remembers. 'He said to him, "Tell me, Eleazar – do
you believe Yahweh was in the baptism of John? Do you believe
that Yahweh was with the great prophet John the Baptiser?"'

'Why did you ask him that?' says Andrew.

'And he could not answer,' I say. 'True?' I turn to Rocky and
he nods. 'Eleazar was silent.'

'I mean, it's not exactly a difficult question.' Andrew persists.

'It was for him, Andrew – and can you imagine why?' Andrew
cannot imagine why and shrugs his shoulders.

'Fish are fish.' He says this when confused, as if something
is settled by these words.

'Think about it. If he said, 'Yes' to me – then why all these
sacrifices? What is their purpose now? Why the money-changers
and the priests in their robes? If John's baptism of repentance
is all that is needed, then the Temple is a ruin, its sanctity
destroyed! Do you see that?'

Miriam sees it. And young John smiles; he also sees it, though
Rocky cannot look at me.

'Yet if he said "No, Yahweh was not with him", then he insults the great prophet. He belittles the hero of the people, for everyone loves John. And so Eleazar did not answer me. He said nothing – though I put my hand to my ear, as if trying to hear. "Have you lost your voice, Eleazar? Most unfortunate! Perhaps you should suck on a date and refresh your throat!"'

Miriam laughs, imagining the scene, but others stay quiet. Joanna says it is a wonder I remain alive and others agree. 'And then I slipped away, I joined the crowd, who were kind and took me to safety.'

There is silence and then Jude speaks up: 'I believe we have gone too far, teacher.'

'I have been going too far for a while.'

'Quite.' He nods as he speaks, as if he has been holding it in. 'Way too far, you know my feelings. And I think others agree.' He is nervous and his unease spreads, though we eat together.

Someone says, 'It is like a last supper.'

Rocky and Andrew have been talking and their fear enters me for a moment. I ask them all to remember me, should anything happen. I love these people, for we have journeyed and had such adventures together – but where have we reached? A room in Jerusalem with fear for walls and again, I sense the horror. So over the bread and the wine, I ask them to remember. 'Do this to remember me, my friends. Share in this meal, for it may be that – like the bread and the wine – I too am broken and consumed.'

And some ask, 'What do you mean?'

We eat in unease. I sit with young John, because he gives me rest, his head on my chest; while the elder John tries to reassure everyone. He reminds us that Nicodemus spoke well of me; he knows Nicodemus, which helps. Rocky draws closer to his brother Andrew and neither can speak with Miriam, who hides herself in the corner. And the taste of wine takes me back; awaking both memory and desire, returning me to long nights with Eleazar, before events took us apart. It is the taste of excitement, of a melting and better land; the taste of two young men who wished to change the world. But here is painful remembering, for this is not as now it is ... the young men grew, the world tastes different now.

Yet something holds us as I look around, some spirit shared – we have travelled all over, after all. We have shared homes, slept exhausted on floors, begged for food, walked mile upon mile, joked with the crowds, fought with crowds, faced wrath and delight, argued and laughed – and we have done these things together. And I remember thinking, *If this is the end and we are driven apart by dark clouds of circumstance – then I will not regret one single day. These people are friends I never thought to have and most surely do not deserve.* And so, with tears in my eyes, I ask them to remember me, in the bread and the wine, to remember this flame-keeper kindly ...

For, in truth, I am overwhelmed as we eat. I am overwhelmed with the heaviness of the moment. Jerusalem is a heavy city, and the Temple, a heavy place ... I wilt beneath their weight. I had felt strength in the afternoon – truly, I had been alive there in the Temple. But here and now, there is only weakness. 'Whatever happens,' I tell them, 'remember me this way, in the bread and the wine. And guard the flame given to you.'

'You speak as if it *is* our last supper together!' says Thomas.

'And if it is, Thomas? Will it have been worth it?'

And no one replies until Rocky says it is ridiculous, that this is not our last supper; though he speaks with unsettled eyes. He did not leave his family and his fishing nets for a night such as this. I feel sadness for him; he is struggling and blusters to cover his way. And now I am up and I know what to do. I take off my outer robe, throwing it aside, take hold of a towel and pour water from the jug into a basin.

'Sit back from the table,' I say, for they are looking at me. 'Sit back! Move yourselves! There is something I must do.' They are slow to move, uncertain. 'Here, see!' I am now kneeling before John with my basin of water. 'So take off your shoes ... take them off! Follow John.' I will start with John, he will not fight and so I take hold of his bare feet and begin to wash – these aching feet, I wash them all, each of them, hard and callused by life – these feet that have walked with me and for me, misshapen and sweaty, striped by the sun, and rough – though Joanna's are softer, and Miriam's so delicate ... I am gentler with them. And some look down and some look away, but all are quiet. 'This is how it is to be among you,' I say, and then Rocky keeps objecting, I thought he might; I have left him until last.

'You will not wash my feet master, but I will wash yours!'

'No, it is better this way, Rocky; better this way. Tonight, I have nothing else to give you and nothing else to promise, but your feet held and washed. So let me wash your feet.'

And now I get up and leave the circle, and the silence continues, though Jude is putting his shoes back on and making quietly for the door.

'You leave us, Jude?' asks Rocky, as he struggles with one of his sandals. His toe is caught in the leather thong; but he wants to know what his friend is doing. 'Where on earth are you going? We were going to sing some songs, and I know you don't have much of a voice, but -' Jude pauses, as one caught out. He had hoped to leave without comment; but Rocky always comments.

'I must go out.' He speaks weakly, his throat constrained.

'Be careful, Jude,' says Joanna. She has often been firm with him. 'Do nothing foolish.'

'We shall let Jude be,' I say, with cheer I do not feel. 'And greet every goodbye. Could be bad news, could be good news. So go well, Jude.' Though his eyes do not reach mine as he slips out into the night.

'Well, that's a bit odd,' says Rocky.

'He always was,' says Levi.

'Milk turns sour with the passing of days,' I say. 'It cannot help itself.'

YESHUA

Gethsemane

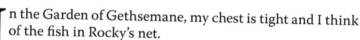

In the Garden of Gethsemane, my chest is tight and I think of the fish in Rocky's net.

There is a place in the net where the fish have nowhere to go; Rocky spoke of it. 'On reaching that place, the fish can swim around as much as they like – but they can't swim out! They live – but they're dead!' He tells it with pride but I feel with the fish tonight. Is this where it ends, the net too tight? My friends sleep, for the dear wasters are shattered as the night wind sighs.

We have eaten together, sung songs of lament and come to Gethsemane, our familiar haunt where either horror or joy will greet us ... for one or other must arrive this evening. Events in the Temple will not be overlooked, I know this. I have kept to the villages, and walked a hidden path; but the Temple always sat waiting and the Temple is the hinge, on which everything opens or shuts. Either Nicodemus ensures they are with me, and the restoration begins; or other voices are heard ...

'Maybe it ends here, John, in this garden; or maybe it starts.' Young John looks at me; he is puzzled.

'Nicodemus?' he asks.

'It is possible.'

'Really?' He does not believe.

'He too wants a new Israel, John. He spoke of a conversation with the priests, with the Sadducees – with Annas even. Who knows? "I will do my best," he said. They may come tonight. They know we gather here, I make no secret of it ... this is my hope.'

'You still have hope after what you did, teacher?'

'I am not your teacher anymore.' John is disturbed by my actions; this is clear and this, my closest friend. I wonder myself if I went too far; though I felt alive there. But did I say or do too much? 'Perhaps I have stirred them to goodness, John,' I say. But his laugh is dismissive which hurts more than any Pharisee.

'Stirred to hate, perhaps. And Jude?'

'Why speak of him?'

'He has left us, Yeshua, he will not be back. The Temple incident, he could not believe it ... maybe others will follow him.'

Anger returns. 'He must do what he must do, John. He has been leaving for a while. Perhaps you have not noticed ... I noticed.'

There is silence between us.

'So we wait for the end,' he says. 'Or the beginning.'

The night is quiet and yes, I wait for Nicodemus. Hope rises in me, pricking the heaviness. He has influence; and Israel could be re-born, born again, with no temple but our spirit. One day we shall have hearts and no rules; for a good heart needs no laws. How can this not be seen? And perhaps he comes now, for surely this is God's will, God's promise – Israel waits for such a day! The gentiles await such a day! We could all be one. And Nicodemus is a serious man. He risked much to speak with me.

Through the olive trees, it is a still and starry night. It reminds me of Nazareth, when I would lie on the roof and gaze at the heavens. We called it 'The Prophet's Room' up there on the tiles ... where a wandering prophet might be housed. Our mother told us every home should have a prophet's room, space for the visitor. And I pray now as I prayed then; I cannot help but pray. Prayer is drawn from me like water from a well. 'Dear father in heaven, your kingdom come and your will be done here on earth, as it is in heaven ... as above, so let it be below!'

'Master, I hear something.' It is Rocky moving towards me. He has woken up, his snoring interrupted. 'Do you wait for someone, teacher? You seem to wait for someone.'

'How would you know, Rocky? You have been asleep.'

'Resting – not asleep; I never sleep.'

Let me be honest with him. 'I wait for horror or joy, Rocky.'

'We don't need to, Master. We could leave now, there is still time.'

'And by leaving run from both? No, I believe I am invited to wait, to yield to one or the other.'

'When did you ever yield?!'

'There is a season for all things. Sometimes we must yield.'

I see movement in the distance, four or five figures in the shadows; they seem uncertain of the way. I see shapes but not faces. Nicodemus is small; I do not see a small man. I continue to watch; perhaps he follows, hidden by his companions. Perhaps members of the Sanhedrin have come here without him, to speak for themselves. I would be glad to speak with them. And then I see another figure, familiar in movement. And I know ... I know in that moment that it ends here in the garden. Nothing begins here ... everything ends. There is only the horror. And I feel the sweat of terror pricking at my skin, as though I bleed.

And I am empty; quite empty of words. So many spoken but now they are gone. I have nothing to say. Words of anger, words of healing, words in parable, words in judgement ... the words rise and fall, they dance and they die ... only I remain. Though who am I now?

'Do you see them, teacher?'

'I see them, Rocky; and you should go. Take the others – certainly take Mark. He is too young.' Mark has become his new friend, a young admirer, which Rocky enjoys. I think it does him good. He looks so lost at times; but when admired, he opens like a flower and remembers what to do.

'I will not go!' he whispers loudly. Their silhouettes are clearer now, they move faster, a torch of fire guides them, men armed with clubs and knives, brazen in the night. 'I'm for taking them on.'

'I think we shall be helpless, Rocky.' But he does not hear me; or cannot believe what he hears. 'Helpless?' he says. I nod and try and calm him. 'It must be so, it must be so.' It hurts me to speak this. I have not asked this of my friends before; and I have not asked it of Rocky. I have asked them to hope, trust and pray, to take nothing for the journey but courage. But I have never called on them to be helpless, which is the only robe now left. 'It ends here in the garden.'

'We shall never be helpless, teacher! *Never.* John! James! Levi! Wake up! Mark – wake Levi up, the lazy toad.'

'It is time to do nothing, Rocky,' but he doesn't listen. He is up and about, doing everything, gathering the band; Levi is cursing Mark, Thaddeus stumbling. But I am moving forward towards the torch light and the figures behind – when suddenly Joanna and Miriam appear through the trees on my left. I hear first the anklets, strange music in the dark – and lamps in their hands, worried faces. I approach them.

'I fear love is not through with me,' I say, and feel tears breaking.

Joanna says, 'Neither are the Temple priests, from what I hear.'

'But love is the more frightening, Joanna; it asks of us the most terrible things. We shall all do our best. And be kind to each other as we fail.'

'My love will never be through with you,' says Miriam; and in that moment we exchange souls through our eyes, where no darkness lives, only union. I hug them both, cling to them both, so grateful, so sad, so alone ... and walk away. I must walk away or cry for a thousand years. I feel the tears; such heaviness of spirit is upon me. And now the men are before me.

'Who do you seek?' I ask.

'Yeshua the Nazarene.'

'You could have come in the light, my friends. No, really. But you arrive in the dark, with swords and clubs, as if I am some bandit! I was with you daily in the Temple and you never laid a finger on me. But here we are and this is your hour with the authority of darkness; I understand. And maybe your shame prefers the shadows.' They are silent for a moment, so I reassure them. 'I am he, the one you seek.' I hold out my hands in welcome. They turn to Jude who appears from the dark. He nods.

'You can trust Jude,' I say. 'We knew each other once, a good knowing; but our paths parted ... for which I am sad.' I look at him. 'Perhaps he is sad too. So Jude, I am handed over by you?'

'Not by me, teacher, not by me.' Jude has hollow eyes like a caught fish, like a fish thrashing, like a fish dying. 'You hand your*self* over.'

'And so I do, and so I do. We must each choose for ourselves and not lay blame at another's feet.'

'You handed yourself over in the Temple this afternoon.'

'I spoke the truth, Jude, which is perhaps the same. But where better for light than the darkness?'

'You must show respect for the law and the prophets.'

'Don't think I come to destroy the law and the prophets.'

'But you *do* destroy, teacher, you do. You dismantle the law and you dismantle us, each of us! What are we to do? You seem to think everything is acceptable apart from the Temple! You let a woman wipe your feet with her hair, using costly perfume!'

He refers to Mary, my friend in Bethany and the best of hosts.

'She used spikenard, Jude ... costly, I agree, but kind. Am I not worth kindness?'

'It stank the place out – I can still smell it.' ·

'You sound as bitter as the aroma, Jude!' Spikenard does stink; it smells of goat and brings all conversation to a halt.

'It is the smell of death, teacher, and if it's death you want ... well, I don't know what you want, or want of *us*. Just what do you want? You say the kingdom of God is within but who knows where? We can't find it. So you leave us as beggars by the side of the road without comfort. You leave us as beggars!'

'Happy are the poor in spirit, Jude – but not the self-pitying. You cry "victim" and fight what is; when all the time you could fall into love.'

In this moment, I feel quite free; a decision is made, an adventure ahead. But Jude rubs his eyes, like a child upset. 'You weren't the answer, you see – not the answer, not the hope I thought ... the hope *we* thought. All of us.' And now he almost smiles, though the smile does not reach his eyes, which is how I remember dear Jude; haunted eyes, with a smile that stopped at his cheeks. 'Why couldn't you just? ... I mean, I thought you could help; and I did my best, really I did, but, well – the Temple? What you did there, I mean ... that isn't going to work. We must *make* friends not lose them. *Make* them!' He looks for help from the sullen faces around him. 'I mean, why are you so hostile, Yeshua? It's just needless, it doesn't get us anywhere. So you hand your*self* over. No one else need do it. You don't even run away now! You sit here in the garden and wait for us. I feel no guilt. Why would I feel guilt?'

I have an overwhelming desire to kiss him; to let him know that all is well. 'Jude, my friend.' I reach out to him. He steps towards me, cautious, holding back. But I do not. I kiss his cheeks, one and then the other and feel his tears; he sobs on my shoulder. I hold him. I cannot judge this man; no judgement is there. I feel such love for him, my fear is quite gone. We release ourselves, each from the other, and he turns and runs into the night. 'So let us go,' I say.

They seem disturbed, those who come to arrest me. Perhaps they expect a fight. My friends gather slowly, but barely know the hour, the day or the place.

'What's happening?' asks Andrew, who is still asleep though standing. And Rocky lunges, grabbing a sword and slashing in the night, until held back by James. I also hold him, this dear madman.

'Remember, Rocky, we must be helpless now – like lambs to the slaughter.'

'I will never be helpless!'

'You will be helpless beyond your knowing, my friend. But fear nothing; we shall all do our best and fear nothing. Shall we go?'

Young Mark runs away and proves a quick fellow; too quick for the soldier who grabs at him. He seizes only Mark's robe, which the boy leaves behind in his hands, running naked into the night, towards the city. And I hear Rocky say to Levi, 'What's going on with Jude?'

MIRIAM

The space man

I cannot sleep. I try to think only well of the future; and how things might turn out for the best. I have always done this; I find it easier, more hopeful. I think of Yesh joking with the crowds; holding children high in the air, to their great delight and eating olives in the morning with cheese. How could anyone harm this man? I hear him laughing as if there is too much joy inside him to be contained.

'Are you awake, Miriam?' whispers Salome. Some of us have returned to her home, where she gives us space on the guest room floor. She lies next to me.

'I'm awake.'

'What are you thinking about?'

'I was remembering a story he told ... the parable of the space man.'

'I don't think I know it. It's not the one about the Samaritan?'

'No, it's different.'

'I heard about *that* story! Lost him a few friends, I hear.' She giggles.

'Then they weren't real friends ... or they wouldn't have left.' I am unable to giggle.

'No one likes Samaritans, if they're honest.'

'That isn't the story I was thinking of.' I love Salome but she can be quite irritating. 'It was the parable of the space man, a new one. He only started telling it here in Jerusalem.'

'Did he think of it here?'

'I don't know where his stories came from. Or when.' I had never wondered, to be honest; but he had a great many. 'He just told them.'

'So tell it to me then.'

'Oh, *I* can't tell it.'

'Tell it!' she whispers excitedly. But can I really tell the story in whispers? I don't wish to wake the others. So I bid her come closer and she shuffles her body sideways towards me. 'I mean, I can't tell it like him, obviously – are you sure you haven't heard it?'

'No.'

'You're not sure?'

'No, I haven't heard it!' This must be the loudest whisper ever.

'OK, OK – so when the space man arrives in Jerusalem, there are problems.'

'Is this the story?'

'This is the story, yes. The space man arrives in Jerusalem and there are problems.'

'What sort of problems?'

'Just let me tell the story, Salome. That's the idea – I tell it, and you listen.' She nods. 'So, as I say, there are problems for the space man when he arrives in Jerusalem.'

'What actually is a space man?'

'*Salome!*' My whisper is a shout. Salome is new to the group. She doesn't understand stories. 'Just let me tell the story – and you'll find out!'

'OK – as long as I do, Miriam. I like stories to have a proper end.'

'So the space man arrives in Jerusalem, OK?' She nods in the Passover moonlight. 'He is a strong man, and he needs to be, as he carries space from town to town across the land. '

Salome giggles. 'The space man carries space? How do you do that?'

'He likes to offer it to the busiest places, knowing that if they lack space, they will also lack joy, tenderness and light. But the space man has trouble today because the High Priest says the space is too large to get into the city.

'It just won't fit,' says the High Priest. 'The Temple is busy and the streets full of worshippers going about their lives. I can hardly stop all these good people for a bit of space! How about making it smaller?'

'You cannot make space smaller,' says the space man. 'It's eternal.'

'But we've a Temple to maintain and a thousand laws to keep,' says the High Priest. 'How can there be space?'

'Without space, there's no tenderness; and without tenderness, there's no light and no life,' says the space man, who stumbles a little, knocked by someone hurrying to prayer.

'We don't need space in Jerusalem – we have the Temple!' says the High Priest. 'We have no call for you, I'm afraid. But you could always try Rome, Rome is a terrible city – they could *definitely* use some space in Rome.'

With the story told, I pause. I hope I've told it correctly.

'Is that it?' asks Salome.

'That's it, yes. Did you like it?'

'I'm not sure the ending's very good.'

'I suppose it's irony. He does use irony.'

'Yes, but what do you think it means?'

I sigh, quietly I hope. I'm not sure Salome understands irony. Or much else. 'I don't think you're meant to explain stories. They can't be squeezed like an orange until the last drop of juice has been extracted.'

'Why not?'

I try again. 'Like you wouldn't try and explain a freshly baked roll.'

'I could explain a roll.'

'You just enjoy the taste, surely?'

'Nonsense! It's about Jerusalem being better than Rome, it's obvious. Hooray for Yeshua! It's *Rome* that needs the space, not Jerusalem, because Rome is rubbish and Jerusalem is brilliant. Did you not see that?'

Salome dreams of a new Israel too; at least she says she does; but she doesn't know how it could ever be, because, as she observes, 'At the end of the day, Miriam, life's not really like that, is it?'

YESHUA

Herod

So this is Herod; though I see him poorly in the darkness. The slave's candle flickers light into the cell and across his smooth and fleshy face.

'You certainly bring people together, Yeshua!' He leans forward and I smell his scented luxury – nard and aloes, more familiar on women, but the rich have their own rules. 'Sadly, however, you bring them together in hate!' He draws back, smiling ... it is the smile of a fox, so the rumour was true. 'The mad Zealots, the dull Pharisees, the unutterably pompous Sadducees, the *dear* Romans, to whom we all must bow very low indeed. They all hate each other; yet nuzzle up like sheep in love in their hatred of you, Yeshua ... quite an achievement.'

'You do not fare much better. I have yet to meet your fan club.'

He is stung. 'I live in a palace, Yeshua. See?' He indicates around him; as if these underground cells are just one further testament to his happy and magnificent life. 'I live in a palace and a palace is better. A palace is where a winner lives. I have a lot of rooms, Yeshua, and some of them are very big while you wander a great deal, you cannot be happy, I wouldn't be happy, a life on the run, a loser's life. That is worse ... much worse, very sad. And now you sit in my gaol, your wandering well and truly done. Pilatus believes so – though he wants me to do the messy work ... the punishment bit, the blood and bones. Don't you hate it when people do that? He passes you on, like mouldy bread. I think I frighten him, he's afraid of me ... he's terrifically afraid of me.'

'You deserve each other. Two blind scorpions, each begging the other for help.' I am already weary of him; and we have only just met. I have been weary of him for as long as I can remember; perhaps before I was born.

'You do know that the Baptiser was here?' he says.

'I do, yes.'

'How you follow each other about! A regular his and hers! And now I hear you're related.'

'We're all related.'

We sit in the fortress at Machaerus; or underneath it, in deep oblivion. I wonder if I shall meet Chuza; but these dark and dripping cells are probably not his domain. The wet stone and iron bars need little care. They smell of piss and shit, and the princely nose winces.

'In this exact cell, if I am not mistaken; an amazing thing. The smell brings it *all* back to me. And I spoke with him, the dear fellow – no, a *good* man – we spoke often. I could hardly have been fairer, really I could not. I talked with him as I now talk with you. I'm not a proud man. I'm a great man ... but not a proud man.'

'So are you a good man, Herod?' He looks askance. 'Do you know Job?'

'Is he the one I sacked last week? That may have been his name.'

'No, that's not ... '

'Very bad man, a thief, not a good man, Yeshua – he had to die, we'll make Israel great, but not with people like him.'

'The Job in scripture. "I put on goodness, and it clothed me; my justice was like a robe and turban. I was eyes to the blind and feet to the lame. I was a father to the poor and

I searched out the cause of him who I did not know." Are
you like Job?'

'I so love the scriptures.' He sits on a silk cushion, brought
by the slave who now holds the candle. The fox-face flickers in
and out of view. 'And you've certainly learned your lines, very
good, Yeshua; I like that. I mean, I had you down as a zealot,
one of the wilderness ones – and let's be honest, nothing good
ever came out of there ... terrible place the wilderness, full of
weirdos and all quite mad. I do *not* like the wilderness. But then
I discover the zealots hate you as well! You tell people to give to
Caesar what is Caesar's, which is not a catch-phrase of theirs.'

'Nothing is Caesar's. Nothing is yours. It was irony.'

'Irony?' He laughs. 'You can't afford irony in Judaea, Yeshua.
It's not a place for subtlety! You just have to kill them ... or
frighten them. Oh, the trouble I have; the trouble I have.'

'The constant victim – fat with privilege, yet somehow a
life of complaint.' But I lose interest in further reply. He must
feel guilty in some manner, to sit here now as he does; there
must be guilt but I cannot help him there. And for a moment,
the candle draws me into a better conversation, a conversation
within – with new yet ancient light. We have talked a while,
the slave's arm tires and the flame dances. It pierces the dark
like a merry knife – new light, yet old, an echo of long ago. The
light sways but it praises God, it makes me smile, a holy spillage
in the gloom ... and I forget the fractured soul who is Herod,
restless on his dunghill of power.

'Why *does* everyone hate you?' he asks.

'Do you speak to yourself?'

'From here on, Yeshua, you're either a dead man, sad but
true – or very lucky.'

'No one is king of their circumstance, Herod, neither you
nor I. No one rules, for events occur like rising waves.'

I think of Galilee. I've been knocked over and near drowned
by events there.

'I cannot rule over other people's hate.'

'Not without an army, perhaps ... though you could keep your
head down, Yeshua, and ease hate away by absence, it might

help you survive ... just a thought, to keep your head down – though perhaps a little late! It would certainly make Chuza's life easier upstairs! Not a talkative man, but always on your side, quietly; yes, I notice that.' Does he know of Joanna? I will not speak of her. 'But instead, of course, you wander and you prod, like a naughty boy goading a bull. You scuttle around Galilee like a beetle, hither and thither, *my* territory. And then make an arse of yourself in Jerusalem, which is definitely that of Pilatus. I don't want to kill Jews – '

'You killed the Baptiser.'

The eyes pass the message. I am hit hard across the face by the soldier. I fall sideways, my chains clattering ... and I recover only slowly. There is a ringing gong of pain in the side of my mouth. Herod watches. 'I'd be very grateful for Chuza, if I was you ... and dear Joanna, of course. It could be so much worse.' And now the fox speaks as if John is not important, that bygones should be bygones, and fresh chapters written. He imagines it all a game, fresh dice in play, though the game has destroyed him. I see this now, his eyes scarred and scared – and the scared become fools.

'Did John keep his head down – and hold it still when your executioner arrived? I doubt it.' I can imagine some struggle. Will I be the same?

'John should not have got involved! What has he to say about my marriage? He should not have taken that tone about my marriage. I'm Herod Antipas! I have a lot of rooms. And he's a loser.'

'So why fear him?'

'I hardly noticed him; truly, hardly noticed him.'

'He had no army and was dressed in rags. So why the fear?"

'He smelt terrible, of course. *Ooh!*' He holds his nose, turning all things into jest. 'He washed sins away in the river, but forgot to wash himself!' I think he's told that joke before. 'I mean, Herodias – she said that he smelt like ... well, it doesn't matter what she said, terrible tongue, terrible tongue, that woman. I mean, I love women, but her tongue – ' A pause I do not fill. 'I did not fear him, Yeshua. He was a mad-eyed outcast, a lank nobody. But here's a lesson life has taught me: when all around wish you dead, you do not give each of them a sword. And John was that sword. There were those who could use him and his complaints. Just as you will be used, Yeshua, don't worry about that. These are not discerning times. I'm told you speak well, people say that, I don't know, I haven't heard you, I don't want to hear you – but don't imagine anyone here gives a ram's bollocks for your words, which are a fart in the Judaean wind and that's it. If, however, they can *use* your words against the Romans, against the Temple or against me ... '

'So you placed his head on the platter.'

'Women!' He laughs as he gets up from his seat. He wishes me to agree, as if Herodias should take the blame. 'I spoke with him, I said, "Best you keep quiet, Baptiser, best you stay quiet in a cave." But not possible apparently! Not possible for John! That's the loser he was. He couldn't keep quiet in a coffin, that one! And neither, it seems, can you, Yeshua ... and in the Temple, of all places? In the *Temple!* On all that is holy, *why?*

'Because it isn't.'

He's getting up, gesturing at his slave to get out the way. The candle sputters. 'A problem in Jerusalem at Passover is a Roman problem, not mine. No Chuza to help you now, Yeshua, because I won't be his dupe, I'm Herod Antipas, I won't be a patsy for Pilatus. He must free you – or do the messy stuff himself!'

MIRIAM

With Levi in the Temple

~

The Temple is busy. It is like a huge-stoned monster devouring people, I feel this now; and some still speak of Yeshua and the things done yesterday; pockets of gossip, though life goes on, no space man here.

'He went mad,' Levi says, shaking his head. 'Didn't quite see that coming, though I suppose the clues were there. It has been building, hasn't it?' And now Yeshua has disappeared, taken in the garden last night; and I have no words. He leaves behind so much anger and Levi says I should not stay, that we are in danger here in the Court of Women, as 'known associates'. It is the nearest we are allowed to the Temple, and as near as I wish to be. The colonnades make deep shadows and I use them to hide, the shadows are kind ... but I do not wish to leave. I find him here in some way; as if leaving here is to leave my love.

'The zealots attack the Romans, Miriam, which is all well and good; it plays well among Jews. But Yeshua attacks the *Temple* – and when you take on the Temple you take on Jerusalem and that's not a battle you can win. Never fight a battle you can't win.' Again he shakes his head; there's much head-shaking at the moment, a sudden plague of it, everyone shaking their head and I don't like it.

I do feel discomfort, there's no question, for I still hear my father: 'Trust in none but God, hard work – and the Temple.' He traded here in Jerusalem, bought and sold in this place – 'a dry city, Jerusalem – and they love their melons there.' And of course he spoke often of the Temple, 'where heaven and earth meet,' he said. 'The plaza – larger than large, that plaza! And the porticos, the columns, the staircases! You'll see it for yourself one day, my girl. You must see the lamp stands in the Court of Women – oh my word! And the colonnades, Miriam – you should see the colonnades! All built by Herod the Great, and he *was* great, you see. A proper Jew he was, building glory in the heart of Jerusalem whilst pissing off the Romans – yet still a traders' paradise. What's not to like? Thirsty pilgrims as far as the eye can behold! Now that's what I call glory!'

But I find no glory here today. Each face speaks accusation and every stone, of death.

'He loves Jerusalem, Levi.' I say this to myself really, and Levi laughs; his face scorns my words, though the scorn is kind in its way. Levi takes me aside, he is not here to hurt but to guide; to ease me from danger, to take me home, though still I resist. 'Yeshua spoke to me of his love for the city, I heard him. He spoke of his sadness at what it had become. There were tears in his eyes, Levi, real tears, as though its people were motherless chicks! He loves Jerusalem with a passion!'

'He disguises it well.'

He pushes me into the corner, not violent but firm; he is more scared than I. He looks around us for danger, a tax collector again and shifty, his good deeds forgotten. 'Jerusalem lives on the sanctity of the Temple, Miriam. You do not understand this, do you? Taking the Temple out of Jerusalem is like taking the fish out of Magdala. There's nothing left. Everything here – *everything* – is built around it ... status, position, income, everything.' His face sweats, his eyes are holes of terror. 'The priests, the craftsmen, look at them! The money changers, the animal sellers, the tanners ... the hostelries that house the pilgrims.' He waves his arms, extending their reach beyond these walls. 'Attack the Temple and you attack the whole city. Do you understand, Miriam? The whole city! He killed himself yesterday.'

'Don't say that, Levi, don't say that!'

He lets go of me and sags. 'Come on,' he says and eases me towards the gate.

YESHUA

What is truth?

'You do not speak, Yeshua – when once so full of words ... so very full, I hear.' I am before Pilatus on his little wooden throne. Good craftsmanship spoiled by its use. A fine chair should hold a fine man, this is my thought, but this chair holds Pilatus. 'A man so full of words now empty, Yeshua?' He offers a queasy smile. 'Are they all used up, like the wine at a poor man's wedding?'

My hands are tied, the cord fierce on my skin. I have soft wrists, James always said this but now I am pushed to my knees, the soldier unkind with his shove. He stands behind me, I hear his armour as he breathes; it has a life of its own, the sword clanking against his thigh. Pilatus appears distracted. His Greek is not bad, he is learning, but he is a chancer, I see this; his fingers tapping his bare knees, his waxy skin. He's as scared as Herod said. It's not wise for Romans to be in Jerusalem at Passover.

'If only you could bring peace, Yeshua – then no need for, well – all *this*.'

'Unfortunately I bring a sword – and seem quite unable to disarm myself.'

'We could certainly help you there.' He smiles at his wit.

'Indeed, we seem already to have done it. I don't see a sword.'

'I'm afraid it's out of your reach. It almost feels out of mine.'

'Nothing is out of my reach.' He is tetchy. 'My *Roman* reach.'

'You have wisely forgotten the ensigns.'

The zealots told me of the ensigns and I am careful to remind him ... the time his soldiers brought ensigns into Jerusalem, imprinted with the image of Emperor Tiberius – and then set them up in Fort Antonia next to the Temple. It was done at night, to keep it secret – as if Jerusalem could ever keep a secret. And when word spread, which it does, like fire, the city was in uproar. Angry Jews then rush to Caesarea to protest, and Procurator Pilatus, this emptiness before me now – he refuses to see them! He turns away from their disgust. From his little throne, he imagines there is no need to deal with these mad men.

But the crowd outside his palace grows; while for five days he continues to refuse a meeting. He hopes they will forget their grievance – always unlikely in Israel, which has store houses full of them and never forgets. And then on the sixth day, he takes to his judgement seat and allows them in. They arrive raging, but he has no plans to listen. Instead, he surrounds them with soldiers and threatens death to any who complain. Only recently arrived in the province, he imagines Judea a reasonable place – or at least one suitably afraid. He imagines it a place where he can pull such a stunt because he has a few spears to his name!

But death held no fear for these men. They bared their necks, lay on the ground and declared themselves happy to die if the ensigns stayed in Jerusalem. What else could they do with the holy city so abused? They would never appease a blasphemer – *never*. So all are now lying down in his palace, awaiting death by sword and spear. And Pilatus on his throne? He need only nod to the soldiers for slaughter to commence – but the nod does not come. He doesn't himself have the neck. Against such rage, such insane commitment, he had no power. He had the ensigns removed from Jerusalem.

Pilatus: 'Every successful commander chooses which battle he must lose in order to win the war. You may have noticed I still sit on the throne, Yeshua, with Israel still ruled from Rome. Who knows where those oafs are?'

Sharpening their knives in the caves probably; I almost think of them fondly.

'If nothing else does, Pilatus will make you a zealot!' they told me when we met. 'He'd make a zealot of a grape!' I see their point; he seeks only power, and loves only himself. Though he says he would like to free me; that this is his desire. 'I would like to set you free, Yeshua. I do have the power.' And now a woman steps out of the shadows behind him, with a well-jewelled neck; though haunted by the seven devils of anxiety in her eyes. Does she wish for a closer look; to greet me even? But I do not speak as the soldier stands, the woman stares, the slaves demur and Pilatus fidgets. He senses the woman; he does not wish her here, but plays the man, firm and strong.

'But I insist you speak!' Only the weak insist.

'I tire of words.'

'The wordsmith tires of words?'

'By our fruits we are known. Words are not real, Governor, they make things up, they pretend.'

'My words are real, Yeshua, quite real!' He speaks to himself, to reassure — as when two dying men each say how well the other looks. 'I say so, Yeshua, and it *is* so.'

He clicks his fingers and asks for cheese. Cheese is brought hastily, with bowing, and set before him on the table by the throne. He smiles, picks it up and throws it away.

'Words,' he says, as if all is quite proved.

I lose interest. I am invited to the festival of debate ... but do not attend. Once I would speak and contest; no one contested like me. But those days appear gone.

'The word "light" is not light, Pilatus. You cannot make your way in the dark by speaking it. The dark will still be dark.' His face queries me, his head pulled back and jutting jaw. 'Words come and go, yours and mine — like ghosts, taken by the wind to who knows where?'

'And the promise to pull down the Temple stone by stone?' He shakes his head, as one in shock. 'I hate to advise a Jew on

Jewish affairs, Yeshua, but, well ... it is words – your words – which have brought you here with strong and determined hands.'

He speaks of another time; I cannot return to the rage I felt then. I wish only to be alone at my lathe, working the wood; there is more truth in a splinter than in this perfumed gallery, slaves within, soldiers without, a woman watching and the anxiety of power on its throne.

'Everyone makes of words what they will, Pilatus. My words cannot change you ... though you could change yourself *by* them.'

'You would change *me*, Yeshua?' His voice rises in delighted surprise. He seems to like the attention.

'No, I would have you change yourself.' He likes this less. 'I am visible before you, but I am not visible.' He squints in mockery. 'You do not see me. Recognise what is in front of you, Pilatus, recognise this moment, this here and this now ... and what is hidden from you will be revealed.' He stares at me; the woman from the shadows steps closer. 'You really do not see what is in front of you, do you?' And now I cannot help it, I start laughing at this scene: a man on a throne; another on his knees; a soldier in armour, a woman made of fear and a slave with a bowl. Who ordered all this? How is it so? Who made him to be on a throne and I on my knees? Who gave one man armour and a wage and another, a bowl which is not even his? I cannot help but laugh. 'You see what is behind you and what is ahead of you, Pilatus, where nothing is revealed. But you do not see what is in front of you!'

'I see this amuses you.' He is cold.

'But *I* see what is in front of me, Pilatus. And do you know what I see? I see a child clothed in a prince's robe and fine-jewelled chains. How happy he must be! Would you not think so? Yet this child, he has no pleasure in his play, for his princely dress fills him with fear. He is frightened that his fine clothes might be torn on a rock or stained by the dust of the world. So tell his mother it is no joy or gain for the child to wear such finery. It denies him joy and separates him from his friends. Do you recognise the child, Pilatus?' The woman from the shadows is aghast; she gasps, and reaches for the throne to steady her. 'We use words for a season, and then the season is past. Only the earth remains ... and truth.'

I hear the horses in the street and soldiers' shouts, 'Get back!'

'And what *is* truth?' hisses the woman, as if this is the only answer she seeks.

'The truth is in the silence.' I feel her eyes. 'So, as Habbakuk declared, let everyone in the Temple be silent.'

Pilatus sits on his throne, she stands behind; both are still. And then truly, the silence arrives. It covers me, like a heavy cloak. I am almost knocked over by it, crushed. I topple sideways, losing balance, the soldier lifting me back up. It is like a rush of wind, like cold air rising from an abyss. I see silence opening before me, and words falling down and away, like broken pottery.

And I do not speak again. He presses me, and eats goat's cheese in frustration. Crumbs fall down his front; he blames the slave. He gets up from his throne, tugs at his robe and paces around. He accuses me of insolence and shrugs at the woman who runs away, back into the shadows.

A soldier strikes me and I fall badly, my arms still tied; I believe my head bleeds. But I have nothing to say. And later, in the mouldy and dripping darkness of the cell, I talk of the wilderness with Barabbas – yes, it is he – who has been beaten; his face swells as we talk. He was taken in Jerusalem. 'I hope you put up a fight,' he says.

'Only in the Temple.'

'You must be mad.'

'While you pose as sane?'

But only one of us will return here; we know this. Tomorrow, according to custom, Pilatus the Chancer will allow the crowd to choose their Passover hero and he shall walk free. He shall be pardoned and walk away, while the other –

'I knew you were trouble,' says Barabbas.

'I have tried to keep myself to myself.'

'You were trouble on a stick. It's why I was kind and allowed you to live.'

'A knife might have been kinder still.' Though I hope for Nicodemus even now; I cannot let go of the hope, it will not retire. I imagine him gathering support even now. The Sadducees, they can arrange things; they can arrange anything in Jerusalem. Though the following day, I step out into the sun from the darkness of the cell. Chained with Barabbas, I am hauled up and pushed before a crowd. I see Pilatus waving to them, as if their old friend and master – no mention of the ensigns. Today he has what they want, with only one name on their lips. 'Barabbas! Barabbas!' is the chant. 'We want Barabbas!'

I let go of my hope in Nicodemus and the Sadducees. The darkness is sudden.

MIRIAM

The awful hate of history

I pace up and down, up and down in the dust.
I pace like a woman with a demon, outside the prison court yard. The price of freedom is my beating heart, thumping and sullen, and everyone an enemy – each soldier and Temple guard; each Sadducee in a hurry; each hunched Pharisee giving advice in the market place, all in cahoots. But I wait for my man; I will keep vigil and pace as I do – and then Rocky arrives by my side, a man I have no wish to see. He has the eyes of a frightened horse, he is turbulent; yet asks me to calm myself.

'Have you killed someone?' I ask. This is how he looks. 'You do not look well.'

'He has been taken,' he says angrily, as if this explains his ridiculous behaviour.

'I know; I was there. You left quickly.'

'And what gain was there in staying? None at all. And there is nothing we can do now, Miriam; nothing. I mean, why are you here? He does not benefit from your support.' I find this an odd message. Is it not odd? 'There's nothing you can do. You should be home – in Magdala.'

'I am home.' I realise this as I speak it. I am surprised at myself and what I say; but I speak the truth. He is my home, this man Yeshua; and I tell Rocky the same. 'He is my home.'

He laughs with empty eyes, as if I am a fool; and as if somewhere else in his mind, a place of fear.

'You should not say such things,' he says. 'They're the words of a stupid woman and Yeshua doesn't need stupid women now.'

'Or stupid men?'

'You don't know what you say, you never did. But I try to help you, believe me. What if they find you here? You'll only betray him – and then what? *Then what?*' He's nodding at me, as if in pain. 'You're no better than the rest of us, Miriam – and not the special friend you imagine, believe me!' I am in shock.

'I ... '

'Stay here and you'll be recognised ... and then followed. We've been seen with him, we're known, you and I...when it's best *not* to be known. Think about it – it doesn't help him if we're caught. What help to him is that, woman?'

'Let me through,' I say, 'I need to see the governor.'

I walk away and he grabs my arm with his hand, which is like a claw. Some call him 'The Claw' – hands hardened and bent from pulling oars and wrestling with nets; he'll leave a bruise, but I pull away, shaking him off; I cannot listen to him anymore.

'Let go!' I say and push forward towards a soldier. I do not know what I have done to offend him. Is it all women he hates – or is it just me? I have liked him – I have tried to like him, hale and hearty Rocky. He carried me to Joanna, after all! But he has pushed me away ever since when I wished to be friends and I do not understand. Levi says to be at peace about it; he says that Rocky is Rocky. But what does that mean? And how can I be at peace when he speaks rudely to me, as if I don't exist?

'Steady there, woman.' I am grabbed by a soldier who I know, we have met. I remember faces, I have always remembered faces, and I wonder: can he help me? It is Marcus, we met in the market place. I was in a hurry; I dropped my basket of fruit. He picked it up and I thanked him. I could have lost it all, I was grateful – before remembering that you should never thank a Roman ... though Yeshua does.

'Oh, it's you!' he says. 'I remember you – the girl who can't carry fruit. And you shouldn't be here.' I am in shock. I gasp. I cannot watch and I cannot turn away. He sees the line of my eyes and I see Yeshua in the court yard. 'Is he your friend?' I nod. 'Oh dear – well, that's the Syrians and the Greeks for you. Not his greatest fans. And a good reason for you not to be here.' I do not know what he means. 'They're your worst local enemy.'

He is covered in blood – Yeshua, my friend. His body tortured and bent, held by soldiers either side; but not in kindness, as I would hold him – held only that the horror may proceed. He spoke of the horror sometimes, and I've seen horror – I have seen much horror, but what is this? And how is it so? My song of a love unknown, ever since I met him; but this is quite another tune. I vomit at the feet of Marcus – and now they mock, and laugh, and kneel... they strike him with staves, on his shins. He cries out; and they laugh.

'Why?' I cling to Marcus, so big in his armour. Can he help me? Can he save Yeshua? He could save Yeshua. 'Why do they do this?'

He looks down at me and smiles disdain.

'These people hate the Jews, woman – and why wouldn't they?' He looks in my eyes, hands on my shoulders, as if to hold my listening. 'Know your history, Jew girl – we Romans do.'

History? What has history to do with this terror? I don't want his speech. I want Yeshua freed. I push forward again.

'I must see the governor ... ' – but he grabs me roughly by the arm.

'They'll do the same to you, woman.'

'I don't care.' He holds me firmly and speaks into my face.

'The last Jewish kings, the Hasmoneans – they conquered, and royally fucked, all the surrounding Syrian and Greek cities. Yes?' He almost shouts at me. 'So don't wonder at this, woman, don't cry "Innocent me!" The Jews made slaves of these people, vassals at best – so these guys aren't friends of any Israelite. They hate the lot of you. Long memories will kill us all, eh?'

He pushes me back again, satisfied in some manner. My arm is sore from his holding and Yeshua lies on the ground; he doesn't seem to move. But they're lifting him again ... he is lifted up. They're putting a robe around him ... but why – why a robe?

'The robe ... ?'

'Someone called him "King of the Jews" – not a clever line.' He speaks without turning to me. He's watching; I think he's enjoying it.

'*He* never said that.'

'Didn't go down well in the barracks. "King of the Jews" – didn't go down well at all, not with the Syrians and Greeks.'

I do not understand this. All those years ago! What has history to do with Yeshua? He speaks for the poor, for the children, for the blind, for the lame – these people are his kingdom! Only this present matters!

'Romans hate the Jews as well, mind!' His tone is mean now; it curdles. 'Sejanus, back in Rome, he's famous for it.' He laughs as he speaks and I see it clear; his kind mask cracks. 'Total Jew-hater, Sejanus! And proud of it...they do like a Jew-hater in Rome. But there's Roman hate – and then there's the Syrians.'

He nods towards the men with their hysterical eyes, forcing some crown on Yeshua's head, his eyes turned to heaven – ripping thorns, blood bursts down his face. 'We tend to leave Jews to the Syrians ... saves us a job.'

Yeshua cries out and buckles, his legs have gone; and when those holding him let go, he falls horribly and sudden, his swollen and blistered head cracking. Tight around him, like a binding, is the robe, a twisted mess of dust and blood.

'"He saves others; but can't save himself!" It's a joke in the barracks.'

I hate Marcus, and I cannot breathe, so how can I talk?

'He doesn't save – only God saves.'

'Not today, darling.'

I make to leave, I cannot remain. 'You will tire of armoured fame,' I say. 'He said that to a soldier, you know? "You will tire of armoured fame."'

'I think he's tired before I have.' And then he laughs again.

The court yard howl is beyond pain, beyond a scream. Yeshua buckles again and I cannot stay. I am revolted at myself, I feel shame; but I walk away and then bend again to vomit. I do not know what to do with my love, for I cannot leave my friend… yet I leave him. And is this to be my last memory of the man? Is *this* our farewell? No justice…no justice. I'd prefer not to live. It is true I would prefer not to live.

And where now do they take my Lord? Where do they take him?

YESHUA

My outstretched arms

The soldier kneels on my arm and cross beam.
I smell his sweat, I smell his groin in my face; binding cloth is tightened around my wrist. It will staunch the blood, slow the death – 'turns two days into three', all know this ... and then the nail lined up, slight pressure on my wrist through the cloth, I feel it – eight inches, I note the nail, flat head, no use for furniture – only cross beams. The pause, the knee still on my arm, holding me down, pain enough, the arm swinging down, but nothing prepares you – my body jerks, I shit my bowels empty, the nail through my wrist, everything swimming, blood everywhere, they move away, dark silhouettes in the morning sky, blocking the sun, changing sides, 'Go away!' – my left arm now, sun then shadow, the clink of armour. These are not Roman, they speak Syrian, they speak Greek, not a good sign, they laugh, they sneer – the other wrist bound, tight binding, hard knee in my arm again, slight pressure to line it up, lining up the nail. I had a good eye, always hit clean, but nothing prepares you, the wrist again, a nightmare of shock up my arm, right the way up, never-ending ... and now I'm being

dragged across the ground, four soldiers holding the cross beam, like horses pulling a chariot, my body lifted, my feet drag, and then suddenly lifted up, bright sun, they climb steps – now everything screams, everything, my shoulders break, this is death, my feet mid-air, looking for a home, the patibulum heaved up onto the stipes, Roman words to remember, my father liked Roman words, made him feel clever, he *was* clever ... the jerk of the cross beam finding its place, held by pegs – strong pegs, my feet find the wooden block, momentary relief, I push up, nothing prepares you – the nail through my heels, eight inches, nailed to the pain, insufferable – 'the expectation that something cannot be suffered', I missed that one, for this cannot be suffered, and this cannot be endured, I disappear ... I look for the cave, look for the light, I try to do this, where else to go? But the cave is flooded, dirty torrents of water smashing through, the corridor flooded, awful water, the light lost and I want only to die and fuck the light. I am poured out like water, dirty water, my bones out of joint, every screaming one of them, my heart like wax, my mouth so dry – my God, my God, why have you abandoned me!

Shapes of people, I see shapes, soldiers smirk. I hear them through the throb, awake and then not, the throb is a noise, a noise of pain, I see them below, they talk and joke, and my cave is dark, I am drowning in the cave but I will not hate, and I will not hate, so forgive them, father, forgive them – forgive Chancer and the Fox, forgive soldier and priest, Jude and Nazareth – yes, even Nazareth, forgive them, forgive Eleazar, they know not what they do; I feel only their struggle, these poor unhappy little men ... forgive them, they know not ...

Ahh! My God and dear heaven, I see my mother and Miriam! I see them now, I think so ... Do I dream? And young John, and Mary, they should not be here, go away! Please, no! They stand near, too near, my mother's head up, staring straight, I try to speak, 'John, take her home with you, please take her home with you' – I think I speak, he must take her home, 'Go with John', I say to her, 'a better family for you, a better son, a better place – and Miriam, don't watch this death, don't watch!'

We made good tables together, my father and I; and good homes, safe homes, foundations you could trust in the rains; and I see him now, bending down to greet a child – glad he is not here, though wanting him here; and that moment when the job was done, 'It is finished, Yeshua,' he would say, 'You can leave it now, you can put the hammer down – or the job's never done. It is *finished*.'

'It is finished!' ... the song is lost or the song is done, my mind is lost, my spirit ebbs, a pain in my side, awful pain, but the light in the cave, I see the light, I have lost my mind but found the light ... the long walk home, back to the light, I feel I dance into the light, such light and into your hands, father, I commit my spirit ... into your hands, into your hands, for here, it is finished ...

MIRIAM

The burial of Yeshua

I walk behind the slaves; though I look only at the palate they carry. I still cannot believe what lies beneath the covering cloth.

And I ask them to carry with care; but Joseph says we must hurry. He is in a rush for the Sabbath approaches when all work must cease – 'We need to get this done,' he says, 'or the body will be unburied and become food for the birds.' And so he shouts at the slaves, which is how it is. Yeshua said the Sabbath is a gift and should not make us sweat with worry as Joseph does now; but Yeshua is dead and Joseph hurries on.

This man is used to giving orders; he does not flinch from the task. I'm told he is a cloth seller in Arimathea, not a town I've heard of. And his fingers, an odd colour; you cannot help but notice, I always look at hands.

'It's the dye,' said Joanna. I had asked her how she knew him, and she just said, 'Chuza uses him.' So perhaps he provides Herod with cloth; and Joanna said he was a follower of Yeshua. 'He gives assistance as and when he can,' she said, in her matter-of-fact way. 'He is a follower.'

And maybe this was so, I trust Joanna; but he was never much seen, too busy with his cloth perhaps ... though he *is* to be seen now, and heard, insisting on speed, when it is too late for that. What is the rush when there is nothing to rush for, when the Sabbath rest means nothing? You cannot rest from sorrow.

He strides ahead, lifting his robe above the dust, and where are the others? I have seen none of them, not one, since Gethsemane – apart from Rocky, and that was some way from friendly. Have they all found fox holes to hide in? I cannot believe they do this. Did Yeshua really have only four followers? One might imagine so! For only four of us were with him at the end, with him at the cross. And yes, where is brave Rocky now? Where is Levi, Andrew, Jude, Thaddeus, Thomas – or any of them? It seems they joined Mark in his hasty sprint away, like snakes escaping a fire; when I wish the fire to consume me whole.

I walk alongside Joseph and tell him: 'Yeshua said the Sabbath was made for man, not man for the Sabbath. Perhaps we invent the rush.' He stops, looks at me and shakes his head, as if I have lost all sense. Then walking again he says, 'We will do this properly,' as if anything is now proper. How can anything be proper ever again?

He has permission from Pilatus, who also buys his cloth. I say that, I do not know he buys it; but these people seem to know each other. He went with Nicodemus to ask for the body. It was brave, I suppose, though late. Such support *before* his death would have been better; support which kept him from death. They beg for merciful permission from the man who showed no mercy.

'I wonder how he sleeps,' I say, thinking aloud.

'Who?' says Nicodemus, who walks with me out of Jerusalem.

'Pilatus.'

'Well, he has been most merciful in allowing us to bury the body.'

'Merciful? He tortured and killed him.'

'It is as it is,' says Nicodemus, though what does that mean? "It is as it is." I don't know what it means – for "as it is", is *wrong*, quite wrong. Yet they bowed and scraped to Pilatus and asked him if they might, with neither fuss nor commotion, give decent burial to the crucified flesh that was Yeshua. 'He did need reassurance,' says Nicodemus, with pride. 'Only to be expected, of course. These are turbulent times – and Yeshua did cause problems at the end. The Temple business, well ... and at Passover time!' Again, he shakes his head. Pilatus had wanted to send soldiers with them, to prevent trickery or trouble; but there was no time; and perhaps Nicodemus smiled his reassuring smile at the Governor. 'It can melt mountains' they say. And so these late friends of Yeshua came to the cross alone to collect the body; and there they found me, standing as one in a trance, as one paralysed.

'Miriam of Magdala?' says Nicodemus, surprised I am here on the hill; surprised I have not fled the scene. But where would I run to? And how can I leave my Lord? 'No one else here?' he mutters, looking around a hill which has long since emptied. 'Well, why would they be?' He answers himself. 'Nothing more to be done and the Sabbath approaches ... probably best if you were gone too, my girl.' It is an order of sorts.

'John has taken his mother to be with him,' I say. 'Young John, I mean – he has taken her. But they were here with me ... they were here at the end, he was not alone. And Mary, the mother of James, she was also ... '

'Poor woman, poor woman,' he says, shaking his head in pained condolence. 'It is not right that a parent outlives their child. No parent desires that ... no parent.' Though it seems to me there are many things not right about this day. But what do I say? I do not speak of Yeshua's hopes for Nicodemus, even to the end in Gethsemane. What good would it do? What good to tell him of the hopes Yeshua placed on his shoulders? But he could have helped, there is no question of this, and as we talk, I resent him and his reasonable smile. Surely he could have done something?

'Yeshua hoped you might save him,' I say.

He is shocked. 'Save him?' He chuckles. 'Yeshua thought that? Well, I could hardly save him, dear girl. Remarkable man, of course – mesmerising, one might say ... yes, mesmerising. He once said I must be born again ... quite a thought, eh? Quite a thought! But not even Yahweh, who can do all things, could save a man who did what he did in the Temple at Passover. No.' He shakes his head and then pauses. 'And we are all exposed, Miriam. Not one of us – but *all*. You must understand that. I sense your indignation, the prerogative of the young. But no survivors are good – that is why they survive. You do see that?'

'I don't understand.'

'This man Yeshua, and the end that he chose ... .' Without looking, he points towards the cross, black against blue in the afternoon sun. 'We are all exposed, Miriam, all of us.' He is uncomfortable, and why wouldn't he be? But he continues as he walks. 'Including himself, of course, this cannot be ignored, that Yeshua must take some responsibility for all this. I believe so. He chose the way and he chose to lead us there with him, a difficult dance for us all. Were it not for Yeshua, we would all be happily at home today ... or at least at home. We would not be worried for our very lives. And should a son force such suffering on his mother? Is that really the way? She will not recover from these events, I doubt she'll recover.' I am bewildered, I cannot find words. We walk on, my mind in chaos. 'I mean, I don't blame Yeshua.'

'You don't *blame* him?'

'He was doing his best, as we all are, in trying circumstances – and yes, his followers – and I include myself, Miriam, I include myself, for I was a follower, in my own way – we did tend to disappear, so to speak, we found other commitments ... only women there at the cross, only women there at the end.' Meaning *no one* was there, this is my sense.

'Three women, one man.' I won't let him forget young John.

'Quite, young John ... but not the best goodbye, is it? It does not cover us in glory. And as for dear old Rocky ... '

'What of him? Have you seen him?' I wish to know where he is.

'Well, a man of such bold promises and high hopes – some say the leader? I did hear this.'

'Probably from him.'

'Yet he ends up denying Yeshua – did you not hear that, Miriam? You may not have heard. But apparently the heroic fisherman denied all knowledge of his master the night of his arrest. "I absolutely do not know him!" ... he kept repeating it across Jerusalem, which is quite a thing really. Wouldn't you say so?'

I am stunned; I have not heard this. *'Rocky?* He denied knowing Yeshua?' I now remember his hollow eyes, his angry hands and vicious tongue when he found me at the courtyard, still fresh from this turning away. But Rocky, how could you!?

Nicodemus: 'No blame though, no blame. As I say, we're all doing our best. It could have been anyone – any one of us. I mean, who wouldn't, in his shoes? Who wouldn't? I don't imagine he's proud. But survival is always a rather sneaky business and he is no different. The trouble is, we either had to be his disciples – or his executioners. There was no in-between on offer, which is problematic. I mean, Caiaphas is a decent enough man, is he not?' I don't know why he asks me. 'I mean, all have their faults, and heroes are few, but he wants only to maintain the sanctity of the Temple and keep the Romans as far from it as possible. And again, who wouldn't, my dear, who wouldn't? So with the Passover crowds to consider, and Rome threatening to strip away their power, he, well – he helps in the death of a foolish young man, and everyone is happy.' I suddenly anger, as if Yeshua was foolish. Does that make Nicodemus wise – this man who watches and hides?

'The soldiers were beasts.'

'But obeying orders ... .one must see all sides, my dear.' He smiles again, smoothing all things over, every crease in the cloth. 'The military survives by obedience, all soldiers know this. Though I appreciate, I don't deny it, the orders did violate Roman justice, this at least is plain.' He looks suitably stern at such misdemeanour, as one might look on a boy who drops an orange from a bridge on a passing farmer. 'I did not mention this to Pilatus, of course! He hardly needs another Jew questioning his army.' He chuckles as if this need hardly be said.

'And I suppose Pilatus also shone in this story?'

'A man who wishes to keep his job? Again, no great crime, my dear – as you would know, if you had ever had a job.' He looks away, aware of the spite he has uttered; and if he is not aware, I am aware for the both of us. 'He is scared, that is all. Scared the Temple authorities will send bad reports to Caesar – oh, he fears this greatly, Miriam, believe me; has dreams about it, I'm told. And he has lost to the Jewish people before, remember; he has lost a number of times. So if he can please them now and again – well, of course he must. He absolutely must. And a good man – for Yeshua *was* a good man, if unwise – a good man is the sacrifice.' He agrees with himself, nodding. 'So really, who comes out well from this, Miriam? We are all exposed – yet who did actual wrong?'

'*I* did not desert him.' I speak with more force than I intend. He looks surprised, a moment of shock – and I'm glad of it! I hope he is stung. Nicodemus imagines he speaks for all of us with his lists of who did what and why. It helps dampen his guilt, like one easing fire with wet cloths. 'Everyone was so – so I am all right.' I see what he does; Yeshua taught me to see the cunning in every human heart. And all the while, he speaks like a teacher, like rabbis I have known, full of explanation yet feeling nothing, and distant to it all. And I cannot be distant. How can I be distant? These are betrayers all. 'I did not once desert him, sir. Not once.'

'But then you are in love, Miriam, is this not so? There are rumours of love between you, and I find that does make a difference. Love can make a fool of us on occasion.' What does he say? Is he kind or cutting? 'But let's at least see him properly buried, he deserves that. We all hold him in our hearts, I'm sure. And perhaps he died for us, in a manner. We might say that, might we not? And it makes it better, gives reason to these events. He died for us, died for us all, that we might see the light ... he did have a strange light within ... well, who knows, who knows? This is not easy for anyone ... '

And it is not easy to remove a man from a cross. You may not know this; and when does one learn and who is there to teach you? Maybe the Romans. But without a ladder or hoist, there is no kind way and we had neither – just slaves. They could ease the stem of the cross from its holding in the ground; I watch them now, heaving up with terrible strain. First they say they cannot lift it and then decide they can. It is touch and go, more arrive to help, they argue with each other, Yeshua is a pale and bloodied blue, almost blowing in the wind, like washing. But then they are unable to hold the tilting wood and it falls backwards. The slaves narrowly escape, but the body jolts and jerks on impact with the ground, quite awful, ripped and torn again. If he hadn't been dead before ...

I watch, though I cannot watch; one nightmare smeared across another. Perhaps I will wake? I would like to wake. I would like to see him washing his face in the morning, laughing with the women in the kitchen, chatting with young John, eating his olives while he spoke – as I have said, he liked olives and ate too many. But I do not wake; there is no such escape this Sabbath eve. They remove the nails, pulling them from limp wrists and ankles and lift the holed body into the casket. I cannot go near; I try but I cannot. And now I walk behind the casket, walking from Golgotha to the tombs. Nicodemus avoids me since our conversation; he has said what he must say. And then the hurrying Joseph turns and tells us we have arrived.

'The tomb is here!'

'They are usually where you left them,' mutters Nicodemus.

I look with reluctant eyes at this end place. It is cut from the rock; cool and dark inside as the sun begins to dip and drop. The slaves lay the pallet down.

Nicodemus says, 'A very fine tomb – and kindly given by Joseph. I believe he bought it for himself ... most generous, really, to give your own tomb for another. May he be much blessed and well-remembered.'

'Let's get him inside,' says Joseph to the slaves. 'Not long until sunset.'

'Please!' All turn towards me. 'Let me help. Let me help carry him.' No one disagrees, so I step forward. I must be near the body, near Yeshua, before he is gone. Joseph calls to a woman who has brought some linen. She spreads it on the ground. I do not take his weight – it is others who lift the carcass ... but I touch; I rest my hand on his cold forehead as his body is laid on the cloth.

Joseph: 'We will wrap the body here, we have ointments.'

'I will do this.' And so it is that I anoint him and rub oil and spice into his crucified skin, broken and ploughed by violence. I cannot believe I do this; I cannot believe the cold. I cannot believe that ... my hands shake, I try and stay calm. Finally, with Joseph tutting and impatient behind me, I fold the cloth over him, slowly, each move a goodbye, fold by fold; and I understand, in this moment, that he is gone, that he is not here. I know it. Yeshua, the man I knew, he has gone ... he has no need of this body anymore. Perhaps I need it, for it is all I have, I stroke it ... but he is not here.

And so his wrapped flesh is carried into the tomb. I walk with them out of the light and into the darkness, the bound body laid to rest on the stone slab. He lies there like a babe in swaddling clothes; and I wrapped him, as one might wrap a child, laid in their cot ... and wrapped in love. One last glance, I cannot leave but I am pushed, kindly eased back out into the sunlight, and they are heaving and grunting, rolling a large stone across the entrance, locking it in place, as is the way, though what will grave robbers find here but the never-ending wounds of love?

And I am walking from the scene, as if into nothing. There is nowhere to go.

YESHUA

Strange waking

There is a fire figure ... I see them, a figure of fire, full of life and colour, orange and purple, green and blue, yellow and red. It dances wild. And then as I watch, a thick crust of lava begins to entrap her, form around her, enclosing. It begins to choke and smother the fire and colour, stifling her life.

And this fire and this crust is a dream, I somehow know I dream; and in the dream the figure is outside its body, separate from it, beating at the crust, trying to break it, to loosen its grip, to give the fire a chance to breathe.

But she beats in vain, for her arms ache and tire; she cries out in vain for there is no one to help and slowly the flickering fire is extinguished. Starved of air, the fire dies, the figure dies, encased in the dark crust, which allows only itself. All life is gone.

Yet the dream stays, I do not leave, I am invited to wait, invited to watch, sensing change, and change there is, wisps of random flame, dancing into life from the fire figures' body ... weak flickers at first, but each encourages another and then another still.

The airless dark, once death's great help, becomes life instead, a path for heat and light in the imprisoning lava. And soon, fractured by the heat, the first crack appears in the crust, and then another ... and then another still.

The fire figure gulps new air, with fresh burning. Purple and red, green and blue, yellow and orange, colour returns, the fire figure lives and the lava crust splinters and cracks. The fire figure burns again ... and the fire figure's free.

My eyes blink in the cool dark. I am with the dream, I am still there, but leaving it. I am breathing, I breathe in and out, I notice this, but with no knowing in my body of where I am and who I am. I am awake, my dream is gone, I do not sleep, I sense I wake, the fire figure gone, and down a path, some memory ... I begin to remember, though this cannot be, but I remember being lifted, hoisted, hoisted up, like a fish on line, I am in terror, I remember rough nails though whether a dream, I cannot tell, and then I remember nothing and know only the present ache – the quiet ache of the wounds, the scorching past, though now almost pleasing, for it is gone, like a passing storm; and with more memory, from where I do not know, another pathway opens. I feel terror again, my body jerks ... but the terror subsides, I breathe again and beyond it is joy, which is a river running through me.

I am breathing joy in the darkness, which seems as light as day; though where I am I cannot tell, no memory here, no memory yet, paths still blocked and still uncleared, though it feels like home.

And I sense binding; it is coarse on my skin and itches; I do not mind. I am aware of being wrapped and bound in cloth, I feel constraint and I begin to move, I push and pull, I am lying down, I come to know this; I am lying down on hard stone – is this my tomb? I am newly aware, awareness dawns, new pathways, this is my tomb, I am dead yet not dead – but my arms are now free, eased from restraint, sweet smells on my body and I feel no fear and slowly, so very slowly, I am sitting up. I unbind the cloth from around me, easy does it, hurting hands ... and can this be? As though death was here but now is washed from my body? Death on a cross, I remember – Oh God, I remember! – fear floods me, a rising torrent of dirty water, I cannot stop it, rising up ... and then passes through, as quickly as it came and such space is left, such open space inside.

As though I died and now I live; and I cannot kill the joy.

MIRIAM

And can it be?

~

I did not recognise him at first; you don't see what you're not looking for.

I had come to the tomb for my own reasons, wishing to get away from everyone and find some peace – though how will that ever be? There's no way back to that place now. And my companions disappoint; no, they frustrate me. How quickly friendship curdles when guilt and terror preside; they snipe and argue among themselves, and sometimes I am the target, though not quite named. And so today, I come out early, the dew still fresh and the air cool, the market place empty; and only the elderly awake in their doorways. They say the old cannot sleep. Well, perhaps they have seen too much?

I just wish to walk; and I just wish to sit, to remember and enjoy this world around me, as he enjoyed the world. The world was his scripture, he saw life in everything and images arise in my mind; images he planted, but which I hadn't seen grow. I see the lilies of the field in all their glory; the patient farmer waiting for the harvest; the suspect builder who's house fell down! He made me laugh. I remember the tiny seed that would grow beyond belief; the angry man woken at midnight by a woman beating on his door, *Bang! Bang! Bang!* – that was a good story! I see the falling sparrows, each known in their ending; the welcomed child and the terrible deaths at Siloam, when the pillars fell. He dared even to speak of those, he spoke of everything, for everything was his scripture – yet at the time, I didn't realise I was listening. I was dreaming, not listening – though it appears I heard it all, when I never heard anyone else.

'Are you listening, Miriam?' my mother would say, and the answer was always 'Yes, of course, I am, mother!' though the truth was, 'No – and why would I?' He must have been clever with his words, though I suppose even these will fade.

And suddenly I am nearing the tomb and I cease my eager walking, stop it dead, as if I am not worthy to be here. Or perhaps I fear something, I do not know. But I struggle to look at the tomb; so I sit on a rock a distance away and feel lonely and quite without weight. I remember, I'd once asked him to share his understanding with me; it is what I had wanted the most. And it returns to me now, a memory freshly coloured.

'Share your understanding with me, Yeshua.'

But he just looked sad and said, 'I cannot share my understanding, Miriam. How can I do such a thing? Understanding cannot be bought and it cannot be shared – only discovered by each for themselves.'

I would happily have paid anything.

'At least give me a word. "Your words were found and I ate them." The prophet Jeremiah said that! He ate God's words ... Levi told me.'

'It is the taste of the words that matters, Miriam, not the words themselves. What taste do they leave in your soul?' I am trying to keep up. Can one taste words like one can taste mullet? 'But from here on, you must find your own words. They will taste the best.'

But I have no soul and, as I sit here, I have no words I just have the breeze, which seems to stroke me; indeed, it is strange how well I feel when all I have done is give up everything I have ever known – as if the world is clean and clear, like the sand as the sea recedes. But on looking up, I am disturbed again, I see something amiss. The sealed tomb –and it may be the light – but it seems unsealed, as if the rock has been pushed a little from the entrance. It cannot be, it must be a shadow, but I need to find out, so I walk towards the tomb. I suddenly wish for company, I am frightened; but there is no one around, this is early, and my heart beats like a great big hammer inside me, because the nearer I get, the clearer it becomes – the tomb is open, someone has opened it, and I'm now turning back, I cannot go on ... and I'm running back to Joanna, she will know what to do; though I find Rocky and John there, and they are angry with me.

'What are you doing out?' says Rocky. 'Have you been followed? You could have been followed.' He is concerned for his hiding place but I am not.

'Someone has taken him!' I am breathless. My voice shakes.
'Taken who?'
'Someone has taken Yeshua.'
'Taken him where?'
'I don't know – but the tomb is open.'
'What tomb?'

I tell them what tomb and they push past me, without a word, they literally push past me, knocking me, and run towards it – though they realise they need me, for they don't know where it is. 'Where do we go?' they ask with impatience, so we're now running together through the Jerusalem streets, I find energy again, and then up into the rough land, Rocky struggling to keep up, but John proving fast – faster than me, and I have taken off my sandals.

'There!' I shout, pointing to the tomb.

'Where?' says Rocky. I think he has sweat in his eyes and can't see; he is wiping them with his sleeve.

'There!' I am pointing again, and John arrives first, but he goes to the wrong one. 'No, the next one!' I am shouting and I follow him, breathless, and we stop at the entrance, a gaping hole.

'Are you sure this is the right one?' I nod. 'Are you absolutely sure, Miriam? It can't be – really.'

'This is Yeshua's tomb.' I think John, too, is afraid; I am certainly afraid and then Rocky arrives and pushes past us both, though he halts in the darkness, and like Lot's wife, he is turned to a pillar of salt.

'He's gone,' he says. He cannot move.

'How do you know?' says John.

'I can see.'

'It's dark.'

'I can see.'

Stepping from the light into the shadows, we cannot see a thing; but Rocky says he can. We both step forward as Rocky withdraws, he doesn't know what to do. And in the gloom, my eyes slowly adjusting, the strangest sight appears – a sight I cannot explain. I see lying on the stone the grave clothes I wrapped so carefully around the dead body; yet there is no body and my stomach churns with the shock.

'We must get back,' says Rocky for he has seen enough, and John agrees, though he keeps staring at the linen and the head cloth, which is separate. 'You wrapped him?' he asks and I nod, 'I wrapped him,' and I don't know if it is awe or horror in his eyes, but he lingers. 'Come on,' says Rocky, 'we need to tell the others,' and again John agrees, though what they are to tell, I do not know; and neither, I think, do they. For no one knows what has happened here. Perhaps they must just do something ... and so they turn and flee the scene. It feels like they flee, as if full of fear, but I remain; they do not wait for me to follow. I watch them running back towards the city, though they move a little slower now, especially Rocky, tired of the sprint; and I wish to run with them but know I must stay. And suddenly I start to cry; tears quite overwhelm me. I don't know why I cry, but something is destroyed, some hope, some plan, perhaps that is the reason. I am so sad. This was to be our place; a place where I could come and sit with him and remember him. A place to bring flowers, to be quiet with the memories ... but that is now ruined, the body stolen and for what reason? Could they not even give him peace in death?

'There's a place where I am not persecuted,' he had once said. 'And that place they will never find.' I remember him saying that, he said it to Joanna and me, when people were attacking him. And perhaps I'd imagined this to be that place, the place that no one would find. But someone has found it – they've found it and taken my Lord and I don't know why and I don't know where they have put him; and I'm kneeling by the tomb, sobbing for a different time, a kinder time; a time when he was here and could tell me what to do.

'Why are you crying?' asks a man with a hoe and I wish him gone. I hadn't seen him and do not wish to speak to him now; he can take his hoe and gardening elsewhere.

'Leave me, please – he is not here.' It will make no sense, I know, but an idea takes hold of me. I am angry. 'And perhaps you have taken him, and if you have, or know who has, I wish to know where he is! You have no right! – '

'Who is it that you seek?' he asks ... and in this moment, the world melts. It is him ... and I cannot conceive anything but foundness. There is no such word, but there it is, *foundness* – the sense of being found, though in what manner, I do not know. 'Miriam,' he says. His smile slices me in half with the sharpest blade. It is Yeshua, he is risen ... he's alive.

'Teacher.' My legs are crumbling, I cannot get up; I try but I cannot move, I sway beneath the rising sun, and I am reaching out towards him, though he moves away.

'Do not hold on to me, Miriam.'

I fall forward into the dust; and he stoops down, picks me up and carries me into the shade; and that is all I know and all I desire. And a few hours later I awake, with the sun high in the sky, to see Thomas and Levi at the cave entrance. They walk around in a daze.

I hear Thomas saying: 'Well, he has to be somewhere.'

YESHUA

Beside the sea

Perhaps others will write of this, they say they will.

They said all sorts of things on the beach this morning, amid their astonishment at seeing me. Rocky promised a book, 'I will write a book of all this, this must be a book!' ... though he cannot write, as Levi pointed out, 'You can clean barnacles off the keel and stand steady in a storm. But you cannot write.'

Rocky does say things. He has never been measured with his mouth; no hand on the tiller there and caught by every wind. Some say he speaks before he thinks, though I say he just speaks; there is no obvious thought on display.

Though their astonishment, bright-eyed and frantic, scarce equals mine; I laugh inside so much, I cannot quiet it. I laugh as they leap from the boat, splashing and wading towards me, half-swimming. I cannot believe it, this scene before my eyes. I am making a fire, the fire is all I need, it is everything – smouldering wood, smoke and embers, heat in the morning chill and the splash and the rush toward me, the wet sunlight, these mad idiots, my friends.

'It's him, it's him,' they shout. 'Yeshua, is it you!? It cannot be Yeshua! Don't be so stupid! Yeshua, it cannot be you!'

I am ripped apart by amazement and joy ... amazement that I am here, that this is so; and such joy at seeing the sea and these wasters again.

They once ran away, it comes back to me, how they all disappeared, though I have lost my capacity for blame, truly; for we are not where we were, Gethsemane feels a long time ago, and now a different space unfolds. They run towards me, soaked through with Galilee wash and shouting, arguing as they approach and I get up to greet them, to hug and to hold – as close to friends as I shall have, though Miriam is not here. And maybe that is best.

'So where are the fish?' I ask. 'We cannot eat surprise.'

'Can you forgive me, master?' asks Rocky, staring at me with wild eyes.

And later he blubs like a child, his head in my lap, beating the ground, his body heaving.

'You're bound to hear,' he said. 'You'll hear from someone.'

'And what will I hear?'

'I said I didn't know you.' He manages to get the words out, between body-shaking gasps. 'And that's that. Anyone who asked, after Gethsemane, anyone who asked me that night if I knew you, they recognised me, they knew I knew you – but I told them I didn't know you. They kept saying it. "You know him – we've seen you with him." They just kept on. And I denied it. I just said they were wrong and I turned on them, told them not to be stupid. I denied you three times ... so what am I worth?'

'Everything.'

And now he is kneeling beside me, a small boy lost. And I feel no blame toward him – I cannot find any blame at all, though he blames himself with the force of a storm. He sobs again, overwhelmed again, begging forgiveness again. But it is Rocky who punishes Rocky. When finally he calms and becomes still, we speak.

'Do you love me, Rocky?'

He is surprised. 'Of course I love you, teacher. You know that, I'd do anything ... '

'Then look after my people.'

'I will, yes.'

So I ask again. 'Do you love me, Rocky?'

'You know I love you. I've just said. Why do you ask? ... '

'Then look after my people.' I stare at him; stare into him. I am wondering who he has, and what he has, inside him.

'I just *said* I will, teacher ... I'll do that, I'll look after them.'

'And do you love me, Rocky?'

'Teacher!' Now he is frustrated. 'This is ridiculous! Of course I love you!'

'Then look after my people.'

'Master, I say I will, I *keep* saying it! I have said it three times. Why do you not believe me?'

I laugh. What else can I do in the morning sun? 'It is not for me to believe, Rocky. Words are hollow and our intentions, a shipwreck; though sometimes they float. So I do not believe you and do not ask me to. I say this for your sake, Rocky. Imagine the terror you would know if I believed you – you would die tomorrow of shame. But here on the shoreline, as you give me your heart, I give you mine.'

He looks frightened.

YESHUA

Manger days

~

'It is *not* a one-mule town, Devira; I have seen at least three. And a dog.'

She raises her eyebrows, a shrug of vague admission. This had been her description, when I asked for the visit. 'One-mule town, Bethlehem.' She has history here, family from way back; though not family she liked. Galilee, through marriage to a herdsman, had been escape for this child of Judaea. 'I didn't mind the distance,' she explains. 'I could definitely live with it.' But I have asked her back, for only she knows the place; the particular place, and I must see it.

'It has grown a bit,' she says, looking around. 'And not for the better ... Bethlehem is *busier* but not better, lost its charm, whatever charm it had ... and no nearer to Nazareth, that's for sure.' She has not enjoyed the journey and has a dismissive air. 'I don't think I'll be back – no, I don't think so.' She shakes her head. 'They can come to *me* now, if they're so keen to see me; they can feel the pebbles in *their* sandals for a change ... not that they will.' We meet in the market place, as agreed. Sometimes she looks at me, and at the wounds, when she imagines me looking elsewhere. But nothing is said, no question asked and they heal a little. Devira continues as if nothing has changed and all is quite normal. We pick up where we left off. 'So where have you come from?'

'Jerusalem,' I say. She nods.

'Dusty old city Jerusalem, eh? Was it dusty?'

'It is dusty, I was warned, a very dusty city ... and so it's good to be free of the place.' And it is good to be free. I have walked it out of my body, I am beyond it now; I no longer feel its claim. 'Just the walk I needed.'

'And whatever else you were, Yeshua – like a trouble-maker, for instance, endless trouble – you always were a walker. Always walked like a mad man, you have. No one could ever keep up with you.'

'I have needed to walk, Devira; I have always needed to walk, to keep moving. The hunted must do this.'

'Hunted?' She does not know what I mean; or chooses not to. She thinks I assign myself undue importance. And even for me, it seems a long time ago, with all sense of the chase now gone, the wolves spent and harmless. Even the nails dissolve in some manner and I find it hard not to laugh. Laughter does spring up inside me, spreading like a fire in the grass, crackling and quick; but I must dowse it a little or Devira will think me strange ... or stranger still.

'Different days,' I say.

'Nasty wounds,' she says, in passing. 'Someone made a mess of you. I won't ask what you've been doing. And don't tell your mother, either.'

'I'm on the mend,' I say and to change the subject, 'There must be some happy farmers between Jerusalem and Bethlehem.'

'Have you ever met a happy farmer?'

'I had no idea. Such joyful crops! I believe I have just walked through Judaea's bread basket. There is rich soil on my sandals.' She shrugs. She does not know what to do with good news. She would prefer a war, a famine, a plague – a problem of some kind about which she can be dour and dry and mutter 'Life's like that'. But I feel so happy, I could have *run* all the way from Jerusalem

– no, I could have run from Nazareth. Indeed, I had to slow myself on occasion, my wounds opening. But freedom does this; it bestows energy – and such light within, the cave so bright!

And I found company along the way, so I had to slow myself then. I was joined by two men on the Emmaus road – a glum couple when we met, full of recent events in Jerusalem and eager to speak of tragedy.

'You're travelling to Jerusalem?' they asked. No, I said, I was on my way to Bethlehem and they applauded the choice. 'Anywhere's better than Jerusalem at the moment – they say even the sky went dark, what with events there.'

'What events?'

Cleopas shakes his head. 'I wonder you do not know.'

'I'm always the last to hear,' I say.

'A near-uprising, apparently, and now they're all in hiding, his followers – and why wouldn't they be?'

'An uprising?'

'Led by Yeshua of Nazareth,' says Cleopas. 'You really haven't heard?' And I am struck hard by his words, as though hit. These men speak of me and my story – yet they do not see me before them. It is as if they speak of another. 'He was a prophet, they say, powerful in word and deed, my friend heard him speak.'

'More than once,' adds his friend. 'More than once … and he didn't take any prisoners.'

'He could be harsh,' says Cleopas, as though apologising for an indiscretion. 'They do say he had a harsh tongue.'

'But some good thoughts, a bit like Hillel – and all encased in a very decent turn of phrase.'

'He attempted an uprising in the Temple, that's what they say, people killed – and he was executed at Passover time, all very quick, so that's that.'

'Crucified,' says nameless.

'Crucified, yes. And now Jerusalem is in lock down, so you're wise to avoid it, Romans everywhere asking "the purpose of your journey, sir?"'

'And they don't ask nicely – but when did the Romans ever? I mean, Yeshua had a mouth on him, prophets do, but … '

'And people had high hopes for that one,' says Cleopas, wistfully. 'I mean, many liked him ... though many didn't obviously.'

'Obviously.'

'And now he's dead.'

His friend nods. 'And maybe for the best.' Cleopas looks confused by nameless. 'I mean maybe he would have disappointed had he lived. That's what I'm saying. I don't know, but he might have done, most do – best to die young, in a way.' Cleopas frowns, he is not so sure, but his friend's opinion grows. 'No, it's sometimes for the best if people die young, I think so. I mean, no one gets better with age, do they? And they can disappoint in later years. I've seen that. So maybe it's better – then people can dream what you *might* have been. The quicker you're dead, the better you get!'

I believe he talks of himself, imagining his best days in the past.

'He said he'd restore Israel,' says Cleopas, eager to be positive again.

'Quite a task,' I say.

'It was a big ask, yes ... too big, probably. Little by little, I always say, little by little.'

We walk together in silence for a while. I feel uncomfortable at the deceit, though I have no wish to declare myself. 'And is that the end of the story?' I ask.

They chuckle nervously; they are embarrassed about something. Neither wishes to take up the story. 'Well, it should be, shouldn't it?' says Cleopas. 'And it probably is – well, *of course* it is.'

'I think we can safely say it's the end of the story,' says his friend. 'Crucifixion. A decent turn of phrase couldn't save him in the end.'

'It's just that ... ' He pauses.

'Is there something on your mind?'

'It's just that – well, no. It really doesn't matter.' He shakes his head roughly, as if he fights something.

'What doesn't matter?'

'It really doesn't matter!'

'Jerusalem is in lockdown because some women say he is alive,' says nameless, interrupting. 'I know, I know!' He holds up his hands to acknowledge the lunacy of it all. 'They say they couldn't find his body when they went to the tomb. *Women!*'

Cleopas picks up the story. 'Apparently the women found the tomb empty and went off to get the men, but when they arrived, well – they found it just as the women had said.'

'Empty?'

'Empty.'

'But no one actually saw Yeshua,' says his friend, as though closing the matter. 'It's not like he was seen.'

'Well, one of the women *said* she did,' adds Cleopas, a reluctant stickler for accuracy. And I think I know who he means.

'One of the women, yes – but I mean ... '

'It would have been quite a thing if they had,' I say. Perhaps I begin to enjoy this. 'Can you imagine it? What if the woman had actually seen him?'

Again they chuckle. 'Bit of a shock to the Romans, eh?' says Cleopas, daring to imagine. 'Well, bit of a shock to Caiaphas as well!' He laughs nervously.

'I mean, obviously someone stole the body,' says nameless and Cleopas agrees. 'So no need for the Romans to worry – unfortunately.'

'Well, quite,' I say. 'But what if they didn't?'

'Didn't what?'

'What if they didn't steal the body? Imagine him being out there ... now.'

'That would be a bit spooky!' says nameless, a little uneasy.

'But good, do you not think? Would it not be good if he was out there somewhere?'

'Not sure – I don't think I'd want to meet him!' He has a loud laugh. 'Bloody terrifying! Anyway, it's not going to happen, not going to happen. Nothing like this has ever happened.'

And now I smile. 'Yet in the prophet Isaiah, the Lord says "Do not cling to events of the past or dwell on what happened long ago. Watch for the new thing I am going to do." Perhaps this is it. Perhaps it *has* happened. Perhaps this is the new thing? Who knows?'

Cleopas is suddenly serious. Is he looking at my feet? He asks me to eat with them; they have found an inn.

'Stay with us, my friend, stay with us – for it is nearly evening and the day is almost over. You must be tired.' I do not feel tired but agree to stay and we go inside, into the cool and dark, a little like the tomb. We order food; loaves and fish set before us – I hear Rocky saying 'sardine' – and wine to drink. Cleopas pays, as one with wealth, but indicates that I give thanks and play the host. He is still looking at me. 'Have we met?' he asks as I break the bread. He is disturbed by something, though again I smile. For what else can I do?

'We have met today, Cleopas, that is for sure.'

He leans toward me and questions. 'What does Isaiah mean, though? You quote the prophet – but what does he mean?'

And so I speak more of his words; lines I know well, though never have I known them as now. 'You know what he says, Cleopas. "Who could have seen the Lord's hand in this? It was the will of the Lord that his servant should grow like a plant taking root in dry ground. He had no beauty or dignity to make us notice him – nothing attractive about him; there was nothing to draw us. We despised and rejected him, as if he were nothing. But he endured the suffering that should have been ours – while we thought his suffering a punishment sent by God! But no, he was wounded for our sins and for our evil. And we are healed by the punishment he suffered."

There is something in his eyes, some dawning in Cleopas; it looks like fear. Though his friend thinks only of the sardine and eats eagerly. I eat a little myself – and think of Rocky, for all fish lead to him. And Miriam. But I chew with no great desire. The light within me is not hungry for food tonight – but hungry for the prophet.

'"He was treated harshly," says Isaiah, "but he endured it humbly; like a sheep about to be sheared, he never said a word. He was arrested and sentenced and led off to die for no one cared for his fate. He was put to death for the sins of our people, placed in a grave with evil men – buried with the rich, though he never committed a crime or ever told a lie.'"

Nameless continues to eat, but Cleopas is in a trance. I cannot stay and soon after this, I rise; Isaiah is almost too alive within me. I explain I must leave them to their night.

'Give my love to Jerusalem,' I say. 'And peace, light and healing to both your households.'

'Your wounds!' says Cleopas, reaching out to me. He does not wish me to go. 'I could not help but notice your wounds!'

'And I notice them less and less,' I say. 'It is true that tears are wiped from our eyes. May it be so for you, dear Cleopas.'

And so I arrive in this little town of Bethlehem, guided by Devira. She is greeted in the street by women, the elder sort, dressed in black and familiar with loss; though she does not stop to chat. And I have no wish to stop either, for we must find the room and I cannot do it without her.

'Are you coming home, Devira?' asks one woman. 'You've been too long in exile. Galilee can never be home for a Judaean.'

'I'm not coming home,' she says, 'But this one is, eh?' She indicates me with her thumb and I wish she had not.

'Who's he, then?' The woman does not think to ask me. She asks Devira, without a glance my way.

'Can a man not visit his place of birth without comment?' Devira speaks angrily, though she has caused the comment. 'And we're in a hurry,' she adds awkwardly and now there is panic in her eyes. She has not played this well.

'He's the scandal boy! I knew it. He'd be that age. And is that why you left us, Devira? Too many secrets?'

'Come on, Yeshua.' She grabs my arm. 'Only bitterness is well-remembered in Bethlehem.'

We walk on, figures in doorways, ambling dogs, the streets rutted by rain, but now hardened. Devira leads, stooped like a warrior marching to war. I feel the gaze on my back, the gaze of watchers, it feels harsh. But I do not turn around – no looking back, for there is no scandal here; though, for a moment, my joy is lost; I feel it slipping from my body. And now we are turning into an alley, closed in and dark, away from the light ... and the intense smell of animal – sheep, cattle and mules; though not as bad as spikenard, nothing could be ...

'This is the door,' she says stopping suddenly and my heart beats faster.

'This one?' I ask. It has no special charm; tired slats of wood on a post, with a damaged hinge. I could mend that.

'Yes.'

We have arrived sooner than I imagined; I am not prepared. 'I've told them we are coming,' she says. 'They agreed, they don't mind.' I nod but I am nervous. 'They did not wish to be here though. When – you know ... it is still spoken of. Thought it better you view the place alone.'

'They wish to be away when the scandal comes to call.'

'You must remember, Yeshua – many wanted her stoned, they felt the town abused by her, as if she came here to hide. It was the people here from Nazareth, it was them who gossiped, so nasty word got round. They felt cheated when she wasn't.'

'I understand; our hosts are afraid.' The hurt passes through me, barely noticed.

'Their guest room was full,' says Devira, pointing to the left. 'No room there – and there was a bit of a to-do about that, I remember your father being angry because he'd booked that room in advance. He was organised like that. But everyone was in Bethlehem then, the world and his wife, what with the census – and people here making the most of their rooms, any space to spare, where money could be made ... I mean, you can't blame them, promising more than they had, so they were double-booked – simple as that. I mean, I told your father to be done with it and go and stay with Zechariah and Elizabeth – your mother's cousin. Well, sort-of cousin ... you know her?'

'She has been mentioned.'

'Decent sort and not so far away, and I mean they'd stayed there before ... but your father said no. I don't know what his problem was, perhaps he didn't want the journey, but he seemed sure, it had to be Bethlehem, he said – so you joined the family in the family room, bit of a squash; but you three were put at the stable end, obviously. Well, two became three soon after their arrival, you being born and that. Oh my goodness, don't remind me! And they said the animals would only come in at night if it was cold.'

'And was it cold?'

'It was very cold.'

'Can I be alone, Devira?'

She shrugs – but I need to be free of her. She talks to fill the space and drown questions. I thank her but leave her behind; I leave her at the doorstep, push open the door and step inside. Closing the door behind me, I stop and I breathe the silence as if this is the holy of holies, sudden quiet; though a very common place. The guest room is to my left, the room my father booked – I sense him again, arguing the case, I could imagine that, my mother tired after the journey; 'What do you mean, no room?! We agreed!' And to my right, neither small nor large, the family room and the smell of baking still in the air, hyssop and yeast. And through the family room, I see the rough door to the stable beyond; and by the door, inside the room, a manger. My legs begin to shake, for it was here, I know it was here; my mother had mentioned a manger, though not to me – to my brothers and sisters, discreet knowledge they could not keep to themselves.

'Mother says you were put in a dirty manger!' Judith had once declared, when she wished to attack me, 'It was all there was. So that's where *you* started – covered in mule spit!' Judith was often vinegar-sour, such an unhappy soul; and I thought no more of it ... until now. And as I look, I see a sturdy piece of work before me, wood kicked and licked by cattle, butted and battered; but standing strong and a safe holding for hay. And was this where I lay? My little skin, my secret room, fresh from the light, my spirit pressed into flesh – thrown into strange company, mother and father far from home; sheep, cattle, chickens and mules ... was this my starting out place? And I feel again my wriggling flesh, the noise and the talk, the terror and the light, the smell of sheep – the big-eyed mule, I have always liked mules.

I fall to my knees by the manger; I bend in memory of this strange beginning and feel again the wood ... and eternity. The cave is too bright; I cannot cope with the light. I am weeping at the manger, sobbing ... but such happy tears. I had to come here; to this town and this place. I had to come and they had to let me in. And perhaps now I can go; perhaps now I can depart in peace? I wipe my eyes, I stay and I stay, and then after a while, I rise and slowly, cross the room, one step after another. I glance back, the manger bed and then turn my face toward the street outside, open the door and begin to laugh.

'What's so funny then?' asks Devira. 'Something in there you find amusing?'

MIRIAM

That fearful room

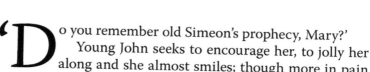

'**D**o you remember old Simeon's prophecy, Mary?'
Young John seeks to encourage her, to jolly her along and she almost smiles; though more in pain than joy ... as if a smile will only bring tears. We have been quieter since she arrived, out of respect. She is Yeshua's mother, after all. 'You have spoken to me of it, Mary,' says John. 'The time you met Simeon.'

We are gathered together; no, huddled together – huddled in secret in Jerusalem, still in fear, and the more so now the authorities rage and spread rumours about the missing body. They say it has been taken by his followers; and seek to take us for the purpose of confession. Some have already confessed, they say, to inventing the resurrection. 'We all have to survive,' as Nicodemus would say.

So the windows around us are covered; and a dark staircase from the street led us here. We attempt disguise with shawls, with heads covered – Rocky entered with a blanket over his head – and have arrived at different times. No one wishes to be seen or found; maybe no one wishes to be here at all. But what are we to do? Word has got around and we must decide on a plan, though no one has a clue. We have heard Yeshua will come; and how my heart longs for it to be so; though no one is sure. How can we ever be sure again, when all is upside down?

I have not seen Mary since the horror, just a week since – but how to measure such times as these? One day is a year. And three years is the bark of a dog. I stood by her through those terrible hours; and she never turned her head from the scene, I swear it, not once. We did not speak, there were no words between us; though she held my hand for a while. Her fingers felt cold; and sometimes I would squeeze them, to offer them life.

And I am glad Joanna is here; she stands by the door. She says she cannot stay long and I wonder if this is her farewell. I so hope it is not, for she is our leader, I would say so; though some will disagree. But without Joanna, there would be no story to tell. 'What is there of our band without Joanna?' Yeshua once said to me. 'And what is there of me without you, Miriam?'

I treasure the words; and hold Joanna in high esteem. But Rocky wishes to lead, this is clear. People like him; or perhaps they simply imagine him their best bet now – though some say he does not care for others; that he just wants their applause; and still his family remain in Bethsaida. But why do I bother with such thoughts? And what does such talk mean anyway – for what is there for anyone to lead except a memory? Yeshua is here but he is not here. Perhaps this is goodbye for us all. I wonder if we shall meet again, there is so little to hold us.

'I used to speak more of the meeting with Simeon,' says Mary, looking at the floor. 'I have not done so of late. And why would I wish to?' She looks haughty, aloof. 'His words to me were like a knife ... a knife in my heart.'

'But Simeon spoke in hope, surely?' John is patient with her. He encourages her to remember and to speak. 'It must seem a long time ago now, but all say this, those who knew him. "Simeon, a good man, he spoke in hope," they say.'

'"Hope," was it?' Mary mocks with her smile. 'Well, perhaps that's what *he* called it.'

'It's what I heard,' says John. 'I wasn't there ... and I know of the sadness since, of course.' We all know of the sadness since. 'But I hear he spoke in great hope on seeing your child Yeshua when he was presented in the temple. Do you remember those days? He felt his long wait to be over, did he not – Israel's long wait! "Lord, now let your servant depart this life in peace, for truly, my eyes have seen your salvation!" There was something about your son, Mary, something about him even then. Simeon knew it – and so did we.'

John is sweet in his kindness.

'But you do not know it all,' she replies firmly, and shakes her head. She then retires into herself again – and who can blame her? We must not lay blame. Though I have told her what I saw in the garden. I have told her how Yeshua lives and how he spoke with me. And she thanked me for telling her – but asked no questions, which one might imagine odd. Does she not want to know more? I think I would want to know.

We sit in silence for a while. No one is at peace, though I wish all of them peace, truly I do. He is risen! I know he is risen – but what does it mean and why do I feel so sad? And some now doubt what they saw on the beach, I know this. Even some here in this room, though Rocky doesn't ... he doesn't doubt. In that way, he is like me: we do not doubt what we saw! We *know!* But we do not understand; and we cannot commune with each other, with some matters in the way, he terrorises me, I cannot escape the feeling.

And then into the silence Mary speaks again, stiff-jawed. She forces the words, Simeon's words and everyone turns. "'Behold, Mary, this child is set for the fall and the rising of many in Israel. He is a sign who will be spoken against, that the thoughts of many hearts may be revealed – and a sword will pierce your own soul too.'" She pauses for a moment. 'And Simeon was right, was he not? He was right about the sword in my heart; for now it is so, now it is so.'

I want to answer, but hold myself back; I feel it is not my place ... though Rocky speaks. 'We did see him, Mary ... on the beach. I know you were not there, how I wish you were ...

but we did see him. We were fishing – casting our nets for the early shoals. He made breakfast for us, he fried the fish. Well, didn't he?' He looks around for support. There are some nods. 'You must believe us.'

Mary smiles again, like cracked wood. She doesn't believe us; I don't think so – as if to believe would be too great a risk. Further pain she cannot manage; she must give up hope, it is the easier way. Perhaps she does not wish him back again, with the trouble he has caused.

And then the door opens on worried glances; a shaft of light cuts across the room and the light brings terror. Andrew moves behind Peter. We thought it locked, and a stone is against it, but the stone moves, and worried eyes watch; for no one imagines themselves safe. Word has gone out, we know this; his followers are to be rounded up ...

It is Yeshua.

People gasp, slump in relief, some rise, some start laughing and I move forward, I smile for Israel – and then pause. I step back ... Mary is open-mouthed.

'Peace be with you,' says Yeshua, looking round. 'Peace be with you all.' I feel excitement in my body, as if I have not been alive until now, as if I have only slept. 'Yes even you, Rocky, you mad man!' Rocky looks surprised. 'May my peace find a home in *you*!'

There is laughter. James enjoys the joke, Levi chuckles, Andrew doesn't and Rocky is bemused, this is clear – as if Yeshua publicly shames him for his denials. These are talked about now, in his absence; and the wound seems opened again in Rocky. He cannot hide what he feels, he never could; his body speaks with a loud voice.

But Yeshua wishes him no discomfort. 'I speak in kindness, my friend. There is nothing now to fear.' And Rocky is calmed as Mary bids Yeshua 'come' with her hand and her eyes. He moves slowly towards her, greeting others as he goes, with bright eyes and gentle touch. She takes his hands in hers, as if to hold him while she speaks; as if he might run away unless firmly gripped. As if he might not be real.

'I need to say this, Yeshua, and you need to hear it. Your father was angry with me when I was with child ... when I became pregnant with you.' Yeshua's eyebrows show surprise; but he slowly kneels to listen.

'And why was he angry with you?'

'He was angry with me because he heard things from the neighbours, wretched people. But what is important, and why I say this, is that when I told him – when I told him what he wanted to know – he believed *me* over *them*. He did that; he believed me. And so when they wished to stone me, for many did – he married me. They wished me stoned, they would have done it, but he married me. He was a just man, your father.'

'I thought him so.'

'I *know* him so! But I have not spoken of him as I might. I should have spoken more. I was too sad, too – *disappointed.*' Yeshua nods and Mary coughs. 'I have not always spoken well of you either,' she says. 'Maybe that saddens me also. Not an easy child ... '

'I wish only mercy for you, mother; for mercy is your home. Judge less and smile more, for all is well. And when you are ready, when you put down your load, as only you can – then truly, you will smile from your heart.' John and Yeshua exchange glances, as some dread eases from her face. She does try a smile, as one nervous of what might occur. John's eyes reassure her.

'And be vigilant!' says Yeshua, swinging round to address us all. He has only just arrived; and we don't know what to think, apart from *'How is he alive?'* But he presses us with these words. 'Be vigilant!'

'We do our best,' says Rocky standing up, as if the leader again. 'We do our best, teacher. We meet in secret, we lock the door ... '

'I do not say be scared, Rocky. I say be vigilant, vigilant as the owl – and allow no one to mislead you.'

'Who could mislead us now?' asks John the Elder – for he does not imagine this possible. 'Yahweh's word has become flesh – and we have beheld it ... in you.'

'Where do you get your lines, John?' asks Rocky. 'Do you dream them up at night with the help of wine?'

'Perhaps you will mislead yourselves,' says Yeshua. 'This can happen. Sometimes we do not need others to mislead us; we do it ourselves.' And now there is quiet. I ask Yeshua if he wishes for some wine, but I can hardly speak – no words come out and I feel foolish. I want only to touch him, as I did in the garden. But he is intent on speaking. He sits on the floor, in the midst of us. People adjust to hear him; I can see only his back, for I cannot move.

'Time is short, so you must listen,' he says. 'These days will change. People will say "Here it is" or "There it is!" – the kingdom, I mean, the energy of God – that is what they will say. "It is here in the field or there by the sea." But know this: first of all, it is *within* you that the son of man dwells.' He hits his chest hard. 'The kingdom of God is *within* you.' He strikes his chest again and then starts laughing, he can't help himself. 'So announce this good news! The sick are healed, the hungry fed, the powerful bowed! Spill the light! Spill it everywhere! But add no more laws, my friends – and no more rules. Our father in heaven, he has had enough of laws and rules! And one day, and this is the promise, we shall have hearts and *no* rules. They will pack up and go home for lack of reason, for lack of purpose!'

'A day some way away,' says Thomas.

'Yet also here right now.'

Is he drunk? Some think this, they tell me so later. 'We did think the teacher drunk – garrulous, distracted even.' But I think he is light rather than drunk; free rather than drunk – and I have seen him drunk, when he bares his soul and speaks of the horror. But he is not so now. Sitting in the belly of our hopes and fears, he is as bright and distant as a star, and so thin. I can almost see through him ... not drunk, but light in spirit. His skin seems to laugh.

And he says to us, 'What am I like to you? Tell me straight. To what would you compare me?'

Rocky says, 'You are like a good angel.'

John says, 'You are like a wise philosopher.'

And then I speak. 'Master, my mouth could never utter what you are like,' and he says, 'Then I am your master no longer, because you have drunk from the same sparkling source from which I spring. This is so.' And my heart sings as he continues.

'Listen, my dear vagabonds – and you will never have to listen again!' He is playful. 'I do not know why gathering you together seemed like a good idea – really, I do not! You are harsh with each other, you compete with each other and you do not understand. You understand nothing. No, really. You wrestle each other for power – and mishear every one of my words. But no matter, for all is new every day. And do you see what you have to do now? Do you see? My friends, I have come to bring fire on the earth, and yes, how I wish it were already kindled. But you will look after this flame; you shall guard it, feed it and spread it. You shall be flame-keepers; and what you need, will be given to you.'

There is silence in the group. Rocky says, 'But we do get on with each other! By and large.' Yeshua smiles, rises slowly and walks towards me. He bends down and touches my hand in the silence. And away from the others, he says, 'I am sorry.'

'Sorry?' I say. I am confused. Why should my lord say sorry?

'For this is goodbye, Miriam – though also my greeting.' I am put into a panic. How can this be goodbye? 'Keep the above within you,' he says, though I hardly listen. How do I even recall these things? 'Keep the above within you and the within above. And you will receive much, for truly, you have angels in your hair. Touch me,' he says.

I take hold of his wrists and kiss the wounds. And then reaching beneath his robe and kneeling forward I bend and kiss his shattered ankles. He gasps ... his smile as sad and happy as a child leaving home for an adventure. He leans towards me and kisses me on my lips. 'My soul friend and my love.' he says. And then to everyone, 'My soul friend, Miriam! We all need friends for our souls! How you will need them too!'

I am a chaos within and then he climbs the ladder to the loft; we watch him ascend. He goes carefully, protecting his wounds, soft and sore against the wood. I notice him wince as he climbs. 'I go to rest, my friends,' he says, but even as he speaks, he cannot speak. He tries again, 'My peace ... ' I almost hear him, but again he struggles to say the words; he mouths them, but no sound comes out. He pauses. 'My peace ... my peace I give you,' he gasps and then hauls himself into the loft.

No one knows what to do or how to converse. Then someone says: 'And when will *we* rest?' I sense the arrival of sorrow in the room; confusion and fear come too. 'They did not spare his life, so will they spare ours?'

'But perhaps we too will rise,' I say and I get up from the floor; I feel I must do this. So I rise and I embrace them all, if they allow – Andrew pulls back a little, and Rocky tenses, so I touch their shoulders instead and begin to speak. Am I the leader now? Though surely Joanna must lead? But she sits quite still.

'We shall not remain in sorrow and doubt,' I say, though my sorrow is great. 'We might be disturbed. But did he not say that those who allow disturbance will marvel and reign over all?'

'It is easily said,' someone makes comment. It may be Andrew; but I am just made stronger by his doubt.

'And I say God will guide you and comfort you ... and me. Has he not prepared us for this? That we become full human now, full of light?'

Mary stares at me, empty-eyed. I decide to turn her heart towards the good; to turn all their hearts towards the good.

'Let us make good of this!' I say. 'Let us make things well which have not been so.'

But Rocky says to me, 'Sister, we know you try to help, that you try your best ... and that you imagine the teacher loves you ... and loves you *differently* from others.' He pauses, he shifts position ... he implies things and looks around. 'So you must tell us, if you can, what you remember of any words he told you ... words which we have not heard ourselves. I mean, many of us have been with him longer than you. We knew him first and he has said many things to us; we know these things. But you say particular words have been spoken to you; words only *you* have heard – you have said this in the past ... though whether there is truth there ... '

Strong feelings of fear arise in me. I feel suffocated, as if this man tries to seal me in. And then strangely, I feel no fear, for I am the soul friend of Yeshua; and I have never run away. When others ran – yes, even those who knew him first, the Galilee crowd, even Rocky – I did not.

'If you wish it, Rocky, I will speak with you of that which has been given to me. It does not grieve me to do so; he said I could share it. But whether you can hear it … '

I have never felt so alone, here in this crowded room … .never so alone and never so strong. I wish Yeshua were here, though I am glad he is not, for he needs to sleep, and I am sufficient. Eyes turn on me, and I speak. I speak of the revelation given. 'Where the nous is, there is the treasure,' I say and try to explain. Perhaps only John the Elder understands, I can see this; only John understands. I try to explain to the others who look at me confused. I explain the opening in the soul beyond our seeing and our feeling, as Yeshua says – a place beyond thought and sense, an opening on the uncreated in each soul, a deeper knowing.

But it is not the time; and they do not understand. I can see they do not understand, and so I go silent. And then Andrew begins, sounding decent and clear, as he always does. Everything is clear to Andrew.

'Tell me, my friends,' he says, 'what do you honestly think of these things she says?' "*She*"? 'I'll be plain, and of course I speak only for myself – but I cannot believe the teacher would speak like this to Miriam, and not speak the same to us. I simply cannot. And no offence to our dear friend Miriam, but I'm with my brother Simon.' Andrew has always called him 'Simon'. He does not like 'Rocky', feeling it lacks respect. 'These are different ideas from those we have known, quite different. So how could he have spoken them – and why? I mean … '

Rocky cuts across his brother. 'It is *possible* our master spoke in this manner to a woman. I suppose we must say that, for anything's possible, as we have discovered. But really … ' and here he shakes his head in violent movements – 'that he should speak with a woman of secrets that *we know nothing of?!*' His voice is incredulous and harsh; a punch in my side. I scream but have no voice. He has taken it from me.

'I think if we knew them, Rocky, they would not be secrets.' It is John the Elder who speaks. Rocky is surprised ... and angry.

'So he prefers this woman over us, John – is that what you say? But then you weren't there at the beginning either!' John the Elder is not easily stirred; he does not swirl like Rocky. He likes things in order. He keeps all things in order and under control; everything in its place and everything with its meaning. And Rocky continues. 'That a *woman* is preferred by our master? Perhaps they kiss, as Phillip says, a good night peck, but do they share thoughts? Is that really what you say, John? As Ben Sira reminds us, "A man's spite is preferable to a woman's kindness; women give rise to shame and reproach." Could he *be* any plainer?' He holds up his arms, questioningly, as if there is no question here. 'So I'm sorry, Miriam, for I'm sure you mean well – oh, you don't need to cry! That doesn't help.'

But it helps me and I do not hold back my words.

'So it is all in my imagining, is it? This opening of the soul – I invent the vision, do I? Is this what you say?' The words somehow emerge through my sobbing – quite how, I do not know, and neither do I care. My anger calms me. 'As if I would lie about our teacher, as if I would do that?'

'Who knows why you say it, Miriam? You mean well, no doubt – '

'And cease from saying I mean well!' I beat the ground where I sit, alone on the floor in the corner.

'Rocky, remember your temper,' says Levi.

'I am quite calm, Levi, quite calm.' His voice rises a little. 'I believe it is Miriam who should watch her temper.' He gets up and strides to the window, away from me, away from the group. 'It is not I who sobs and screams.'

'Remember your temper,' repeats Levi, 'and do not speak in this manner because she is a woman.'

'*Hah!*' Rocky is surprise and scorn.

Levi: 'For that is how our adversaries are, Rocky, they speak thus – all glad they are not women; all grateful to God they are not so. But we are not to be as they are. Does our master not say that?'

Rocky turns away; he returns to the covered window.

'You've been with the poor for too long, Levi. Who thinks so?' He turns around to face us, pretending to laugh, pretending to be jolly. 'Who thinks Levi has been too long with the poor? And too long with women perhaps, who knows!?' He looks around; some look uncomfortable. He breaths deeply, he is shaken like a rattle.

'If the teacher holds her worthy, who are you to reject her?' asks Levi. 'That is all I say.'

'I do not reject her.' He does reject me, I've always known it. He has always been awkward with me. 'I do not reject her. I merely question – '

'The teacher loves her more than us, Rocky.'

'That's ridiculous.'

'He knows her well, we see that. He knows her very well.' Rocky shrugs, Levi quietens, hesitates, like one stumbling on a disturbance. 'What if the call to be full human really is our good news?'

'Our call, Levi, is to heal the sick and preach the kingdom.'

'But what does that mean?' says Levi. 'What *is* the kingdom?'

'I see it as quite obvious,' says Andrew. 'All must repent ... '

I start to climb the ladder. I have moved back to my corner and I start to climb the ladder to see Yeshua. I have to do this, I can do nothing else. I wish him to be down among us again; things will be different then. I do not like to argue or to hear them argue; and nor can I be with them. I know he sleeps, he must be tired; and I will not wake him. I will let him sleep; though as my head arrives in the loft, I cannot see him in the gloom. My eyes are blind from the candles below; I know he will appear. But he does not appear, even when my eyes find sight.

He is not here in the loft ... he is not here. He is gone ... and I am overcome. My legs become loose. I lose my balance and sway in the dark. I buckle, I cannot take this in. He is not here. My breathing is shallow; I seek to calm it but feel only tears ... spilling, hot tears. 'No,' I say, feeling with my hands through the straw. 'No, no, *no!*' I climb slowly back down the ladder. I do not know what I do; I am too much in shock. People talk among themselves, Rocky is bent forward, I remember, his head is in his hands, as if tired and spent.

'He is gone,' I say, and then I say it again, because some seem not to hear or carry on talking. 'The master – he is gone.'

MARY

The sword withdrawn

I thought it was young John; I sensed someone there and I assumed him returned. He does move quietly around the place.

'Mary,' he says and I carry on with my sewing, the cleaning done; and lunch already prepared. I earn my keep. And then there is quiet, a deep quiet, the sun shining on my feet and I feel his hands on my shoulders. I don't turn, there is no need; they are kind hands, hands that know me, I like them, if that is allowed. John would sometimes do this by way of greeting, touch my shoulders or my arm; though his words now are strange: 'I come to take the sword from your heart, Mary; it is time the sword is gone.'

And before I can speak, because his words trouble me, I feel something pull inside and know a strange sort of melting. I feel my bones to be melting, a shell inside me melting, like wax in the sun and an easing of pain – pain I did not even know was there. I experience some torment removed, though what torment, I could not say, and the feeling of mercy – a deep pool of mercy, I am somehow swimming in it and laughing, even as

I sit by the window. I quite forget where I am or who I am with – something I never do. But here is a peace I have not known and my being in happy turmoil.

'No more the sword, Mary,' he says, 'for all is done well. In a world you do not have to make for yourself, is a mercy you do not have to make for yourself. Go free ... as above, so below.'

And if I may say it, for it seems a foolish thing, I feel the sun in my heart, which is not how I speak, yet is what I feel, and as he removes his hands from my shoulders, I turn around ... but there is nobody there.

And later, John tells me he was at the shoe menders at the time of this visit; and that whoever came, it was certainly not him. And I still ponder these things in my heart, as one somehow young again and ready to play. Do I really write that? This is not me, for I have never been so. Yet I truly believe I am allowed to play!

MIRIAM

From here on

I do not think so much of Yeshua now, though he is in all my thoughts, like light through a window. He is the light in my thoughts; but not the thoughts themselves.

I remember he once told me that the Baptiser was all he thought about until, in the wilderness, he became Yeshua. And when he became Yeshua, he no longer needed John or thought of him as he did. And likewise, Yeshua was everything to me; until I found Miriam. And now I do not need him in the same manner; though I need him still, the free man, every day.

I will not love another; I could not do that, for who else is there? With Yeshua, this restless swift found a place to land. But he also gave me nous, and nous need not cling; it is its own knowing, not borrowed from another. And I learn that the company of another isn't security and kisses aren't contracts and love does not mean leaning. I discover that I can endure, that I really do have worth – though sometimes I cling and cry for him to be with me again.

I hear stories of Rocky busy in Jerusalem, though he now calls himself Cephas. And news also of Yeshua's brother James, who is also in Jerusalem and speaking up for him, I am told ... well, what can you say? 'He comes to the relationship late' – I can hear Yeshua say this. And I'm told these things, and more, by Joanna, who lives near me in Tiberias, this new town on the shore of Galilee, 'where I still feel him,' she says, 'and the fish market is good.' Pushed away from the group, she lets them be; and maybe she is angry, I think she is, resentful of what has occurred. And she speaks of another arrival in Jerusalem, a man called Paul, who I do not know. He too is a follower of Yeshua, though how he is so, I do not know. He was not one of the group – but perhaps he too lived in Arimathea? (I am unkind, I know.) Oh, and apparently they argue, Rocky and Paul. They argue a great deal, and must go their separate ways for everyone's sake. Rocky believes Paul should be more Jewish, and Paul, a former Pharisee, thinks he should speak more with the gentiles!

'Neither backs down, they cannot do it,' says Joanna.

'And you should know, Joanna!' I say, laughing. 'For when did you ever change your mind?'

'Yeshua changed it,' she says. 'He gave me a different mind.' And there she says it all.

But it is the men who now preach, even though I preferred Joanna's words. Both the younger and elder John spoke well, as did Levi – and Thomas made me laugh, and Susanna was sharp. But such times are passed; they passed with Yeshua and these are different days. The spring flowers in Galilee are still beautiful; as were the days and the times he created; though difficult as well. But these things are no more, though daily, when I can, I pick a flower to remember.

It may be that I will never recover. I told you of my shock on climbing the ladder to find him gone; and recovery is slow. The group have not met since that day, though young Mark tells me he will write all things down and Rocky will tell him what to write. The elder John also says he will record what we saw, 'for Rocky's is not the only telling of the story. Though if I record everything, Miriam, and all that was done – well, not even the world could contain the books that would be written!' We must hope he contains it somehow.

Young John still looks after Mary, who seems to flourish ... and even smile! 'She was like a child at play,' said Joanna after one of her visits. 'I was quite taken aback, her eyes sparkle. In truth, I had forgotten how beautiful she is, Miriam. "That I should be so lifted up, so chosen!" she said – but didn't explain anymore.'

I find deep happiness in this awakening in Mary, as if she comes home to delight; and I believe that Yeshua rejoices too – for how can he not?

Jude, however, died by his own hand, by wretched rope, we hear; and this saddens me much. I still hear Yeshua's screaming words from the cross, 'Forgive them father, they know not what they do!' And you will ask how he could he say such a thing, when they seemed to know very well what they did – particularly the Syrians, I saw them. Yet I hear these words always, again and again, and know he spoke them to Jude above all others. He spoke to us all, but surely spoke most to Jude? Yet in his fear, poor Jude could not receive ... and imagined himself beyond the reach of love.

About others, I do not know; though Joanna tells me of new followers in Jerusalem, that the group grows, and that they call themselves 'The Way', as if starting again. I do not know how this is so – for who do they follow? And whose way is it? Yeshua is not here and he is not known by these people; they never knew him. So perhaps it is Rocky's way they follow or James – or perhaps it is the mysterious Paul. I believe there are different camps, as there were when he was alive.

Though I shall live alone, with my window shutters of light blue – yes, I found some through a trader from the east. Berenica saw them in the market. They speak of blue Galilee, which laps the Magdala shores; and so they speak of him. And here alone I will write quietly of this life and death and rising: 'The Gospel of Miriam of Magdala'! How does that sound? And perhaps I will find sense here; though sense is hard to find. Nothing is plain and nothing is changed – yet all is quite re-arranged, as if there is a large hole in the sky. And is this the kingdom come? That a man might rise and conquer death's cold hands?

That one, and therefore all, might one day rise and live again in love? And that we are given our nous as friend and guide for this difficult journey, to help us towards full human?

I cannot tell. As I say, these are strange times – though I begin with my morning shout, 'He is risen!' Yes, this is so! I open the shutters and shout it to chickens of Magdala who cluck in merry agreement! And still I smile as I remember that oddest of days, which began with the empty tomb: 'He is risen!' I shouted it at everyone that morning, for it was hardly the stuff of whispers. How could I not shout? And I, Miriam – the first to see and meet that risen man! Though now I tremble that such things occurred. And doubt. For how could it have been so? And was it really so? On some days, even I can doubt what I saw and knew and touched. This is the trouble with memory; I do know it can lie.

And that is enough for now. What are words anyway? They cannot hold the moments I remember; though my body holds them well, a better holding, for the body never lies. And as darkness falls on my small town, I hear the wind stirring the water. I close the shutters and light a candle – with every goodbye we learn, this is true. He once kissed my lips and my wound, as I kissed his. So let gratitude free me for today and not imprison me in a past now gone. He is here with me now in the scent of cassia and camel's thorn, in onycha and myrrh ... and in the laughter. He is risen. He is here.

And I hope I have done right, I feel so. For soon after our loss, soon after he was gone, I travelled from Magdala to Nazareth to greet his family, to tell them of things, to wish them well; it seemed a journey I must make. And as soon as I saw it lying there, pushed to one side, I knew I must ask; I could do no other. To my joy they said 'Yes' and I carried it home. So hanging in my room, on the wall between the door and the shutters, is the sign:

Yeshua: Carpenter/Builder/Restorer

You will understand, dear reader. And while you may not applaud, I still save cockroaches; though maybe they save themselves.